SEE MORE OF YOUR FRIENDS

A Novel

ELISS KACEY

Flight Risk Press Trade Paperback Edition
Copyright © 2024 by Flight Risk Press. All rights reserved.
Published in the United States by Flight Risk Press
ISBN 979-8-9921829-1-0 (trade paperback)
ISBN 979-8-9921829-0-3 (Ebook)

LIBRARY OF CONGRESS CATALOGING-IN-PUBLICATION DATA
Title: See More of Your Friends: a novel
Author: Eliss Kacey, pseud.
Rights and Permissions: Flight Risk Press
LCCN/Date: TXU002462064 / 2024-12-08

elisskacey.com
flightriskpress.com

To my Beloved. You are my favorite person.

TABLE OF CONTENTS

CHAPTER 1

A TALE OF TWO THREESOMES

Eric stands in the muted glow of a dimly lit public restroom. The muffled undercurrent of music and woozy, intoxicated voices seep through the narrow perimeter of light that surrounds the locked door. His hands grip the cold edges of the bright white porcelain sink, eyes clenched shut, as a swirl of emotions move through him. He was hoping the alcohol would calm his nerves.

Beads of sweat pearl at his hairline, his breath is shallow, throat dry. His chin lifts to meet his reflection in the mirror, and his dark undereye circles make him look older than his 44 years. He can see his heartbeat pulse in the pale blue vein of his right temple when a loud pounding comes through the door.

"You done in there?"

"Just a minute!" Eric counters with an unsteady timbre in his voice. His gaze drifts down to his left finger and settles on his wedding band. With a deep inhale and sharp exhale, Eric unlocks the door to face the unknown ahead.

❧

One month prior.

The residential block is lined with mid-century homes; some modernized, some restored, all immaculately maintained. Yards are weedless, green, and mowed, hedges are evenly trimmed, kids travel in packs of two to three according to age and mode of transportation—grade school kids on bikes, teenagers on skateboards, the younger ones pass by on scooters. Most homes have at least one, if not two, newer vehicles in the driveway. Neighbors pass by on the sidewalk with strollers or well-groomed, leashed dogs, occasionally waving or nodding hello, a few stopping to make polite conversation on this warm, sunny Sunday afternoon.

Eric is in his driveway, in swim trunks and shirtless, his hard work at the gym showing as he dips a bright yellow sponge into a bucket of bubbly, soapy water. Anita Ward's *Ring My Bell* streams through the wireless speaker as he lengthens over the hood of his SUV, arm moving in circles in time with the beat. His back muscles articulate, making a pleasing diamond shape with each extension and rotation. His chestnut brown hair glints gold in the sunlight.

I love this song, Jules thinks to herself from across the yard. She is in a white tee shirt and cutoff shorts, shoveling soil into the garden boxes she built. She is already anticipating the work week ahead and is making various mental lists of everything that needs to get done—conference calls to be scheduled, which clothes need to be dry cleaned, setting up time with the accountant… Looking up for a moment to brush her dark hair away from her forehead, she takes in the sight of Eric, and the noise in her head begins to quiet. He still gives her butterflies, still makes her heart race, even after more than a decade together. Removing her work gloves, she slides her sunglasses over the bridge of her nose, chin tilted down, eyes fixed. "You get that car nice…and clean."

Eric responds well to the attention. He flashes Jules a broad grin, slows down, and elongates his circles. Foamy suds drip down the slope of the hood as he squeezes the sponge. Standing upright to rinse the soap with his hose, he combs his fingers through his hair and meets Jules' gaze with a cocked eyebrow. "See something you like?"

Jules, bubbling with excitement on the inside but cool and collected on the outside, walks slowly in Eric's direction. Her silhouette reveals her lovely figure, and her voice drips with suggestion, "Why, yes. I…do."

When Jules comes within touching distance, Eric steps backward in teasing, tantalizing slow motion. He maintains eye contact, matching her stride, leading her to follow him. Their chests rise and fall with anticipation, the electricity between them intensifying with each step. Together, they trace a path up the paved driveway, across the plant-lined front walkway, and toward the concrete landing. The past several days have been hectic with work, and they have wanted each other, badly, all week. Jules catches her slightly trembling bottom lip between her teeth.

Eric breaks, unable to resist Jules any longer. He pulls her close, and their bodies collide in a passionate, breathless kiss. They stumble through the heavy teak front door, which barely closes behind them as Eric presses her against the entryway wall and then to the living room sofa, hands roaming over every inch, setting her skin on fire wherever he touches. Her tee shirt and cutoffs pool at her feet.

Jules responds with equal fervor, pressing her body against his, making quick work of undoing the buttons of Eric's trunks. Her lips find the soft curve of his neck, trailing lower to his collarbone, biting, licking. Eric grips a fistful of Jules' hair, pulling her to meet his gaze before nibbling at her earlobe and whispering moans into her ear.

"Please," Jules urges, pulling his hips toward hers. Eric just smiles, teasing, pushing against but not into her, savoring her impatience. Their bodies move against each other with escalating urgency until Eric breaks again and thrusts inside of her. Her back arches, and their breaths hitch, intermingle, as their rhythm changes. Jules' muscles grow taut around Eric, and he glides deeper into her, pressure building within both of them. Jules peaks, quickly followed by Eric, and they collapse, spent.

Eric buries his face in the crook of Jules' neck as she wraps one arm around him, kissing the side of his cheek, holding him close. They lay like that for a while longer, Jules running her fingers through Eric's hair, enjoying the relaxed weight of him on top of her. "That was nice," Jules coos as she shifts out from underneath him, taking his hand and curling up next to him under a throw blanket.

"Indeed," replies Eric with a kiss on her forehead, tucking under the blanket with her. His thumb traces the contour of Jules' wedding band, a smaller version of the one he has on his left finger. Daisy, their 4-year-old border collie, emerges from the back bedroom, toy in mouth, taking her place next to

Jules. Jules' heart swells in moments like these, when all three of them are together, the little family they created.

The three have lived in this home since Daisy was a puppy and, over these years, have made it their own. The living room has cream-colored walls, a deep-cushioned, contemporary, cocoa-colored sofa, an oversized teak and glass coffee table, and a soft, neutral area rug partially covering the refinished hardwood floors. There is a symmetrical pair of linen-shaded floor lamps just behind the sofa flanking a modern, wooden sofa table topped with a basket of Daisy's toys, a green-handled pet lint roller, some colorful coasters that look like postcards that they collected on various travels, and a stack of Eric's recipe books. Centered on the wall in front of the sofa hangs a mounted flatscreen television above a matching modern console table that holds two framed photos. One of Eric and Jules on the courthouse steps just after their wedding ceremony. Eric is in a tailored navy suit, crisp white shirt with the top button undone, no tie. Jules wears a form-fitting, cap-sleeved white shift and holds a small bouquet of dark red roses. Jules' head is tilted back, laughing, and Eric's face is beaming, watching her. The other photo is of Daisy, mid-air, catching a royal blue plastic frisbee.

Eric reaches for the remote, turns on the TV, and flips through channels, stopping on a scene featuring a very attractive couple lounging poolside, him in a swimsuit, feet dangling in the water, her on a chaise sipping a drink in a bikini. A catcall of a whistle emerges from Eric's lips, "Damn, he's hot. Look at that chest."

Jules turns to Daisy in mock exasperation, "Daddy has such a type." She turns back to Eric with a coy smile,

"And she's gorgeous." They both break into an easy, familiar laugh.

"Any hits on the app?" Eric asks.

Jules reaches for her phone. "Let's see... Straight guy, straight guy, straight guy... Straight guy who wants to choke me... Ok, here we go," she reports, "a couple!" Eric's interest is piqued. "Normal?"

Jules scrolls through the profile. "They seem normal. Good shape, attractive. Complete sentences. No typos." After a brief pause, Jules adds, "She's bi. He's straight."

"Of course he's straight." Eric sighs, shoulders slumping. "All of them are straight. We can't be the only bisexual couple out there..."

Eric and Jules talked about ethical non-monogamy for years, even before they got married. But to date, it had only ever been a theoretical exercise. While her love and attraction to Eric is undeniable, Jules ached to be in a relationship with another woman again and experience parts of her sexuality she couldn't readily express with him. Eric, equally attracted to women and men, longed to experience aspects of himself and his sexuality that didn't quite fit within his relationship with Jules. He had fleeting encounters with men and women before settling down with Jules but very few actual relationships. There is a great deal Eric remains curious about, ways in which he wants to feel intimacy and connection. Despite scrolling the apps looking for compatibility, they hadn't yet found what looked like a good fit for both of them, and despite being open with one another on their inclinations, neither wanted to take any action that would hurt the other or their marriage. This had become a deep source of frustration for each of them over the years as the urges grew stronger. For Jules, in particular, the yearning was growing too difficult to bear.

"I know this is hard," Jules sympathizes, squeezing Eric's hand, "but we've got to start somewhere. How would you feel about me starting a chat? See what they are like? We can consider it practice." Jules raises Eric's hand to her lips, searching his expression. *If only we could start actually meeting people*, Jules thinks, *maybe we could begin finding couples to connect with*. "Would you be ok with that?"

Eric doesn't respond but also doesn't pull his hand away. His initial instinct is always reticence, a feeling in his gut that just isn't quite right. But he also understands Jules' perspective. How will they ever meet other couples if they aren't willing to make contact? After a few seconds pass, his reluctance softens, and he gives in. "Yeah. Sure, I guess. Let's see where this goes."

Jules perks up at Eric's concession and plants a kiss on the back of his hand. Eric gives her a half-hearted smile as he stands to walk to the kitchen, his expression falling the moment his face turns away. Jules reaches for her phone to start typing her first message.

Afternoon spills into evening, which spills into night as Jules sits up against the tufted fabric headboard of the bed she shares with Eric. The bed is flanked with matching night tables, each topped with shaded ceramic lamps. Eric's holds an alarm clock with backlit red numbers, a soft, quilted eye mask, and the dangling cord of his phone charger. Jules' holds her own clock and a stack of paperbacks she's collected from airport newsstands. Jules' laptop screen casts a blue glow that reflects in the lenses of her reading glasses, and Daisy snoozes at her feet, her chest rising and falling with each light snore. Eric emerges from the bathroom in his heather gray jersey pajama bottoms, pulls back the covers, and tucks into his side of the bed. Jules senses his discomfort.

Setting her glasses and laptop on her night table, Jules turns toward him, placing her hand on his face. "Hey," she whispers, thumb caressing his cheek, "what's going on over there?"

Eric responds with a slight shrug but doesn't pull his face away. Jules continues, "I love you. Your emotional support means everything to me."

"Supporting you is what I do," Eric murmurs, avoiding her gaze.

Jules gently guides his chin to face her. "Us. You're supporting us." She locks eyes with him, soothing but intent on making her point. "We'll take this at our own pace. Okay?"

"Okay," he says as their eyes meet, though his voice remains unconvincing. "I'll come around. I know how badly you want this."

A sparkle of mischief flickers in Jules' eyes as she navigates them back to safer territory. "This afternoon was so sexy," she teases.

"Yes," a slow grin spreads across Eric's face, "it certainly was."

Jules reaches to switch off the bedside lamp. "Sweet dreams, my love," she whispers.

"Sweet dreams."

~∽~

Early dawn light paints the kitchen window as Eric starts the day. He makes a pot of coffee while Daisy lies at his feet, her tail thumping a steady rhythm against the cabinets as he pours her breakfast into the bowl.

Jules interrupts their routine as she strides into the kitchen, radiating power and grace in her carefully tailored black suit. Eric halts, coffee pot suspended in mid-air. "You take my breath away."

A smile lights up Jules' face as she closes the distance between them, leaving a soft kiss on his lips. "Funny," she teases, a glint in her eyes, "I was just thinking the same about you."

She settles on a leather cushioned stool at the marble kitchen island. "What's your day look like?"

"Gym, then the office. Just paperwork today. I shouldn't be late," Eric says, placing a steaming cup of coffee in front of her. "How about you? No boxing class with Beth and the girls this morning?"

Fingers circling the rim of her favorite 'World's Best Dog Mom' mug, Jules checks the time on her phone. "No boxing with the girls today. I have an early staff meeting. I'm hoping to catch up with them at the coffee shop after. The rest of the day should be straightforward, and I should be home by dinner." Sipping her coffee, she lets out a contented sigh. "Mmm... This coffee is delicious. Thank you for spoiling me."

"Spoiling you is what I do best," Eric says with a grin.

"I'm a lucky girl," Jules remarks with a flirty glance over the lip of her coffee cup.

Eric chuckles softly. "That makes two of us."

Jules rises, ready to leave, and casts a glance over her shoulder. "I'm off. I love you."

Eric smiles. "I love you more."

⤝

Jules starts her workday in a sleek, glass-paneled conference room. Immaculate upscale furnishings gleam under cool-hued recessed lights. The far wall showcases an elegant, backlit metal sign bearing the name of the private equity firm where Jules, known professionally as Julia, is a partner. The firm occupies the top floor of one of the most sought-after boutique office buildings downtown, with extra-high ceilings, expansive windows, and highest-end finishes.

Seated in camel-colored leather chairs around a polished wood rectilinear conference table are six men, all associates, ages spanning from late twenties to late thirties, and Jules. The only other female presence in the room is the reception-ist, who busily arranges breakfast on the sideboard. As the men engage in their pre-meeting patter, Jules silently reviews her notes and wonders if it will be another blue shirt bingo day. So far, her colleagues are sporting four pale blue button-downs, a blue check, and a tone-on-tone blue golf shirt.

"Tough workout this morning," Will boasts. "The talent at the gym was, shall we say...distracting."

"I'm jealous," Seth counters, gently rubbing his shoul-der, "I'm still nursing this injury."

"You're always full of excuses, Seth," Hunter ribs, sharp-tongued, drawing laughter from the other associates.

Their banter stops as Peter strides in, his shock of silver

hair contrasting against his light pink Brooks Brothers collared shirt. He takes his seat at the head of the table, Jules situated to his right. "Good morning, team. Let's start with Project Bronco. Where are we with diligence?"

Darn, Jules thinks to herself, her expression unchanging. *So close to a bingo...*

Hunter doesn't hesitate. "I've got high hopes for this one. This could secure us a stronghold in the Midwest. We should seize this."

"I second that," Will adds. "They've got the territory and client base to catapult us to the top. I'm with Hunter. We should move quickly."

"Exactly." Hunter leans forward, elbows on the table. "We have competition. If we hesitate, we'll lose the deal."

"Let's take a beat." Jules' words hang in the air as all eyes turn in her direction. "I understand the potential benefits, but we haven't completed due diligence. We need to get a handle on their financials. Their balance sheet is messy, which could impact our return."

Hunter repeatedly taps the end of his pen on his notepad. His neck reddens, and his head shakes with a barely perceptible no. He takes a deep breath and sneers at Jules, "We need to move swiftly." Will and Seth are quick to back him up. "Very swiftly."

Peter intervenes. "I'm with Julia on this one. We need to take a knee, and I need to look at the numbers. Full diligence report and financial projections in my inbox by COB." Hunter flings his pen and leans back hard in his chair.

Peter's phone rings, and he reaches to answer, ignoring Hunter's outburst. Covering the mouthpiece, Peter says,

"Alright, everyone. Back to work. Julia, can you hang back a minute?" Jules remains in her seat as the room empties and Peter takes his call. While she waits, she reflects on the path she's taken to get here.

Jules had a blazing start in the workplace, starting out as an analyst at one of the country's most prestigious investment banks. Quickly making her way up the ranks, she was responsible for billions of dollars in investment and had one of the strongest performing teams in the industry. She was widely known for her sharp intellect and keen decisiveness when it came to deals. She met Peter when they were on opposite sides of a transaction, and he quickly recognized Jules' talent. Jules was both firm and ruthless, depending on which side of the negotiating table you were on. She was always prepared; some would say overly so. She would plan, anticipate every scenario, set traps, and win. Work has always been a highly controlled game of skill for Jules, with very little, if anything, left to chance.

After years of professional courtship, Peter convinced Jules to join him as a partner at his firm, where Jules could be more hands-on with the portfolio companies and growth strategies. For Jules, this was an opportunity to test her skills in private equity, including fundraising and strategic partnerships, which would expand her skillset. At the time, it felt exciting and new.

Jules enjoys the professional relationship she's built with Peter over the years. His reputation in the industry is impeccable, and he brings the same level of analysis to deals as Jules, which is why their financial performance is in the top right quadrant year over year. Jules finds their disciplined approach and stellar performance quite satisfying, particularly for her competitive nature. While these qualities are something they each valued in the associates they brought on board, some of the more recent hires, like Hunter, Will, and Seth, are more instinct-driven and haven't quite settled into Peter's and Jules' way of doing things. This introduced a new challenge to Jules, as Peter often relies on her as the voice of reason, which some of the associates interpret as a threat. Some days she handles this challenge better than others, but over time, it has become long in the tooth. Differences of opinion are always welcome in the teams Jules manages. Ego-driven decisions, however, are another story.

Jules' phone lights up with a message from Beth.

Missed you in class today. We're downstairs in the coffee shop. Can you join us?

Jules replies: **Be down in a few. Start without me,** and puts her phone in her pocket as Peter finishes up his call.

"I may have a partnership opportunity for us with a new firm in town," Peter starts. "They've brought on some stellar talent, and here is what I know about them." Peter shares the details he's gathered and looks at her. "I need you to do some research. Find out what you can."

"I'll see what I can do," Julia assures him.

"Thank you, Julia. I know I can rely on you."

Jules stands, collects her things, and heads straight to the elevator to meet Beth and the girls.

Tucked around a cozy table at the bustling coffee shop sit Beth, Kyra, Madelyn, and Claire, each dressed in casual, post-workout attire. Coffee after boxing is a weekly ritual and a time for everyone to catch up. Beth is Jules' best and dearest friend. They've been like sisters since they met in business school. Beth is comfortably in her later forties and radiates a confident warmth and natural beauty. Around Beth's neck is a gold link chain with three gold charms: an "A" for Alex, Beth's second husband; an "M" for Mason, her 11-year-old son from her first marriage; and a "K" for Kevin, her 18-year-old stepson from Alex's first marriage. Beth is the only mom in the group and has a strong maternal energy about her. She also has a searing sense of humor.

The third in Jules' and Beth's inner circle is Kyra, who is an animated bundle of effusiveness. Her dirty blonde hair is in a messy ponytail, hairline still damp from the morning's workout. She just turned 40, and her infectious laugh amplifies her attractiveness. Kyra works in sales, has never been married, nor shows any interest in settling down. Energy like Kyra's is too big to contain.

Madelyn and Claire are close with one another and know Jules, Beth, and Kyra from the gym. Madelyn is a year older than Kyra, attractive with sharp features and short, reddish brown hair. Following the end of her last relationship, she moved into the one-bedroom apartment up the street from Claire and came to know the other women through her introduction.

Claire is the youngest of the group, in her late thirties, and has a certain girl-next-door quality. She never misses a chance to flash her white gold engagement ring and wedding band. Claire married Jerry almost a year ago after an extended engagement. She had been planning her dream wedding since she was a little girl, and her pink rhinestone keyring says "BRIDE."

As Beth winds up the laces of her boxing gloves and stows them in her tote bag, she looks towards the other three women. "Ok, ladies. Workout is over. Now catch me up."

Madelyn turns to Kyra, tone heavy with envy, "I don't know how you do it. You always find the best men to date."

"I don't know about that…" Kyra shrugs, a modest smile tugging at her lips.

"The men I meet have so many issues and such high expectations. I just want something stable," Madelyn complains. She has a pattern of meeting men, getting very attached, and then the relationship fizzles.

"Y'all," Claire joins in, glancing at her rings, "I'm so glad I'm not on the dating scene anymore. Married life suits me just fine. I don't know what I would do without my Jerry. Wouldn't you agree, Beth?"

"I agree. It's great being married to Alex. He is the best man I know," Beth adds.

Madelyn rolls her eyes.

"I could hear that eye roll from across the room," Jules says with a smirk as she approaches and drops into the seat next to Kyra. Beth passes Jules an almond milk latte, one sweetener, just how Jules likes it. "You're my heroes. Thanks for this," Jules lets out with a sigh, taking a sip of her drink. "Intense day up there. And it's barely nine o'clock."

"Must have been important. You never miss class," Kyra says.

"I needed to be in early. Deal team meeting on a new transaction," Jules explains.

"I never get used to seeing you in your work clothes," Madelyn comments. "You look so serious."

"It's her armor. Protects her against the sausage fest she works in every day." Beth winks at Jules, and the other women laugh.

"Speaking of," replies Jules, "how are the boys, Mama? Any new Mason moments lately?" Jules is like an aunt to Mason and Kevin.

"My goodness," Beth responds, shaking her head and already giggling. "Who knew being a mom to an 11-year-old boy would be so hilarious? I ran into one of the other moms last week. Turns out the boys are getting curious about girls. In her search history was the phrase 'sexy babes,' but they forgot the 'e' in 'babes,' so up turned a bunch of videos of 'Sexy Babs', which, for the record, is my new role-playing name with Alex." Beth ends with an animated eyebrow raise as the table breaks out in laughter.

"Too funny!" exclaims Claire, the rest of the women nodding in agreement.

"Alright, ladies, my turn," Kyra announces to the group. Pausing for dramatic effect, Kyra sighs. "I think I'm in love…"

Jules shares a look with Madelyn and Claire. "Uh-huh."

"We've heard this before," Madelyn adds.

"We sure have," Claire nods, sipping her coffee.

"It's different this time. John gets me. He's sexy as hell. Doesn't have a ton of baggage. I really like him," Kyra gushes.

"This sounds promising." Jules smiles over her coffee cup. "What do we know about this guy?"

"He's been with the same company for years and works downtown. Never been married and doesn't have any kids. He lives out near you guys," Kyra motions to Beth and Jules. "His house is freaking amazing." Kyra takes a sip of coffee and continues, "He's introducing me to his best friend, Charlie, from college. She's going to be in town for the weekend. I can't wait to hear what he was like in school."

"Charlie is a she?" Claire blinks.

"Calm down, Claire. She's gay. Very gay. They used to go to strip clubs together," Kyra explains. "No need to sound the alarm bells."

"So, when do we get to meet this John?" Jules asks.

"Slow down there, Jules. I'm not ready for that," Kyra replies.

"Now let me get this straight," Madelyn interjects. "You can meet *his* friends, but he can't meet yours? You just said you were in love!"

"Patience, my dear," Kyra scolds playfully in return. "You know I'm not one to rush into anything." She quickly shifts focus towards Jules. "Meanwhile, can we talk about you and Eric?"

Jules swallows hard at Kyra's question. "I guess now is as good a time as any."

"Alright, then. How's your 'experiment' coming along?" Kyra encourages.

"What experiment?" Madelyn asks.

"Whew, um." Jules takes a deep breath. "Eric and I are exploring dating other couples," she says, tone uncharacteristically nervous.

"Excuse me?!" Claire nearly chokes on her coffee.

"Wait. What? Separately? Like swinging?" Madelyn stammers, just as confused as Claire.

"Not really swinging. We are looking for more of an ongoing connection. Eric hasn't been with another man, and I haven't been with another woman, since before we got married. We would like to find other bisexual couples that we can get to know," Jules clarifies, her voice becoming steadier.

Beth reaches over to give Jules' hand a supportive squeeze.

"Wait…y'all are…gay?" Claire asks.

"Bisexual," Jules corrects gently.

"So…poly?" Madelyn asks, trying to understand.

"Ethically non-monogamous," Jules replies.

Madelyn shakes her head. "Sorry. I'm trying to wrap my head around this. You want to date other people? How is this the first time we're hearing about this?"

"I guess there was never a good time to bring it up before. Beth and Kyra have known about us, but we don't generally talk about it. You never know how it will be received, and…" Before Jules can finish, Madelyn blurts out, "Does this mean you have orgies?"

"And you get questions like that," Jules deadpans, keeping her cool. "Ideally, we would date other couples together, but it's not necessarily limited to that."

"But you're married," adds Claire, also shaking her head. "How do you date other couples?"

"Well… We are figuring that out. We are hoping to find couples we can connect and have a good time with."

"You mean sex? Are you serious?" Claire's jaw drops.

"I have a hard enough time finding one person at a time

to date," adds Madelyn, rolling her eyes again and taking the information in. "Have you guys done anything like this before?"

"This is new for us," Jules explains. "It's a little scary, but mostly exciting."

"How did you know this about each other? I had no idea either of you were bi or open or—what did you just call it?" Madelyn asks.

"Ethically non-monogamous." Jules reiterates.

"So... Monogam*ish*?" Madelyn asks.

Jules laughs lightly. "Yes. ENM works, too."

"I guess I'm less surprised about you, Jules," Madelyn continues. "I would have never guessed it about Eric."

"It came up early in our relationship and was a big part of how we knew we were right for each other. It was the first time each of us could be ourselves."

"Don't you worry, he'll run off with another man?" Claire asks.

"I don't. None of these things mean we aren't committed to each other. This is about expressing other parts of ourselves," Jules replies, tone firm. Responses like Claire's bring out a mix of weariness and defensiveness in Jules, which the group picks up on and quickly grows quiet.

"Well, I think it's awesome," Kyra breaks the silence. "You two are always looking for ways to keep things fresh and interesting."

"It's more than that," Jules says. "It's core to who we are. It's especially tough when you are both bi—no one really sees you. It's been a real struggle to find community. Beth and Kyra have always been supportive, but we are looking for couples who are more like us. It's one thing to be accepted. But we've never felt like we fit in."

"I hadn't really thought about it like that," Madelyn adds. "You two look straight from the outside."

"We do. And even when we come out to people, they have a hard time relating. We are looking for more people we can be ourselves with. We are done with being invisible. I can't do it anymore," Jules says, a hopeful smile re-emerging.

Beth leans in. "Well, I'm thrilled for you guys. Alex and I always have your back."

Jules nods toward Beth, thankful, and then turns to the other women. "Thanks for letting me share. Coming out to you like that was a big deal for me."

With no further comment on Jules' announcement to the group, Madelyn abruptly shifts topics, "I'm, um, happy for you, Kyra. John sounds really nice." She then turns to Jules. "Listen, Jules, would you mind if I come over tomorrow night? I could use your input on a new work project."

Jules is happy to be changing subjects. "Of course, Eric is making dinner. Drop by around 6." Jules' phone buzzes. "That's my next meeting. I've got to head back up, ladies. Kyra, I hope we get the chance to meet John one of these days now that you're so deeply in love." Jules winks and blows a kiss to Kyra as she stands to leave.

"I need to get to work, too. I'll walk out with you." Beth stands as well, and the two women exit, leaving Madelyn, Kyra, and Claire.

Madelyn's eyes open wide. "I didn't see that coming."

"Me neither," Claire adds.

"What coming?" Kyra asks.

"I thought they were happy," responds Madelyn, taking a sip of her coffee.

"And they're married!" Claire exclaims. "What Jules is talking about—that's just not something you do when you're happily married!"

"Hold on a minute. They are absolutely happy. What's making you say that?" Kyra asks.

Madelyn is quick to jump in, "I've only ever heard of people being open when things aren't going well. They start looking outside of the relationship to get their needs met. This just sounds like permission to cheat."

"That's exactly what it sounds like. I can't imagine being ok with it." Claire nods in agreement. "Back when I was on the dating scene, I'd meet these men who could only meet during the week at lunchtime or in these out-of-the-way bars or restaurants. Seriously, just say you're married, for crying out loud. Cheater, cheater, pumpkin eater."

"Alright, you two. I've had about enough of this. I get that it's not traditional, and it might not be right for other people—you especially, Claire. But it's part of who they are, and they want to find ways to express it. I'm all for it." Kyra glances at her watch and stands up. "I have to run. See you both in class next week."

Claire and Madelyn exchange a long look as Kyra departs.

⁊

Jules stands inside the elevator of her office building, doors still open to the ground floor. Dylan, fresh-faced, just out of college, and Peter's only son, steps in just as the doors close.

He's grown since she's seen him last. He's now almost a foot taller than she is and has filled out considerably. Still boyish in the face but with the body of a man.

"Dylan," Jules greets, "That's right. Today is your first day."

"Julia," Dylan says with a nod.

"I'm sure your dad will be happy to have you on the team," Jules continues as the elevator ascends. There is a moment of silence before Dylan responds.

"I can hold my own." Dylan's tone is sharp, almost aggressive.

"I'm sure you can," Jules responds, unfazed, as the elevator doors open to the well-appointed lobby area. Dylan steps out of the elevator first. He takes the last gulp of his coffee and leaves his empty cup and dirty napkin on the receptionist's desk. Jules stops in her tracks. "Aren't you going to throw your trash away?" she asks.

Dylan shrugs, "I just did," and makes his way down the hall toward Peter's office. Jules shakes her head as she turns to walk in the opposite direction. *Just great*, she thinks to herself. *He'll fit in perfectly.*

The remainder of the day moves quickly, and Jules drives home as the sun begins to set. Traffic is unusually light as she glides along the streets, moving from city blocks to residential neighborhoods. Jules parks in the driveway and steps through the front door to find Eric in the kitchen, Daisy at his feet, tail thumping at Jules' arrival.

"You're a sight for sore eyes," she says, setting down

her work bag, removing her blazer, and taking a seat at the island.

"Hi, gorgeous," Eric greets, pouring a glass of wine and sliding it over to her. "Tough day?"

"Long day." Jules exhales, still decompressing. "Started the day by pumping the brakes on a new deal which is never fun. It's awful being the only adult supervision in the room."

Jules isn't quite sure when the shift happened. When her career turned into glorified, well-paid babysitting. Despite the private school pedigrees, this new crop of associates is hasty and presumptive with their work, and Jules finds herself spending a disproportionate amount of time fixing broken models and triple-checking diligence findings before signing off on deals, creating a dynamic that Jules does not care for. Like she's a grade school teacher checking student work. And for the associates, unused to having their work corrected, it's causing insecurities, which show up as micro-aggressions, all pointed at Jules.

Her professional superpower is seeing potential. In companies. In colleagues. In opportunities. It's what's driven her to succeed. But now, it all seems to feel flat. Her loyalty to Peter and uncertainty about what she wants to do next are what have kept her in her current position, but her professional boredom is becoming hard to ignore.

After a few sips of wine, Jules continues. "I'm also doing some behind-the-scenes recon for Peter on a potential new partner firm. We'll see where that goes."

"You have a lot on your plate."

"Par for the course," she acknowledges, turning over the day in her mind. "Do you remember Dylan? Peter's son?"

Eric nods yes, and Jules continues, "I remember when he was a freshman in high school. He started at the firm today as an associate."

Eric half-teases, "You're outnumbered."

"I've always been outnumbered," Jules responds with fatigue and less subtle defiance. She pauses for a sip of wine, not letting her frustration ruin the evening. "Enough of that," Jules says. "What about you?"

"I had a good day. I got a lot done. I'm at Avendale tomorrow so I will get to see Sam." Eric is a social worker with over a decade in the profession, specializing in elder care. He is widely considered one of the best aging care specialists in the area. Working with individuals and their families at advanced stages of life is something Eric always felt called to, and it gives him a sense of meaning and purpose. Even under difficult circumstances like reductions in funding and programs, Eric remained confident that he was making a difference.

Eric's professional demeanor is both comforting and disarming, but he is by no means a pushover. He knows when to be firm, fights hard for his staff and clients, and has developed into a strong leader. While his job has turned supervisory over the years, he still makes space for casework for some of his favorite clients—most notably Sam.

Jules softens, work tension dissipating. "Please send him my best," she says. "On the social front, I got to see the girls today for coffee. Kyra is in love…"

"Is that so?" Eric smirks as he lights the stove, a blue ring of fire coming alive after a few clicks.

"She really seems to like this guy. And she's meeting his friends. It sounds promising."

Half joking, half skeptical, Eric adds, "We'll see…"

"Also," Jules continues, "Madelyn is coming for dinner tomorrow night. She has some work stuff she wants to talk about. I said it was ok."

"Of course. I'll pick up extra on my way home."

Jules stands. "You're the best. I love you. I'll get out of these clothes and set the table."

"I love you more," Eric replies. "Dinner will be ready soon. We'll make it an early night. I'm going to the gym before work tomorrow."

The alarm breaks the early morning quiet, and Eric is quick to silence it. He takes extra care not to disturb Jules, still deep in sleep. Daisy yawns, stretches, and trots behind Eric to the kitchen while he puts the coffee on, leaving out a mug and a love note for Jules. Dressed in workout gear, he kisses Daisy on the head and locks the front door behind him.

The gym is wide awake, alive with the morning workout crowd. Music pulses from Eric's earbuds as he logs miles on the treadmill, flanked by runners on each side, racing to their own personal soundtracks.

Eric finishes with a sprint, running hard and breathless before slowing to a walk to cool down. Toweling off and looking up, he can't help but notice the new face at the gym in the free weights section. He's olive-skinned with jet-black hair and, while new to the gym, not new to working out. His muscles flex under his workout clothes. Eric has to stop himself from staring.

After a shower and while dressing for work, Eric spots

this new guy noticing him back from across the locker room. Their eyes meet for just a second before Eric's cheeks grow warm, and he, suddenly and atypically shy, looks away. Eric smiles to himself as he finishes dressing, the thrill of the attention rippling through him.

Eric can't remember a time when he wasn't attracted to men. To people, really. His sexuality didn't discriminate. Choosing one gender over, or to the exclusion of, another never sat well with him. And yet, time and again, he felt internalized pressure to pick—woman or man. Never women and men. Until Jules. The acceptance he found with Jules made the world make more sense—that life could be a both/and instead of an either/or. This feeling wasn't limited to who Eric found sexually attractive. It was masculine and feminine. Caring and being cared for. Hard and soft. The space created by and within his relationship with Jules enabled a broad spectrum of emotion and experience, a place that felt comfortable and safe. Mostly.

From the beginning, Eric and Jules were open about their sexuality, and while the container of their relationship could not, and is not expected to, fill every need, neither of them experienced anyone else intimately since they got together. Experiments in non-monogamy in prior relationships had not gone well for either of them, resulting in a trail of bad breakups. To date, their openness existed in conversation only. A little edgy, a little dangerous, but nothing either of them ever acted upon. Not in real life.

They would fantasize together, talk in great detail about scenarios they wanted to explore, which added dimension and thrill to their relationship, curiously and counterintuitively sharpened by undertones of jealousy and envy—all part of the emotional mix. The satisfyingly dissonant feelings of possibility, pleasure, and insecurity heightened the sexual tension between them. Unspoken questions of 'Would you, could you, touch anyone else, be touched by anyone else, love anyone else, like you do with me?'

They deleted and rejoined the apps, testing the waters to see if they could find anyone compatible. But nothing ever happened. Nothing ever went anywhere. Which is why Jules' latest persistence caught Eric off guard. He's seen what happens when Jules sets her mind on something. Very little, if anything, gets in her way.

Eric finds this exciting—the prospect of actually engaging with others. But it also makes him nervous. Sometimes Jules' determination, even when well-intentioned, can cause emotional casualties. Other people's needs, other people's feelings, sometimes get overlooked. *I'll take her at her word this time*, Eric convinces himself. They will go slowly and navigate this together.

Eric's thoughts are interrupted by Alex, Eric's best friend, and husband of Jules' best friend, Beth. "Hey, man," Alex greets Eric with a handshake and a one-armed hug, "heading to work?"

"Yeah, just finished my run. How's it going? How are the kids? Mason still doing baseball?"

"Yes, he loves his little league team. I almost forgot how bad those cleats smell," Alex replies.

Eric laughs. "Ah, to be a smelly pre-teen! How was Kevin's last day of high school?"

"I wept." Alex shakes his head. "I can't believe I have a college freshman."

"Gosh. Congratulations, man."

"Thank you." Alex nods. "He's been asking about you. Wants to know when he'll see his Uncle Eric next."

"He's such a good kid." Eric smiles. "Tell him I said hi, and Jules and I are looking forward to celebrating his graduation at your house."

"I definitely will." Alex checks the time on his watch and shifts the conversation. "I'll let you get to it. Catch you later."

"See you soon. Have a good workout." Eric high-fives Alex and heads out of the locker room.

∽

A few blocks away is Avendale Assisted Living, one of the locations Eric is responsible for that provides care and assistance for aging adults. Avendale is Eric's favorite facility. It's a sprawly, converted Victorian with powder blue hydrangea bushes and a painted porch. Leaded windows are crowned with panes of stained glass. Some of the early risers have already claimed their rocking chairs for the day, and Eric greets them with a warm smile on his way into the building.

Eric bounds up the steps to the staff offices. Desks are filled with manila folders, outdated computer equipment, and framed photos of families, pets, and past vacations. Casual greetings are exchanged, and then Linda, who has worked in Avendale for over 30 years, arrives with a cupcake box.

"Linda, my love," Eric teases, "are those what I think they are?"

Linda bats her eyelashes. "Maybe…"

She hands Eric a cupcake, who takes a bite of the red velvet and rolls his eyes up to the ceiling. "Linda, you have done it again. Now, if you'll excuse me, I need to be alone with the rest of this cupcake."

Linda cackles with delight and takes her seat at her desk. "Here, take one for Sam," she says, "and don't you eat it!" Eric tips his head in gratitude, then cracks a mischievous grin.

"I make no promises," Eric replies as Linda's laugh follows him down the hallway.

"Hey, cupcake. I'm glad you're here today. I need to talk." Vickie, the Executive Director of Avendale, stops Eric mid-bite before he heads downstairs to meet Sam.

"Vickie! For you, the world. What's up?"

"Let's chat in my office," Vickie says, leading Eric down the hallway. *Not good*, Eric thinks as he takes a seat in front of Vickie's desk and she closes the door behind them. A new finger-painted picture of a rainbow is held to the beige metal filing cabinet with a magnet—the latest artwork from Vickie's granddaughter. Vickie has run Avendale for years and is a solid member of his team. She's dedicated and resourceful and takes pride in her work. She is the definition of service-driven, and both the staff and residents love her.

Vickie walks around her desk, takes a seat in her well-worn vinyl chair, and looks Eric squarely in the eyes. "There's no easy way to say this," she says. "I don't think I can do this job anymore."

Eric takes in what Vickie just said. "I'm listening," he says. "Tell me what's going on."

"This last round of state audits nearly killed me. I feel like we go from one audit right into the next, and it's impacting our ability to care for the residents. We are already understaffed, and rumor has it more budget cuts are coming. I won't be able to fill my open roles, and I can't keep overworking my people. I come in early. I stay late. I do what I can to help make up the difference. But it's taking its toll on me. My blood pressure is through the roof, and I've had to up my medication. My doc says this isn't sustainable. And…"

"And?" Eric maintains eye contact with Vickie.

"And I agree," Vickie replies.

"Ok." Eric nods. "What do you want to do? Are you resigning?"

"I want to think through my options with you." Vickie's tone softens. "I don't want to leave this place. I love this place. I love the work we do. But I can't keep working like this. I need help."

"Alright," Eric says. "I'm here, and I've got your back. I will do whatever I can. One question, though."

"Yeah?" Vickie asks.

"Why did you wait till it got to this point to tell me? You know you could have talked to me."

"Eric," Vickie says, "I know how hard you work. Avendale is just one of the facilities you're responsible for, and I also know the others don't run like this one. You have enough on your plate."

"Yes," Eric replies. "But you are a priority. Not just Avendale—you. Have you started thinking through what you would need to make this workable for you?"

"I started to, but when I found out more cuts are coming…" Vickie's shoulders slump, and her bottom lip begins to quiver lightly. "I felt hopeless. It's like the state wants us to fail."

"Oh, Vickie." Eric leans forward. "I'm so sorry. Thank you for raising this with me and for your candor. I will be honest with you. Cuts are coming. But I think we can get ahead of some of them. Let's put our heads together and see if we can come up with something workable for you. I don't want to lose you, and I will do whatever I can to get to a solution. Fair?" Eric extends his hand to Vickie.

"Fair," Vickie replies as they shake on it. "Now go visit with Sam. He's been looking forward to seeing you all week."

⤸

Sam stands in the front room, eyes framed in thick glasses. Once thick on top, his salt and pepper hair has grown thinner over the years that Eric has known him. His posture curves slightly forward, but his gait is strong and steady, and the walks he takes with Eric have become somewhat of a ritual. His features brighten as Eric approaches and asks, "Ready to get some fresh air?"

"Absolutely. Let's go. The park should be lousy with birds right now. And give me my cupcake."

Eric and Sam walk side by side down the ramp and to the park. They take a seat on a metal bench in an oak tree-shaded spot, and Sam pulls a bag of birdseed from his pant pocket. Eric starts, "It's been a few weeks. How are you?"

"You know me. No complaints. I have food to eat. A roof over my head. And enjoyable conversation with you.

What else could I possibly need?" Sam's reply brings a smile to Eric's face.

"And how's the poker game going?" Eric asks.

"You lose some, you lose some." Sam shrugs and Eric laughs. "What about the enchanting Ms. Camilla, who I saw you with the last time I was here? You still have your good eye on her?"

Sam snorts. "Always. She's a charmer. We play backgammon. Sometimes, she lets me win," Sam says with a wink.

"She must really like you," Eric says with a chuckle. "She never lets anyone win."

Their conversation lulls briefly as birds gather to peck at the seed Sam spreads, and he asks, "What about you? How's that fetching wife of yours?"

Eric takes a deep breath before responding, "She keeps me on my toes."

"Do you like it on your toes?" Sam asks.

Eric smirks. "Most of the time."

"I remember when you were still just dating. She drove you crazy. Women do that." Sam shakes his head.

Eric's tone takes on a note of seriousness. "She's in this phase now where she really wants to come into herself. It's hard to explain. It's like a growth spurt but with her personality. She wants more from her career, more from her personal life. I want to support it. Support her. It's just hard to know what she needs. It's hard to know if I'm being a good partner for her…"

"You love her," Sam observes.

"More than anything," Eric responds.

Eric's phone buzzes with a text notification, a heart

emoji from Jules, which brings a smile to his face. Before Eric can put his phone away, another message pops up. This time from Jules' friend Madelyn.

Looking forward to seeing you tonight.

Eric shrugs and puts his phone back in his pocket, not giving Madelyn's text another thought.

✍

Nestled amongst Scandinavian-designed, neutral office furnishings, Jules and Dr. Emily Layton, in their respective seats, mirror each other—hands resting on laps, eyes closed, breathing in a synchronized rhythm. Dappled light streams through the office windows, which are curtained with finely woven fabric. Dr. Layton's extensive psychotherapist credentials and accolades are tastefully framed and hang handsomely on the walls.

Dr. Layton has been seeing Jules and Eric as a couple for years. Dr. Layton is widely recognized for her expertise in relationship growth and enrichment, specialties that resonate hard with Jules and Eric, who've built a life around their marriage. From time to time, Dr. Layton sees Eric and Jules individually when one or the other needs a safe space to process their feelings and talk things through.

From Dr. Layton's perspective, Jules and Eric are an interesting couple—well-educated, well-off. They are both late bloomers, not coming into their own until they were in college, away from their parental units. Eric is the warmer of the two, at least initially. He has an approachable and easy way about him, which hides some of his darker tendencies. Eric feels more comfortable with a food processor than a lawn mower and takes primary responsibility for making their house a home.

He also has limited personal relationships outside of his relationship with Jules. He is quite close to his childhood best friend, Alex, who provides Eric with a strong sense of support, shared memories, and common history. Eric sees himself as an uncle to Alex's kids, a role that brings out a paternal side in him. He cherishes being 'Funcle Eric' and feeling part of an extended family.

Jules is more reserved. When she warms up, her wit and intelligence shine through. She takes the lead on the household finances and major decision-making and is highly ambitious, particularly in her career. But, as is common with ambitious people, Jules is seldom, if ever, completely satisfied. It was Jules who signed herself and Eric up for Dr. Layton's enrichment course and is the one actively seeking opportunities for them to grow as individuals and as a couple.

The subject of the couple's unexpressed bisexuality and ENM inclinations became a prominent theme in recent months. Dr. Layton wondered how these repressed parts of themselves would surface; when fantasizing about their desires was no longer enough. Although they both had previous same-sex relationships, bisexuality as a label is, at the same time, too big and too limiting for each of them in different ways. Emotional connection is the primary driver of Eric's sexuality, regardless of gender. Jules' sexuality is driven by her desire for personal freedom and power, without any constraints.

Eric had a few sexual encounters with men in college and in graduate school. Nothing that rose to the level of a relationship. Jules had serious romantic relationships with women in the past, and Eric feels certain that if he wasn't in the picture, she would be with a woman. While Eric prides himself on how well he knows Jules' body and his ability to give her pleasure, Jules' prior relationships with women remain a tacit source of insecurity for him. Dr. Layton suspects this is also a source of Eric's self-editing—restraining those parts of him he thinks Jules might find too aggressive. It remains unclear if, how, and when these parts of Eric will get expressed.

Jules has her own version of self-editing—self-censoring the vivid scenes she plays out in her head to protect Eric's feelings. Despite the couple's open lines of communication, each has subjects that are off-limits. Undiscussed. Particularly when it comes to ENM, neither of them had a clear idea of what it would look like in reality and kept some of their urges bottled up. In one-on-one sessions with each of them, Dr. Layton sensed that the pressure of these undiscussed needs and desires was building, especially for Jules, who, as of late, was seeing Dr. Layton on her own more frequently.

"On the count of three," Dr. Layton's soothing voice fills the space between the two women, "we will open our eyes, present, grounded, and ready for our session. One... Two... Three..."

Both women flutter their eyelids open, and Dr. Layton, in her soft yet firm manner, meets Jules' gaze. "Shall we pick up where we left off?"

"Yes. I'm ready," Jules affirms.

Dr. Layton briefly scans her notes. "Last session, you

and Eric were open to the idea of exploring additional aspects of your sexuality. In real life. How is that going?"

"Well… We got the app, and I have been looking for couples to meet. There is one couple that I just started chatting with. She is bi, he is straight, but they are the most normal couple I've found so far." Jules goes on to explain how challenging it has been to find other compatible couples.

"Is Eric part of the chat?" Dr. Layton asks.

"He knows the chat is happening, but he's not taking part. He's reluctant because the guy is straight. I understand his concerns, but…" Jules folds her arms over her chest, "I just want to start meeting people."

"I'm hearing frustration."

Jules nods her head in acknowledgment. "I guess it is frustration." After a brief pause, she adds, "Actually, it's anger. Not at Eric. At the situation. I have suppressed these parts of me for so long. *We* have suppressed these parts of who we are for so long."

Dr. Layton encourages Jules to say more.

"We have our safe haven at home where we can be ourselves. I can show my masculine sides. Eric can show his feminine sides. We can talk about our turn-ons and turn-offs. It's normalized in our house but nowhere else."

"Do you want to open the relationship so you can each see other people?"

Jules stands and walks over to the window before continuing. "Not completely, no. That would be too difficult. I'm afraid of what it would do to our relationship. But I'm also afraid of what this…this not doing anything is doing to our relationship. Eric and I—we have a life together with its own dynamic. One we have worked hard to achieve. I need somewhere to put this energy that won't break what we have. And he needs it, too."

"Why now?" asks Dr. Layton. "You've known about these parts of each other the whole time."

Jules takes her seat across from Dr. Layton. "It's hard to explain. I think it's a mix of feeling like our relationship is strong enough to act on these urges and feeling like I don't want life to go by without having these experiences and knowing these parts of myself. I feel willing to undertake some risk and put ourselves out there without as much fear about what other people might think or how this might impact our careers. All I know is that something has shifted in me, and the need to act on these feelings is only getting stronger. I just wish I knew what I was doing."

The evening sets in, streaking the sky with hues of gold and orange. Soft music fills the kitchen, punctuated by the sound of Eric's chef's knife chopping vegetables to prepare for dinner. Daisy, true to form, nestles at his feet, hoping for some food to drop. Eric is lost in thought, mulling over his earlier conversations with both Vickie and Sam.

"It smells wonderful in here," Jules announces as she walks in through the front door, leaving her bag and keys in the entryway. She has a dozen bright red roses wrapped in brown paper.

"Hi gorgeous," Eric responds, looking up. "Are those for me?"

"They are for you. I know they're your favorite."

Eric takes the flowers and buries his nose in the blossoms. "Thank you. They're beautiful. Let me get them in some water." Eric carefully lays the flowers out one by one, trims the stems, and arranges them in a vase.

Jules takes a seat at the kitchen island and watches him. She can tell by the look on his face that something is weighing on his mind. "How was your day?" she asks.

"Rough day," Eric responds. "Vickie almost quit on me."

"No!"

"Yes. We are asking too much of our people, especially her. I've got to figure something out."

"What are you going to do?" Jules asks.

"I don't know yet." Eric shakes his head. "And more budget cuts are coming, which isn't helping."

"Oh, babe," Jules says. "I'm sorry."

"Yeah. Me, too," Eric says. "And it gets worse. Vickie sat me down in her office and told me she was feeling hopeless about her job. That she feels like the state wants us to fail. She's dedicated her whole career to what we do, and she's one of the best we have. Not only are we screwed if she leaves, but I don't know how I would motivate anyone to replace her."

Jules reaches out to squeeze Eric's hand. "If anyone can figure this out, you can."

"I really hope so. What about you?" Eric asks. "How was your day?"

"I had a session with Dr. Layton today," Jules replies.

"Want to talk about it?"

"Nothing new or surprising," Jules dismisses. "Just trying to figure all of this ENM stuff out." Jules tilts her head down and rubs her temples. "I wish I knew what I was doing. I have this drive in me to do this, to explore. To find ways for us to be more fully expressed." She looks up to meet Eric's eyes. "But I have no idea what that looks like."

Eric empathizes. "I get it. I really do. You're not the only one who is frustrated. I wish I had an answer, but I don't know how to do this, either."

Jules steps around the island and reaches around Eric's waist, pressing a comforting kiss to the back of his neck. She chooses a fruit-forward Sauvignon Blanc from the wine rack, fills a glass, sits back down, and picks back up on the conversation. "I've been chatting with that couple on the app."

Eric looks up, tentative but also intrigued. "Yeah? Anything interesting?"

"I think so. They seem to have some experience dating other couples—not just one-night stands," Jules offers.

"That's what they all say." Eric stirs the vegetables, pulses some basil in the food processor, and puts a chicken in a roasting pan.

Jules lets the wine sit on her tongue before swallowing and then responding, "I think I want to meet them."

Eric's head snaps up. "Meet them? Are you sure? He's straight. This doesn't feel like a fit."

Jules' tone takes on a harder edge. "We just said this is wearing us both out, and what we've done so far isn't working. We need to put ourselves out there and start actually meeting people." Jules takes a breath before continuing, "I know it's not perfect, but I want to do this. I want us to do this. Can we just start seeing what other people are like?"

The background music amplifies the silence that falls between them as Eric works through his internal resistance. His logical brain knows she is right, but the tightness in his gut suggests otherwise. His logical brain wins. "Alright. Let's do it. Set it up."

Jules, pleased, leans over the island and kisses him. "Yes! Thank you."

The doorbell rings, and Jules announces, "That must be Madelyn. I'll get it." She opens the front door to find Madelyn standing under the glow of the entryway light, in full makeup, wearing a short, black dress with spaghetti straps and white and black python-printed heels, holding a bottle of wine in each hand. Jules cocks her head to the side and raises an eyebrow. "That's quite the look. I thought you were coming from the office to talk about work."

Madelyn shrugs nonchalantly, high heels clicking against the floor as she strides in past Jules. "I stopped home to change. Yum, it smells so good here. Is that pesto?"

Before she can give it any more thought, Jules' phone buzzes. She glances at the caller ID and calls out, "I'll be right in. I have to take this."

Jules steps into another room while Madelyn takes a seat across from Eric at the island. He hands her a glass and a bottle opener. "Hi, Madelyn. Haven't seen you in a while. How are things?"

Madelyn pours herself a glass. "Really good. Busy, you know. The usual." Madelyn's gaze drifts over Eric as he bends down to check the roasting chicken. "You're looking great."

"Flattery, my dear, will get you everywhere," Eric responds with an exaggerated flex of his biceps. "Jules said you wanted to come by to chat work?"

Madelyn swallows a big gulp of wine. "Yeah. Work. Jules always has the best advice."

"It's that big, sexy brain of hers." Eric checks the pots on the stove. "Dinner is just about ready. Can you help set the table?"

"Happy to," Madelyn beams.

Meanwhile, Kyra and John sit in a high-back booth at one of the trending new restaurants across town. Wine glasses are half full, and small plates of warm olives and fresh bread rest in front of them. There is a lit votive candle in the middle of the table, creating a pool of warm light against the white tablecloth, complimented by the dramatic, hanging light fixtures overhead. There is a hum of lively chatter from the surrounding tables and upbeat lounge music streaming through the speakers. The dinner rush is in full swing, and the clatter of pans echoes off the tile walls of the open kitchen.

John, handsome and still boyish despite a little gray in his temples, exudes a calm confidence. His green eyes sparkle and are fixed on Kyra in her low-cut black dress. John checks the time on his phone. "Charlie should be here in a few minutes. I can't wait for you to meet her. I think the two of you will get along great. She and I met our first week in college. We struggled through Calc 1 together. Our professor was, like, a thousand years old and wasn't going to spend his limited time left on earth explaining concepts to us. She found us a tutor, and we split the cost—we were both broke back then. It saved us from having to repeat the class."

"She's a clever one."

"She is. She's had my back ever since. And I've had hers."

"Did you ever date?"

"Charlie and me? No. She's always played solidly for the other team."

"Got it. Does she have a job lined up here?"

"She works for herself. Consulting. She keeps odd hours, but she sets her own schedule. Her clients are all over, so she gets to decide where she makes her home base. She does quite well for herself."

"Nice."

"Very."

A petite woman with dark hair, shaved on one side and long on the top, approaches the table and gently interrupts, "Excuse me, beautiful people. May I join you?" Her button-down shirt is crisp and white. A colorful tattoo peaks out from under one sleeve. She is strikingly attractive.

John's face cracks into a massive grin as he rises, wrapping Charlie in a hug that lifts her off the ground. "There you are! I've missed you so much." Releasing Charlie, John turns toward Kyra, "This is my best friend, sister from another mister, the one and only Charlie."

Charlie reciprocates John's greeting with a smile that lights up her face. "I've missed *you* so much." Turning her attention to Kyra, her eyes linger. "My," she pauses, seemingly lost for words, "John told me you were gorgeous, but… truly, you are stunning."

Kyra's cheeks flush pink with the compliment as she slides over, patting the seat next to her. "It's so nice to meet you. Please...sit." She reaches for the wine bottle and pours Charlie a glass. "I hear you moved back into town."

Charlie picks up the glass of wine and the conversation thread. "Yes. Just recently moved back. Still getting settled into my new place. I found a spot close to John."

Kyra smiles in acknowledgment. "It's so nice to be close to friends."

Charlie tilts her head in John's direction. "Especially this guy. We were inseparable back in the day."

John's smile widens. "We were each other's wing person."

Kyra raises her eyebrows. "Is that so?"

John nods, chuckling, "Yes. Often. We learned each other's types really quickly."

"Did it ever get complicated?" Kyra asks. "Like if you both fell for the same woman?"

Charlie and John answer simultaneously. "That hasn't happened."

"Nope—never."

Back at Eric's and Jules' house, Eric, Jules, and Madelyn sit around the dinner table, mid-meal, plates half empty. Their conversation is sporadic and hesitant. Eric and Jules have nearly full wine glasses. Madelyn drains the last of hers and generously pours herself another before attempting to jump-start the conversation. "Eric, this meal is fantastic. I hope you'll share your recipe."

Eric throws a questioning look at Jules, his eyebrows

creased slightly. Jules responds with an imperceptible shrug, as baffled as he is.

"So, Madelyn, you mentioned wanting to discuss work. How can I help?" Jules asks.

"Right, work." Madelyn hesitates before responding further, swirling the wine in her glass. "Actually, before we get into that… I was hoping we could talk a bit more about your, um, experiment…"

Jules nearly chokes on her food.

"Our, um, what?" Eric asks.

Jules turns to Eric, quick to explain. "Kyra has been encouraging me to come out more, especially among friends. It came up at the coffee shop yesterday, and I told the girls about it. About us."

"I see," Eric replies, surprise evident on his face.

Madelyn leans in slightly, her movements unhurried and deliberate. Her fingers glide over Jules's wrist, a light, teasing touch that lingers. Her gaze locks onto Eric's, a playful glint in her eyes. "Yes," she says, her voice low and smooth, "I'm very curious about how it all… works." Her lips part slightly as she draws out the last word.

Back at the restaurant across town, Kyra, John, and Charlie are cozy in their booth, plates empty, conversation flowing. Charlie and John pick up right where they left off, sharing stories of their college adventures like no time has passed. As the wine glasses empty, the stories become more animated, their gestures more expressive.

"…and then this guy over here looks in the rear-view

mirror to see his girlfriend in the car behind him, and he's totally busted!" Charlie exclaims, head tilting toward John. John's cheeks flush, remembering the night in question, as Kyra's shoulders shake with laughter. Passing servers offer small, curious smiles.

Kyra, wiping tears from her eyes, turns to John. "You were quite the wild one in college!" she teases.

John responds with an exaggerated gesture. "I don't know about that. I was definitely getting myself into trouble, though."

Charlie chuckles, taking another sip of her wine. "You couldn't keep yourself out of strip clubs!"

John, grin widening, "I kind of still can't."

Kyra leans in, eyes sparkling. "I like them, too."

Charlie raises an eyebrow, a smile stretching across her face. "That makes three of us."

John raises his hand, signals the server for the check, and reaches for his phone to order a rideshare. "So, um, since we're all in agreement, I know where we're heading next. You know," he says, glancing towards Charlie, "for old times' sake."

Caught off guard, Jules and Eric stare at Madelyn, her statement floating like a provocative dare. Their surprise is mixed with a sense of intrigue, an unspoken curiosity lingering beneath their initial shock. Neither of them experienced a threesome before.

Madelyn wastes no time. She lifts her hand to Jules, her fingers lightly tracing the outline of her face before leaning in to kiss her. Eric, still seated, watches. He is intent, fascinated, and growing increasingly excited. As Madelyn breaks from Jules to make eye contact with Eric, a new dynamic takes form.

Eric stands and navigates his way around the table. He begins by kissing Jules' neck, his lips traveling upwards until they meet hers in a heated exchange. He then turns his attention to Madelyn, their lips meeting, slow at first, then more urgent.

Jules watches the scene unfold before her, a spectator and participant in this unexpected turn of events. There is uncertainty, yes, but there's also a thrill that radiates through her. This is new, this is unknown, and, for now, it's all going well.

The rideshare driver takes Kyra, Charlie, and John, crammed into the backseat, to a semi-industrial part of town and drops them off in the poorly lit parking lot of an old brick warehouse building. The building is painted black, with blacked-out windows, and the only signage is a magenta neon cowboy hat perched above the door, which is guarded by two very large bouncers, also dressed in all black. As they approach the entrance, Kyra, Charlie, and John feel the music before they hear it. John flashes a membership card and pays the cover for all three of them.

Inside is a world of color and sound. Flashing red, fuchsia, and purple LED lights bounce off the mirrored walls, and the music is a mix of country and electronic with a sinewy, sultry bass line. Spread out across the vast, white lacquer stage are adult versions of carousel animals, beautifully sculpted and mounted on brass poles that would rise and fall in loose time with the music. Servers wear neon-colored thongs, tasseled holsters and pasties, cowboy boots, and matching hats, indulging guests with a table dance when the right amount of tip money is flashed. The stage dancers, in various states of undress, writhe on the backs of the carved horses, show off their acrobatic skills on the poles, and collect ones, fives, and the occasional twenty from the fingers of their rapt audience.

Kyra, John, and Charlie are in their own world, bubbling with laughter, sugary cocktails, and shared excitement. John's arm wraps around Kyra while his eyes fixate on the dancers all around them. A dancer approaches with her focus on Charlie, using the sway of her hips to wiggle into her lap. Charlie spreads her legs, making room for the dancer to get closer as Kyra watches, curiosity gleaming in her eyes. Charlie and the dancer move to the rhythm, bodies flirting with the pulsating music. As Charlie glances back toward Kyra, their eyes lock, a palpable tension between them. The dancer, picking up on the connection, doesn't miss a beat. She reaches out, extending an inviting hand to Kyra. With only a slight hesitation, Kyra moves out from under John's hold and meets Charlie in a bold, unanticipated kiss. The sight captivates John. He watches, arousal coursing through him.

"Let's take this back to my place," he says, signaling the bouncer to call a taxi to the front.

✧

Jules is now pressed between Eric and Madelyn. Madelyn's fingers navigate the buttons of Jules' shirt, and her gaze flicks between the couple, a sly smile plastered on her lips. With a small step backward, Madelyn slides down the spaghetti straps from her shoulders, her dress cascading to the floor, leaving her fully exposed to the eyes of Jules and Eric.

Re-approaching, Madelyn's aim becomes clear. She glides towards Eric, pressing up against him, their lips meeting in a passionate kiss, igniting a fire within him. He kisses Madelyn back hard, his tongue finding hers, her arms coming up to grip the hard muscles of his back.

⚘

The front door to John's house swings open, and Kyra, John, and Charlie tumble inside, laughter bouncing off the walls. John pulls off his shirt in one swift motion. Charlie helps Kyra out of her dress, their eyes gleaming with an implicit understanding.

The playful encounter escalates as laughter gives way to soft gasps and whispered words, clothes slipping off and landing in scattered piles across the floor. The room is alive with heat and anticipation, a tangle of limbs and desire. Charlie and John guide Kyra to the bed, laying her down with tender hands, their touches both teasing and deliberate.

Kyra's breath hitches as Charlie's lips trail across her collarbone, feather-light but electric, while John's hands explore the curve of her hips, his fingers pressing into her skin. A low hum of pleasure escapes Kyra's lips, her hands instinctively fisting in John's hair, pulling him closer, while her other hand roams over Charlie's soft, warm skin, making her shiver.

The energy between them intensifies, a rhythm forming as the three become more entwined, each movement sparking a ripple of pleasure that seems to echo between them. Their breaths mingle, the air thick with the scent of skin and the sound of soft moans. Charlie's laughter melts into a satisfied sigh as Kyra's nails graze her back, and John's lips find Kyra's neck, murmuring something she can't quite hear but feels deep in her core.

John shifts, positioning himself between Kyra's thighs, his movements both confident and reverent. "You feel so good," he murmurs against her skin, his voice thick and unsteady as he gives in to the moment. A shudder rolls through him, breath catching, before a deep, guttural moan escapes his lips. His body tenses, his face reflecting the satisfaction coursing through him, before collapsing between the two women, chest heaving with aftershocks.

Charlie and Kyra exchange a look, a small, knowing smile passing between them as John's breathing slows. With a triumphant grin, he drifts into sleep, his body nestled against theirs. Kyra brushes a lock of hair from John's forehead before she turns back to Charlie, lips curving into a smile.

The night isn't over yet.

Charlie and Kyra continue on, exploring each other, tasting each other, each achieving multiple peaks of satisfaction. The hours wane, and the women curl up in a sweet embrace, Kyra tracing gentle patterns across the light brown freckles on Charlie's nose, forehead, and cheeks while John snores contently beside them.

⁊

Back at Jules' and Eric's, the dynamics have taken a turn. Madelyn's full attention is on Eric, leaving Jules sidelined.

"Madelyn, I had no idea you were bi," she says, attempting to slow things down.

In response, Madelyn unzips Eric's pants and sinks to her knees. Looking up, she replies, "I'm not," before taking Eric all the way into her mouth. Eric's satisfaction is obvious from his reaction, a sharp contrast to Jules, who watches from a few feet away, visibly upset.

"What do you mean you're not bi?" Jules presses, tone rising.

It's unclear if Madelyn doesn't hear the question or is actively choosing to ignore it.

"What do you mean you're not bi?" Jules' voice climbs in pitch. "Take my husband's cock out of your mouth and answer me."

Madelyn's lips break contact with Eric, eyebrows knitting together in surprise. "Whoa, Jules—take it down a notch. I thought you and Eric were into this."

"You need to leave, Madelyn," Jules retorts, her voice unyielding.

"Jules!" Eric interjects.

"Now!" Jules' voice echoes around the room, leaving no room for negotiation. Madelyn rises, slipping her dress back over her head. She glances back, realizing things went too far. Regret flashes across her face.

"Jules… I'm really…" she begins, but Jules cuts her off. "Out!"

As Madelyn exits, Jules puts her shirt back on and moves towards the kitchen. Her body slumps onto a stool at the island, head cradled in her hands. Eric follows her, buttoning up his pants, his expression a mixture of confusion, frustration, and concern.

"What was that?" he asks, struggling to understand.

"What do you mean, what was that?" Jules answers, her voice shaking, tears welling in her eyes. "We agreed we'd go slow. That was not slow."

"I wasn't the one that escalated it," Eric counters defensively.

"You didn't slow anything down," Jules snaps back.

"It kind of felt right. I thought you were feeling it, too," Eric argues, matching her tone.

"I was not," Jules states flatly.

"Clearly."

Turning her back to him, Jules tries to maintain some composure. "She was all over you. I had to just sit there and watch. She was using me to get you turned on—she's not even bi, did you not catch that?" Jules' voice trails off, hurt lacing her words. "You just let her."

Eric stammers, "Babe, I'm sorry. It happened really fast. I don't know what I'm doing. I don't know what *we're* doing."

Jules' tears flow freely. "I have no idea what we are doing, either. I want us to be able to do things like this, but that was too much. I wasn't ready." Her voice cracks, "I... I wasn't prepared."

"Come here," Eric pulls her into his arms. Jules doesn't reciprocate and breaks away. "I felt so shut out. So disconnected from you. I... I don't know how to do this." Jules' voice cracks.

"That makes two of us," Eric responds. He approaches

Jules once more, drawing her into his arms again. Slowly, Jules begins to soften, her arms gradually encircling him in return. He rocks her gently, side to side. "I'm sorry it, um, *went down* like that," Eric says.

A half-sob, half-laugh escapes Jules. "Not funny."

Eric kisses her forehead and whispers, "I fucking love you."

CHAPTER 2

OPEN-ISH FOR BUSINESS

It's only been a handful of days since the encounter with Madelyn.

Jules paces back and forth in front of the windows in Dr. Layton's office, eyes red and swollen. She opens and then closes her mouth, struggling to find the right words.

"Take your time," says Dr. Layton. "I know this is hard for you."

Jules' upper spine curves forward, and she drops her head. She can't remember ever feeling so overwhelmed and uncomfortable with emotion, not even when her parents split up.

Jules grew up an only child, and her parents divorced right before Jules graduated high school. She remembers the years before the divorce as quiet. Silent. Unlike some of her other friends' parents, there was no arguing. No fighting. No communication. No love.

Jules couldn't pinpoint when exactly her parents stopped loving each other, but she could remember when it became unacceptable to show any emotion. It was like someone turned the volume off in her home. Meals were eaten in silence. No friends over. No radio in the car when she was taken to or picked up from school. Even the television was watched on low volume. Jules came to understand that silence was her parents' way of keeping the peace.

Jules made some pocket money working over summer break, and when the noise level in the house dropped to zero, she got herself a pair of headphones. The best she could afford. She created for herself an inner world of music, a soundtrack for her imagination. Jules would lie back in her twin bed, stare up at her ceiling, and let her mind roam. She would lose herself in the stacks of books she checked out of the library and let herself be moved deeply by the characters. She found between the pages an emotional range that did not exist in her household and often wept into her pillow as she approached the last page, happy or sad outcome notwithstanding. She would picture the narratives like a movie in her mind. On occasion, she would add herself to the story and reimagine the endings, scored with the music streaming through her earpieces. Sometimes, she got the guy. Sometimes, she got the girl. Sometimes, she got her heart broken.

In a sketchbook she kept tucked in between her mattress and box spring, she would sketch her favorite scenes between journal entries and cut out poems and quotes she collected and pasted in with a purple glue stick. She would draw and fantasize about who she was crushing on at the moment, the conversations they would have, where they would go on their first date. If her feelings were strong, her mind would wander to what they would do together if left alone. What they would smell like. What their lips would taste like. What music they would be listening to in the background.

Jules felt very comfortable in the world she built inside her head. It was the only place she felt safe with her feelings. It was far less lonely than the world that existed outside her childhood bedroom door. This began a pattern for Jules. When emotions were new or became difficult, she would retreat inward, turning her feelings over and over until she could make sense of them. Sometimes, this happened quickly. Sometimes, it took longer.

When Jules addresses Dr. Layton, her voice is shaky. "It happened so fast… I know this is what I said I wanted, but…I wasn't prepared."

Dr. Layton responds from her seat across the room, "I understand."

"And Eric," Jules drops down on the tailored sofa, "he just let her do it. He let it escalate. Like I wasn't even there. I can't get the images out of my head. I'm so angry. I feel so stupid."

"Have you spoken with Eric about how you're feeling?" Dr. Layton asks.

"I can't. I'm not ready. I haven't sorted myself out yet."

In his own separate session with Dr. Layton, Eric unpacks his side of the story. "We didn't have any ground rules. I understand that better now. Eric's gaze shifts downward, recalling the details of the evening. "And Madelyn, well, it was like she was on a hunt. I was so turned on by the attention, to be wanted like that by someone else. Someone new." He pauses, taking a moment to compose his thoughts. "I'm not even sure if it was me she wanted. Or to mess with Jules. Or both. Madelyn has always been flirty, but I didn't see this coming. I feel like I should have seen this coming."

Dr. Layton nods, encouraging Eric to say more.

"I'm so mad at myself, and I'm so mad at Jules." Eric's voice is raw. "I know it's not rational, but Jules is the one who wanted this. To explore more. I apologized for what happened, and I thought we were okay. Or, at least, ok enough. But we're not. Her walls are way up, and she isn't talking to me." He swallows hard, eyes meeting Dr. Layton's, searching for reassurance.

Eric was familiar with Jules' pattern of shutting down in the face of uncertainty and emotional discomfort. When she's unsure what to say or how it will come out, she stops communicating. Eric recognizes what it is when it happens, but it doesn't change how it makes him feel: alone, insecure, and abandoned.

"I don't know how to fix this, Dr. Layton. The not speaking to me… It's making me nuts. I know she needs time, but I feel so shut out and isolated. I don't do well when I feel like this."

"You were there, Claire," Madelyn chews on her thumbnail, her tone a mix of defensiveness and irritation. "Jules said they were into this kind of thing, did she not?"

"Yes, ma'am. She sure did," Claire confirms.

The women sit across from one another on Madelyn's couch, two full glasses of wine between them, while Madelyn shares the details of her night with Eric and Jules. "I don't see how this is on me, how suddenly I'm the bad guy. One minute, they were totally into it, and the next…"

"So, what exactly happened?" Claire asks.

"Well," Madelyn takes a big gulp of her wine, "after Jules made her announcement at the coffee shop the other morning, I got to thinking. I've always wanted to have a threeway, and Eric…"

"Eric is so darn handsome," Claire interjects.

"He is," Madelyn agrees. "And he's such a flirt. I can't help but think that this whole ethically non-monogamous talk is an early warning signal of the demise of their marriage. I mean, really? Who does that? I'm not going to let an opportunity like Eric pass me by. So, I came home to change after work and put on the spaghetti strap dress."

"Ooohhh, you look so good in that one…"

"I do." Madelyn winks. "So, I get there, and Eric and I are drinking wine while Jules is in the other room taking a work call. Eric was making dinner—a man who can cook is so damn sexy. We flirt and drink, and when we all sit down to dinner, things start to…you know, heat up."

"I don't know, Madelyn. Tell me." Claire's eyes are eager with anticipation.

"Well, it started with me kissing Jules," Madelyn says, "which, by the way, Eric was totally into. And then he and I started kissing, and everything was going well. Really well. I felt him connecting with me. It was so hot. But when I took him into my mouth…"

"Wait. You what?!" Claire interrupts.

"I went down on him, and Jules lost it," Madelyn responds flatly.

"Madelyn! Of course she lost it. Did you talk about doing that beforehand?"

"No," Madelyn's tone turns defensive, "but if you were there…"

Claire shakes her head. "I don't think so, Madelyn. That seems really aggressive and sort of unsolicited."

"Well, Eric didn't seem to think so. He was hard as a rock."

Claire sets her wine glass down and gives Madelyn a disapproving glare. "Madelyn, he's a man. Of course he was hard as a rock."

"I think it was more than that, Claire. I felt a spark. A connection. I feel bad about Jules, but she kind of brought this on herself."

"Have you spoken to him?"

"I've messaged him. No response."

"Well, I wouldn't expect one if I were you," Claire says.

"We'll see, Claire. I know what I felt."

Later that evening, after supper, Claire sits, spine erect, in the floral print-covered armchair in the living room she shares with Jerry. She is in a bubble gum pink satin robe with a feathery collar. The feathers match her pink, kitten-heeled mules and her open lace pink eye mask. Jerry is on all fours, naked except for a black leather collar and a black leather dog mask. His head lies in Claire's lap while she pets him.

"Mama loves her puppy, doesn't she?" Claire murmurs.

Jerry pants in return.

"And Puppy loves his mama, isn't that right?" Claire continues.

Jerry pants a little harder.

"Good boy. Now, what that silly Jules and Eric did, inviting Miss Madelyn into their sex life with that filthy threesome sex talk? That is not something we do, is it, Puppy?"

Jerry doesn't respond.

Claire's expression turns serious as she wraps her fingers around the inside of Jerry's collar, making it taut around his neck. "Now listen here, Puppy. Mama does not like strays. Not one little bit. Puppy understands what Mama is saying, right?"

Jerry lifts his head as he braces against the tension, his panting straining. Claire pulls harder until Jerry goes breathless. She releases, and his head falls back into her lap.

∾

Kyra sits on one side of the back booth of a half-empty bar facing Jules. Cocktails sweat in the tall glasses in front of each of them. The atmosphere is heavy. Jules absentmind-edly stirs her drink with a straw, the ice cubes clinking around the glass, eyes cast downward as they wait for Beth to arrive. Kyra has never seen Jules this despondent before and isn't sure what to say.

Kyra is the youngest of three, the only girl. She came along later in her parents' life, the unplanned-for cherry on top, they would say. She is especially close to her middle brother, Tommy, who, like her, hadn't yet settled down and showed no signs of doing so. Thank goodness for her eldest brother, who is married with two children, taking the pressure off when it comes to grandchildren. Kyra shined in her people skills—a ten out of ten on likability. She met Jules and Beth at the gym in boxing class. Jules was intense, all business once her gloves were on. Beth spent most of her time making jokes. Kyra overheard one of her jokes in class one day and couldn't help but start giggling. The laughing was contagious, and soon, half the class was bent over and cracking up. Beth loved it, and before long, she and Kyra became friends, quickly followed by Jules.

Jules had been a pleasant surprise. Despite her tough exterior, Kyra found her to be soft underneath. Unexpectedly sensitive and empathetic, Jules became an excellent friend. She was caring, astute, and didn't mince words when it came to advice and sorting through problems. Jules supported Kyra through countless breakups and just as many rebounds, always patiently and attentively listening. From Kyra's point of view, Jules' relationship with Eric was extremely special, one of the few positive examples Kyra got to see up close. When Jules came out to Kyra about their sexuality, it made Kyra feel very close to her, very trusted.

Kyra and Jules had been out for a coffee when Kyra opened up to Jules about a woman she had been seeing. Kyra liked the woman well enough but wasn't looking for anything serious, and certainly not anything exclusive. The woman not only wanted Kyra to herself but was adamant about Kyra no longer dating men. Kyra wasn't ready to end the relationship, but she wasn't ready for these constraints either and didn't take well to the ultimatum. Jules listened, offered her support, and then confided in Kyra that she and Eric were also bisexual with non-monogamish tendencies, but hadn't really done anything about it since they got together.

Years went by after that conversation, and when Jules told Kyra that she and Eric were thinking about dating other couples, Kyra was thrilled. It was an opportunity for Kyra to support Jules the way Jules had supported her. Kyra suspected there would be bumps along the way, but not like this. Not right out of the gate.

"Sorry I'm late," Beth says, taking the seat next to Kyra. Reaching out, she takes Jules' hand and gives it a light squeeze. "How are you doing, my friend? Things getting a little easier?"

Jules barely squeezes back. "Talking to Dr. Layton helps."

Kyra shifts in her seat, her brow furrowing. "Well, Madelyn feels like a total asshole."

Jules and Beth respond in unison. "She is a total asshole."

Kyra holds her hands up in a gesture of surrender. "I don't disagree. At least she knows what she did."

"Yes. At least she's a self-aware asshole," Beth adds with her characteristic sarcasm.

"Always seeing the bright side, Beth," Jules retorts, her face breaking into a weak grin.

"There it is!" says Beth. "There's the smile we all love."

Jules blows Beth a pouty kiss. Beth always knows how to make her feel better. Jules exhales heavily and attempts to shift subjects. "What's new with you and Alex? How are the boys?"

"We're good," Beth replies. "Worried about you guys. Eric told Alex you haven't been speaking."

Jules casts her eyes downward. "This is unfamiliar territory. It's so tense right now. I thought I was ok, but I'm not. I can't get out of my own head, and I don't want to say anything that will make things worse."

"I get it," Beth says to Jules. "I know how hard it is to think about someone you love having feelings for someone else. Even, like in your case, if it's fleeting. You were there when it happened to me."

"Wait," Kyra interjects, "I don't know this story. What happened?"

"We were in business school," Beth says, facing Kyra. "Mason was just a toddler when my ex fell for someone else. Not just temporary, either. He left me for her. Left the family we made together for her. He didn't just screw her, he screwed my whole life. I wasn't sure I was going to be able to complete the program. I could barely get myself out of bed."

"Of course you were going to complete the program. I wasn't going to let you drop out because of what he did," Jules adds.

"And I am very grateful to you for that," Beth says. "The point is, I know you're hurting, but it's not the same. You are the center of Eric's universe. Whatever he might have felt in that moment, whatever it is you think you saw, it's nothing compared to what he feels for you."

Jules shrugs, averting her eyes. "Please, I need a break from talking about this."

Kyra reaches into her bag and pulls out a tin of THC gummies, which she passes to Jules. "Here, take one of these. It will help." Sensing Jules' reluctance, Kyra adds, "Don't worry. I'm driving. I'll get you home safely."

Jules relents, takes one of the sugary gummies out of the tin, and swallows it. Kyra offers the tin to Beth, who politely declines and steers the conversation to Kyra. "What's going on with you and your new friend, John?"

Kyra's face lights up, and she squeals, "Girl, he is so fucking hot!"

Jules leans in, grateful for the uplift in mood. "Tell us the good stuff. And don't leave anything out."

Kyra also leans in and drops her voice to a whisper. "It's getting more serious, I think. I see him almost every night."

Jules grins and looks at Beth. "New relationships are so sweet."

"So sweet," Beth adds, smiling at Kyra. "You have that new relationship energy."

Their conversation flows more freely as Kyra shares further details about John and the time they've been spending together.

"You're gushing," Jules teases. "Like, really gushing. I don't think I've ever seen you crush this hard."

Kyra widens her eyes. "I know, right? He's got a brain. He works out…"

Jules gives an approving nod.

"He's got a steady job, a place of his own, and…a wild side. Like me." Kyra lets the last statement hang.

"What do you mean?" asks Beth.

Kyra drops her voice again. "We had a night. Me, John, and Charlie. It was so fucking hot."

"Charlie? As in John's best friend?" Jules asks, surprised.

Kyra grins and nods. "That's the one."

Beth tilts her head back and laughs to herself. "God, my life is so boring."

"That's close to home, girl. You be careful," Jules warns, but Kyra shrugs it off.

The women continue sipping their drinks and chatting, and after about thirty minutes, a wave of calm washes over Jules. Her shoulders relax, and her whole countenance softens. "Mother of Pearl, Kyra. These gummies are strong. My whole body just started tingling."

Kyra rubs her palms together. "My evil plan is working. C'mon. Let's get you home."

Jules' head leans against the passenger side window of Kyra's car, eyes glassy, smile serene. Kyra drives through puddles of warm light cast by overhead street lamps. The music in the car is soft. Easy. For the first time since the encounter with Madelyn, Jules' breath is deep and not shallow.

"How're you doing over there?" Kyra asks, stealing a glance at Jules.

Jules smiles wider in response, cheeks flushing. They ride together like that, with just music in the background, until they reach Jules' and Eric's home. Pulling up in front, Kyra steps out of the car and walks Jules to the front door.

"Go make things right," Kyra says with a serious tone, followed by a peck on Jules' cheek, who steps inside and locks the door behind her.

The house is quiet, save for the low hum of the refrigerator. Only the kitchen lights are on, and Eric sits at the island, shirtless and scrolling on his phone. Daisy is curled up by his feet. He looks up at her arrival. Their eyes meet.

Without breaking eye contact, Eric slides off the stool and onto his hands and knees. Slowly, like a cat, he crawls across the room toward Jules. He circles her feet then stops, kneeling in front of her, facing away. He is physically close to Jules but not touching.

Jules can feel the warmth radiating off him. Her breath deepens, and the tension builds. A moment passes, and Jules presses her legs against Eric's back. This is their first physical contact since the encounter with Madelyn. Eric releases a loud sigh, and his shoulders drop. Eric has learned, over the years, to give Jules space to process her feelings, but it's not without sacrifice. Jules' retreats into the far corners of her mind take an emotional toll on Eric, leaving him feeling alone, longing. Moments like these, her re-emergence, feel to Eric like homecoming. His insecurity lifts, and it's as if he can breathe again.

Another moment passes, and Jules' hands find Eric's neck and shoulders. Her strokes are soft, and he lets some of his weight press back into her. Emboldened and clumsy from the effects of the gummy, Jules grabs a fistful of Eric's hair and pulls.

"OUCH!" Eric winces and pulls his head away.

Jules' eyes widen, and she lets go immediately. "Oh, God. I'm sorry."

Eric shakes it off, "It's ok. It's ok." He resumes his position, and they stay there, collecting themselves, each wanting to continue, each wanting more contact.

Jules takes another deep breath and, with a more

measured touch, grabs Eric by the hair again. Bigger fistful this time, not as abrupt. A groan of pleasure escapes Eric's lips as he tilts his head back. Stepping to the side of him, Jules pulls him by the hair back down to all fours and leads him to the sofa. With a subtle tug, she guides his torso upward so that his upper body lies flat over the ottoman, bent at the waist, knees and shins on the floor.

She takes in the sight of him as he lies in front of her, letting time stretch out. His back muscles are tense with anticipation, his face turned away. He twitches when she makes circles on his back with her fingertips, light at first, then with increasing pressure. Feeling more confident, she leans down over him.

She presses her mouth against his bare back, gently grazing his skin with her lips and then teeth. The hiss that escapes Eric's lips is encouragement for Jules to continue. She takes his flesh between her teeth and bites softly. Eric's moan changes, taking on an achy quality. Jules bites harder. Eric's spine arches and trembles as she alternates between biting and kissing.

Eric can no longer keep still. He flips over and pushes Jules onto her back, expertly dragging her shirt up with his teeth and, through her bra, takes her nipple into his mouth, biting back. Jules feeds his urgency, raising her skirt, and widens her legs. Eric, hunger now in his eyes, pulls down her panties, unzips his jeans, and slips in, filling her entirely. Jules lets out an audible exhale, and her fingers dig into his shoulders. She holds him there, and they make love fiercely, eyes never breaking contact.

"I'm so sorry," Eric breathes out, voice strained.

"I'm so sorry," Jules echoes.

"I love you," Eric continues, pushing into her harder.

"I love you more," Jules replies, pulling him closer. Eric's body shudders, and Jules holds him in her arms, feeling the hot wetness fill her. Their breath slows, and their bodies untangle to lie side by side, facing one another.

"I didn't mean for it to go that way." Eric's voice is quiet but steady.

"I know," Jules replies. "I didn't either."

"We should have talked beforehand," Eric says.

"I know that now." Jules nods in agreement. "It happened so fast. I got caught off guard."

Eric's tone firms, "I get it. I really do. I'm sure it was hard for you. But you can't ignore me like this. It's too much."

"I didn't know what to say, and I didn't want to make things worse. I was so angry. I'm still angry," Jules rebuts.

"I know. I am, too. But I wouldn't have agreed to do this if I knew you were going to shut me out." Frustration lies heavy in Eric's reply.

"You're right," Jules murmurs, "I'm sorry." Her fingers trace patterns on his bare chest.

"Me, too," Eric responds, his hand covering hers and pressing it against his heart.

"I missed you," Jules whispers.

"I always miss you." He stands, hand never leaving hers. "Let's go to bed."

They make their way to the bedroom, fingers interlaced, Daisy trotting closely behind.

Morning light filters into the bedroom after a night of deep, restful sleep. Eric stirs and opens his eyes. Jules lies facing him, already awake and watching him.

"Uh-oh," are his first words.

"Good morning," Jules greets him.

"Mornin'," Eric responds tentatively.

"I want to keep going," Jules announces.

"How do you mean?" he asks, brow furrowing.

"I'm not going to let Madelyn ruin this for us. We started down this path for a reason. I don't want us to bail after the first setback."

He rolls onto his back, forearm covering his forehead as he processes what Jules is saying.

Jules continues, "I know this was fucked up, but I don't want to stop. I want us to figure this out. Figure out ways we can express these parts of ourselves."

Eric lets the weight of Jules' statements settle in. "I do, too," Eric eventually says. "But I need to know that we are going to keep the lines of communication open. This only works if we are open and honest with each other."

"I understand." Jules nods her agreement.

"And we have ground rules," Eric asserts.

"Absolutely," Jules concurs.

"So, what exactly do you have in mind?" Eric asks, turning again to face her.

"I still want to go on a couple date with Miles and Elena. From the app," Jules answers.

"The straight guy?" Eric raises an eyebrow.

"I know he's straight," Jules acknowledges. "I just want to meet them. I want to see what other couples are like. Worst-case scenario, they can give us some advice on how to make this work."

Eric goes quiet. Again, his logical brain understands what Jules wants to do, but his gut is reluctant, and after what he just went through with Jules, he doesn't feel like he can tell her no.

"Ok," he finally responds.

"Ok?" Jules confirms.

"Ok," Eric repeats.

"Thank you!" Jules exclaims, leaning in to peck Eric on the cheek. "I'll set it up when I get a break at work today."

Jules slips out from under the covers, steps into the bathroom, and turns on the shower, leaving Eric alone in bed. He turns onto his side and checks his phone, a text notification from Madelyn from the night before prominent on his home screen. Without a word, he puts his phone face down on his night table and sits up to start the day.

Jules is immaculate in her navy blue suit, the first to arrive in the conference room for the morning team meeting. She looks over her notes while Will, Seth, and Hunter file in, sharing the highlights of the night before, Dylan just a few steps behind. Dylan, without being asked, shares details from his evening, his pitch a little too loud, overbearing. The receptionist, efficient and silent, sets up the breakfast and coffee service for the group before discreetly exiting the room.

"So, Julia, are you going to kill another deal for us today?" Hunter sneers.

"Only if it's a bad one," Jules counters without looking up from her notebook, her tone level.

Seth snorts, pointing at his buddy. "Ha! She got you, dude!"

"It's not always about the numbers," Hunter retorts, trying to regain his footing.

"Actually…it is." Jules leans back in her chair, locking eyes with Hunter. The room quiets, tension building as Jules and Hunter hold their gaze. She wasn't expecting to spar professionally this morning, but since it was happening, she would enjoy it.

"Hey, Julia. Can you grab me a coffee?" Dylan interrupts, his words slicing through the silence.

Hunter, Will, and Seth freeze. Jules doesn't flinch. She shifts her gaze from Hunter to Dylan, meeting his stare head-on.

Peter enters, completely unaware of the dominance struggle at play. "All right, everyone. Let's get started."

Dylan looks away first, a smug smirk on his face, as the meeting proceeds. Each team member reports on the status of their respective projects, coming to agreement on next steps. Peter adjourns the meeting, and as the associates file out, Jules notices the crumpled, used napkin Dylan left behind on the conference table. She rolls her eyes to herself and looks up to find Dylan watching her, the same smug smirk on his face.

As Jules stands to leave, Peter asks, "Julia, how is that research we talked about coming along?"

"I should be finished soon. So far, your instincts are correct. They would be an excellent co-lead for us on this deal, which would help us de-risk and free up significant capital. I have a little more research to do to confirm, but it's looking good."

"Do you think it's a go?"

"I'm reserving my opinion until my research is complete, but early indications are a yes. I think this will be a big win for us if everything checks out. Our competition will never see this coming."

"Great, Julia. I look forward to your conclusions."

Across town, John and Kyra share a quiet morning in John's kitchen. Kyra is at the breakfast table, wearing one of John's t-shirts, hair still mussed from sex and sleep. John busies himself making coffee, then sits down opposite Kyra, a mug in each hand.

"I could get used to these lazy mornings," John comments, taking his first sip.

"Me, too," Kyra replies, her smile warm over her cup.

"So, um, how was your visit with Jules and Beth?"

"It was good to see them. It always is. They wanted to know more about you, of course. I told them all the good stuff," Kyra responds, a playful note in her voice.

"I can only imagine…" John's cheeks lightly blush. "How's Jules? Is she doing any better?"

"I think so. That encounter with Madelyn was rough for her. For both of them. No one really talks about when threesomes go wrong," Kyra responds.

"Do you think they go wrong often?" John asks.

"Probably. Especially for people like Jules and Eric—it's more than just play for them. Threeways get so glorified, but sometimes real feelings are involved," Kyra continues.

"I guess I never thought too hard about it. That's never been an issue for me." John shrugs.

"How many have you had?!" Kyra's eyes go wide.

"Not tons. But more than a few. Always casual," John confesses.

"Always two women?" Kyra prods.

"To my knowledge, um, yes," John replies, his eyes meeting Kyra's.

Kyra lets a moment pass and then continues, "You know I would be ok if that wasn't the case."

"I appreciate that," John acknowledges. "But that's not my thing."

"I get that… I get that. It is my thing, though," Kyra's eyes stay locked on John's.

"What do you mean?" John asks.

"I'm bisexual," Kyra states.

"That was obvious the other night," John teases lightly.

"Well, yeah. But it's important to me that you understand. I'm interested in both men and women—not just casual," Kyra explains, her tone serious.

"Ok," John acknowledges, non-plussed.

"Ok?" Kyra asks.

"So, you have relationships with other women. I'm ok with that."

"You're ok if I have relationships outside of… Wait, what

is it that we're doing here?" Kyra probes, a light tone of teasing in her voice.

"I'm ok with you dating other women. That doesn't bother me. Men, though, I want that to be me," John affirms, resolute.

"My only man, huh," Kyra murmurs, a slow smile spreading across her face.

"Yes," he confirms, his gaze unwavering.

Kyra moves closer to John, smoothly sliding onto his lap.

"So," Kyra asks, "does this mean we're going steady?"

"I believe it does," John responds with a twinkle in his eyes.

They lean into each other and kiss, the taste of coffee still fresh on their lips.

⤲

Eric is at the gym, intensely focused on lifting weights. Alex is by his side, matching his rhythm. "Hey, man," Alex says, his gaze fixed on the mirror, "stop me if I'm out of line, but Jules has been pretty open with Beth about what's been going on with you two lately. Are you guys ok? Are you and Jules back on speaking terms?"

"Yeah. We are working through it, and things are getting better. It's been tough, though," Eric replies, the strain of his workout echoing his sentiment.

"I'm sure," Alex acknowledges, grunting as he completes another set.

Their conversation lulls as they continue their workout; the only sounds are the clatter of weights and footfalls on treadmills.

"What was it like?" Alex asks, unable to contain his curiosity.

"With Madelyn?" Eric clarifies, pausing his weights for a moment.

"Yes, with Madelyn," Alex repeats, his gaze meeting Eric's in the mirror.

Eric's response is thick with complex emotion. "I have so much conflict about this. On the one hand, it was so sexual. So hot. Jules and I have never had an issue with that, but to have someone else desire me like that. It was... intoxicating,"

"Damn."

"Yeah. Until I realized what it was doing to my marriage. I think she thought she was some kind of unicorn. More like an interloper. That woman was on a mission. I was a means to an end," Eric continues, his expression grim as he restarts his lifting.

"Have you talked to her?" Alex asks, matching Eric's rhythm once more.

"To Madelyn? She's texted me. I'm not responding. I have nothing to say," Eric states, his voice firm.

"That's probably smart," Alex comments and, after a beat, adds, "I don't think Beth and I could do it. Especially after what we went through in our last relationships. That may make us dull..."

"It's not dull. It's just not you guys. If we're being honest, I'm not entirely sure it's for us, either. But Jules is determined to continue down this path."

"I guess I'm wondering how you're approaching it. Other people, I mean. How do you handle jealousy?" Alex continues. "I would be out of my mind if Beth had an interest in anyone but me."

Eric halts his movements for a moment. "I don't have a real answer for that yet. It's hard. Your brain tells you that you can set up all these rules and guidelines to protect the heart. As if that's even possible." Eric resumes his exercises. "We're not doing this just for the thrill of it. It's more complicated with us. And neither of us wants something that's just casual. So, yeah. The jealousy is real. And hard."

Alex nods, taking the information in. "Is it worth it?"

"What do you mean?"

"All these feelings? The impact on your relationship? Do you think it's worth it?"

Eric drops his weights and mulls over the question. "Don't know yet. I'm not clear on what I want out of it. I'm not sure Jules is clear, either. But when she sets her mind on something…"

Alex nods in understanding. "I get it. Beth is the same way."

After a moment of silence, Alex picks the conversation back up. "I couldn't handle Beth having a relationship with anyone else. Being unfaithful."

Eric turns to face him. "That's the thing. It's not infidelity in the way that you're describing. It's part of who we are. I understand where you're coming from and why you feel that way, but this isn't a reflection of the relationship being incomplete or broken or not being enough. It's about what each of us needs as individuals." He gives Alex a small smile. "But, to your point, it doesn't make things any easier."

"I can see that," Alex says, bringing the topic to a close and shifting subjects. "What are you guys up to tonight?"

Eric shakes his head. "We have a date."

"Good god, your life is interesting," Alex says, shaking his head to himself.

"Not so fast. The guy is straight. Jules insists we meet them to see what other couples are like. So more like a potential new friend courtship."

"Huh," Alex says.

"Yeah," Eric nods in agreement. "I have my reservations. The last thing we need right now is another debacle."

Out of the corner of his eye, Alex sees Jerry, Claire's husband, approaching. Jerry has always been a little awkward, saying the wrong thing at the wrong time, butting in on conversations. He married Claire "under duress," he often jokes, even in front of her. He was extremely effective at making the people around him uncomfortable.

"What debacle?" Jerry interjects.

Eric is already annoyed. "We were just finishing our conversation, Jerry."

Unfazed, Jerry grins and says, "I like conversation."

Alex redirects, "How are things with you, Jerry? And Claire?"

"I'm good. You know, working out." Jerry flexes. He then turns to Eric, a mischievous glint in his eyes, "Hey, uh, Eric? Claire tells me you had an FFM with Madelyn. Way to go, brother. That's awesome."

Eric is taken aback. "That's none of your business, Jerry."

"Seriously, Jerry," Alex adds, tone stern.

Jerry holds up his hands. "Whoa, guys. I'm just trying

to be supportive." Jerry grins, clearly unaware of the tension in the air. "I mean, Claire and I are straight and all, but a threesome, man. Living the dream."

"Enough, Jerry," Eric snaps.

Alex follows, "You're an idiot, Jerry."

Jerry is unable to stop himself. "I mean, c'mon. Isn't it every guy's fantasy? G on G. Especially those two. So hot. Jules with that ass. Madelyn with those legs…"

"You're being really inappropriate." Eric is on the brink of losing his temper.

"I'm just happy for you, man," Jerry responds, still aloof. He opens his arms to hug Eric. "Bring it in, man."

Eric sidesteps to avoid him. "I've had enough of this," he says curtly. "I've got to get to work. Alex, thanks for the talk."

"Always, man," Alex responds, shaking his head at Jerry.

Eric grabs his dumbbells and walks over to the rack to put them away. He bumps elbows with the new guy from the locker room the other day.

"That guy is the worst," the new guy says, tilting his head toward Jerry. "Swears he's straight. Then invites you to wrestle."

Eric cringes and breaks into a laugh. "He's clueless."

"You have a great laugh," the new guy compliments, making Eric blush, a pregnant pause filling the space between them.

"Thanks," Eric stammers, suddenly feeling very self-conscious. "I'll see you around."

The workday comes to a close, the day turns to evening, and Eric and Jules are driving in Eric's SUV on their way to an upscale, out-of-the-way bar across town to meet Miles and Elena, the couple from the app. Eric is in his dark denim straight-leg jeans, freshly pressed white button-down shirt, brown leather belt, and brown lace-up shoes. Jules is in a plum-colored cocktail dress with three-quarter sleeves and a hemline just below her knees. Her yellow-gold earrings and delicate necklace provide a little bit of sparkle, and her loose, dark hair falls just below her shoulders. Jules is touching up her make-up in the passenger side mirror when, hand trembling, she accidentally drops a brush. "I don't know why I'm so nervous."

"I'm nervous, too," Eric confesses from the driver's seat.

"We're just meeting for drinks. There's no pressure for anything more," Jules says to reassure herself as much as Eric.

"I think that's the right way to approach it," he agrees.

"I'm just really curious about how this all works," Jules shares as she flips up the visor and puts her makeup bag away.

Eric signals, turns into the lot, parks, and shuts off the engine. "Well," he says, "we're about to find out."

The bar is dimly lit, noisy, and packed, but all Jules and Eric can focus on are the two people sitting across from them. Miles is tan and handsome with a lean, athletic build. Elena has a warm, inviting smile that lights up her face. Silence stretches between the two couples, thick and uncomfortable, until Miles breaks it. "It's nice to finally meet you in person. And thank you for looking like your profile pictures," Miles says, his expression endearing.

Jules follows up with a question, "People don't always look like their photos?"

"Sometimes the photos are a little...dated," Elena responds.

"Or touched up," Miles adds.

"Or dimly lit," Elena finishes.

Miles leans slightly forward in his chair. "Let's just say it's not always the most accurate representation of who you are meeting. But not in your case..."

"You're both very attractive," Elena affirms, also leaning forward.

A blush creeps onto Jules' cheeks. "Thank you."

Silence settles like a curtain again, a little less awkward this time, and Eric takes the opportunity to speak up, "We're usually not this nervous. As Jules probably mentioned, we're pretty new at this."

Elena nods, her expression soft, "Yes. It's quite charming, really. There's no need to be nervous around us. We're very friendly."

"We appreciate that," Jules says with an exhale, starting to relax for the first time all evening.

"I remember when we were first starting out," Elena reflects. "It wasn't easy."

"It was like learning a new language," Miles adds. "All these new labels, new acronyms—what you're into, what you're not into."

"Everyone starts out thinking they are up for anything," Elena comments, eyes twinkling.

"Oh yes," Miles agrees with a hearty laugh, "until someone tries to pee on you."

Jules and Eric start to giggle.

"You laugh," Elena smirks. "I had to get a new carpet."

Miles continues. "It's tough in the beginning. We had a great first experience, which made it easier to keep going. But after that…" Miles trails off.

"Goodness, after that, we had a few fiascoes," Elena adds.

"Please share," Jules requests, her curiosity piqued.

"We'd be here all night," Miles replies. He takes a sip of his drink and turns the focus back to Eric and Jules. "Tell us more about yourselves. What called you to the lifestyle?"

Eric considers his words before replying, "I'm not yet sure we're in the lifestyle, but we are both bisexual. I'll let Jules tell her own story, but mine started when I was young."

Eric realized he was different from the other kids when he was twelve and away from home at sleepaway camp. Boys slept in bunks on one side of the lake and girls on the other, but they would come together during the day for camper activities. There were sports, games, and, best of all, arts and crafts. The arts and crafts room was large, with big, rectangular windows facing the lake and white Formica shelves overflowing with rainbow stacks of construction paper, markers, crayons, paints, plastic cups full of brushes, colored pencils, and half-used-up bottles of Elmer's with twist-to-open orange caps, filmed with scabs of dried up glue.

Eric was particularly fond of arts and crafts time because Elizabeth, a twelve-year-old girl from a few towns away, was always at his table. She could draw and paint, and they would collaborate on stories that Eric would make up, and she would illustrate them like little comic books. They made a good team.

During the annual camp scavenger hunt, the campers were put into teams, given colorful maps, and set out in search of the treasures the counselors hid for them. Eric was dispatched on a solo mission to locate a clue near a stand of pines, and as he rounded the corner of a tree trunk, he found Elizabeth looking for the same clue. The competition was on, with both Eric and Elizabeth searching high and low, both spotting the hidden clue at the same time.

The fluorescent pink egg, a remnant of Easter, was tucked into a tree branch, and the two ran towards it, Eric reaching it just before Elizabeth. Already a gentleman, he offered to share the clue, not just claim it as his own, and, in exchange, Elizabeth rewarded him with a kiss, half on his cheek, half on his lips. She took a step back and turned to run to rejoin her team as Eric ran his tongue over where she'd kissed him. It tasted like watermelon bubble gum, so sweet it was almost soapy. A warmth took root in his stomach, and there was a stir in his shorts as he, too, turned to run and rejoin his teammates.

Eric floated like a cloud for the rest of the day, still smelling the watermelon flavor sticky on his face. He wouldn't wipe it off, wanting it to last as long as possible. His scavenger hunt team placed fourth, and after the awards ceremony, when the boys were sent back to their cabins to change for supper, Eric caught a glimpse of his campmate, who had already stripped down to his underwear. The same warmth he felt when Elizabeth kissed him took hold in Eric's stomach; the same stirring took place in his shorts, and he quickly turned away, hoping no one saw him look. Eric laid awake that night, staring at the ceiling from his top bunk, turning over the events of the day and these new feelings in his body. He felt mostly excited but also very confused.

The pattern would repeat for Eric through the rest of middle school and into his high school years as he found himself attracted to both girls and boys. He knew it was 'normal' for him to like girls in this way, just as he tacitly understood that it was not 'normal' for him to also like boys.

Eric's parents were schoolteachers. His father also coached baseball and was known for being strict, well-loved by his players, and delivering winning seasons year after year. Parents with high expectations for their child athletes would choose Eric's father's school district with hopes that they, too, would have recruiters with scholarship dollars scouting at games and following up with offers. Eric's father was firm, with a strong sense of what was right and what was clearly wrong. Gray areas did not sit well with him.

Eric's mother, on the other hand, saw only shades of gray. She recognized and appreciated the nuances of daily life and showed limitless empathy for her students, her husband, and Eric, the apple of her eye and her only child. Eric got his good looks from his father and his heart from his mom.

He continues with his story, "When other boys were crushing on girls, I was crushing on boys and girls. I understand it better now, but back then, it was confusing. I felt like I was the only one who had feelings for both. One day, after school, I found my dad in my room waiting for me. He'd found my porn magazines, saw that I was looking at both men and women."

"How'd he take it?" Miles asks.

"Not well," Eric admits. "He told me that there was no middle ground when it comes to sex. That I'd have to pick. There was no room for discussion."

Eric's relationship with his father was never the same after that. While Eric's parents were still alive and in good health, Eric recalled that day in his bedroom as the day he lost his dad. Eric never again felt comfortable around him, and not another word was ever spoken about Eric's sexuality or preferences. The distance between them created that day remained unrecovered.

Jules wraps her arm around Eric, bringing his focus back to the present, and looks at him with tender eyes.

"So, I shut myself down. Completely. I still struggle with the shame, isolation, and abandonment I experienced from that time. It still hurts," Eric confesses. "When I went to college, I dated mostly women. That was certainly the easier thing to do. But I couldn't ignore my feelings for men and, from time to time, I would have sexual experiences with them. My dad put fear in me, though. I thought if I was transparent about my sexuality, I would be rejected."

Jules opens up, following Eric's lead. "I was a late bloomer, but when I started developing feelings, they were usually for girls. I couldn't really do anything about it until I got to college. I had a crew there, all lesbian and very serious about it. I thought I was a lesbian, too. But every now and then, a guy would catch my eye or flirt with me. I liked it. When I told my crew that I was going out on a date with a man, it was like I committed a crime. They told me I was betraying them. Betraying lesbianism. Betraying womanhood. I was forced to choose—my sexuality or my community. That infuriated me. Here we were, fighting for choice and self-expression, just not mine. I can barely remember the guy I wanted to date, but the price of dating him was my friends, my identity."

Eric fast-forwards the story. "I was in the last month of my grad program, which was a few buildings down from the business school. This hottie," he nods toward Jules, "would study on the picnic benches."

Jules smiles, remembering. Despite the number of years that passed, the memory of meeting Eric for the first time stayed fresh in Jules' mind. She hadn't done much dating in B-school; her focus was on studying and landing her dream job. But there was something about Eric, the way his brown hair framed his face, bangs a little too long. His eyes were bright, and he couldn't stop smiling when he talked to her. She was not looking to meet anyone so close to graduation but found that her pulse quickened when he approached her. In fact, it was the most excited she'd been in a long time.

"It didn't help that I became a bumbling idiot just thinking about talking to her," Eric adds, his face lighting up at the memory. "So, I got my nerve up and walked over. She was buried in textbooks and looked up at me. Her first words were—"

"Are you lost?" Jules interjects, laughing.

"That Jules charisma... I told her no, I was exactly where I wanted to be, sat down, and we started talking."

Jules found conversation with Eric easy. He was in a master's program to become a social worker because he wanted to help people. He'd dated before but hadn't really had a serious romantic relationship. He was smart, funny, and charming. Despite their different fields of study, they had a great deal in common. They were both fit, enjoyed being outside, and were looking forward to graduating. They read a lot of the same books, listened to a lot of the same music, and liked the same kinds of beer.

"The chemistry was immediate," Jules continues. "The chat turned into drinks. Then dinner. Then more drinks. We ordered yet another round of beers, and I decided I wasn't going to hide who I was. I didn't want to be in another relationship where I had to hide parts of myself. So, I told him, on our first date, that I was bi."

"I'd never been so relieved in my life," Eric adds. "I had no idea how much tension I was carrying around with me until, in that moment, I let it go."

"He told me he was, too, and it was like something clicked. I didn't feel like I was going to be judged or oversexualized. I didn't feel like I needed to hide this part of myself. It made for a great start to our relationship."

Eric looks at Jules, mirroring her affection. "With the exception of a really shitty threesome, we've been monogamous. We love and accept each other's sexuality, but we haven't really expressed it outside of the relationship."

"I want us to be able to express it. That's what this is

about for us," Jules concludes, relief washing over her after saying the words out loud. A quiet settles over the group.

Miles speaks up first. "I feel very honored that you shared your stories with us."

"Me, too," Elena echoes. "Thank you for being so open about yourselves."

Jules and Eric let out heavy sighs. "Thank you for listening. We've never really shared like that before," Jules says, sounding a little breathless. "If you'll excuse me for a moment. I'm feeling a little flushed—I need to…"

"I'll join you," Elena offers, standing up.

As the two women walk towards the ladies' room, Miles turns to Eric. "I want to hear about the shitty threesome."

⟊

The restroom is down a long hallway, away from the noise of the bar. It has three stalls, and the walls are lined with glossy, jade-green tile. Jules emerges from a stall and washes her hands in a glass vessel sink with a gold-tone faucet. Elena appears from another stall, their eyes meeting in the matching, mounted, gold-tone-framed mirror.

"I'm sorry you had to go through that," Elena says.

Jules sighs, shaking her head slightly. "It was a different time then. Although, I'm not sure it's much easier now."

Elena's reflection looks thoughtfully back at Jules. "I think what you are doing is brave. I know you found each other, but many people live their whole lives with all of this desire in them. And it is hot, and beautiful, and raging. And they don't know what to do with it. So, they ignore it. Or repress it. Or it comes out in ways that aren't exactly healthy. You're facing it head-on."

Jules holds Elena's gaze. "I hope I don't get punched in the face with it."

Elena laughs. "There is no guaranteeing that. Consider it part of the adventure."

Turning towards each other, the women lock eyes. Elena gives Jules a warm smile and says, "We really like you. We'd like to get to know you better. No pressure. This is our first date. But we'd like to see you again if you and Eric would like that."

Jules smiles warmly back. "I would really like that. Let me talk to Eric. I will let you know."

"That went better than expected," Eric admits on the drive home. "I didn't anticipate sharing like that."

"I know. It felt good, right?" Jules beams.

"It did." Eric nods in agreement. "I didn't think I would feel so comfortable."

"I'm proud of us," Jules declares. "For putting ourselves out there. For telling our stories."

"It felt good to be so..." Eric searches for the right word.

"Open?" Jules fills in.

"Yeah. Open," he agrees, and the conversation lapses into an easy silence.

After a moment, Jules speaks up again. "When we were in the ladies' room, Elena said they'd like to see us again. I told her I'd talk to you about it."

Eric furrows his brow, his earlier reticence swelling back

up to the surface. "I don't know, Jules. They are very nice, and it felt good to speak freely, but he's straight. Not hetero-flexible. Straight. I don't know where this goes for me and don't know how I feel about that."

"I'd like to see them again," Jules presses. "I don't know that this goes much further, but tonight felt so good."

Eric again feels pressure, like he can't say no. A few seconds pass, and he says, "Alright."

Jules brightens, "Really?"

"Let's see where it goes."

CHAPTER 3

SOMETIMES YOU'RE THE PIGEON, SOMETIMES YOU'RE THE STATUE

KYRA ROLLS OVER and opens her eyes to find John standing, bare bottom facing her, rummaging through his dresser drawers. She smiles to herself and sits up in his king-sized bed, white cotton sheets and summer weight comforter gathered around her. She stretches her arms over her head in a yawn and asks, "Hey, cutie, what're you doing?"

John turns to face her, holding up two tee shirts, a dark green one with the phrase 'Eat, Sleep, Ultimate, Repeat' written in black, all capital letters on the front, and a lime green one with a picture of a silhouetted person diving for a frisbee. Both look well-worn and soft from a thousand washings. "Which one do you like?"

"Definitely the dark green one."

John nods in agreement and puts the other one away. "I'm excited for my game today."

"I can tell." Kyra is enjoying John's enthusiasm. It's like she can see a glimpse of what he was like as a boy.

"Alright. I'm going to jump in the shower. Can you, um, ring Charlie to make sure she's up and knows where to meet us? Northwest corner of the park by the playing fields. Eleven o'clock."

"I'm on it," Kyra replies.

John, Kyra, and Charlie have become inseparable. They do movie nights at the local theater. Meet out for weeknight trivia after work. Accompany each other on errands. Do game nights at John's. Not more than a day or two passes without a hangout. While there has not been another encounter like the night Kyra and Charlie first met, there continues to be both innocent and not-so-innocent flirting between them. Their fingers playfully touch in the popcorn container at the movies. They briefly hold hands under the table at trivia. On one occasion, Charlie stole a kiss on the lips from Kyra during game night when John was in another room. Kyra's heart would race in these moments, and her mind would flood with rationalizations. *This is all in good fun, and I'm not breaking any rules. Not technically anyway...*

Kyra reaches for her phone, pulls up a list of recent calls, and taps 'video' for Charlie's number.

Charlie hears her phone ring with the incoming call and pads from the bedroom of her new apartment to the kitchen counter to answer. She is still in the form-fitting gray boy shorts and loose white tank top she slept in.

Her new place is a welcome fresh start. Brand new with floor-to-ceiling windows that flood light over the white walls, chevroned hardwood plank floors, and exposed brick accents. It's a perfect backdrop for her modern furniture and the art pieces she's collected over the years. She's mostly unpacked; only a few boxes remain. Being back in her hometown has been better than she expected. Old connections re-established. New connections forming. The distance between here and her old life feels good, feels right. Charlie smiles and thinks to herself, *Yeah, coming back was the right move.*

She picks up a tangerine from the fruit bowl on the counter and sees the video call is coming from Kyra. Charlie props the phone against the bowl and, voice still gravelly from sleep, says, "Good morning, beautiful."

"Good morning back." Kyra smiles widely into the phone. "What are you up to? Are you even dressed yet?"

Charlie rolls her eyes and grins. "I have clothes on, thank you very much."

"Whatcha got there?" Kyra asks.

"Tangerine," Charlie responds as she tucks her neatly trimmed thumbnails into the rind of the fruit.

There is a break in the conversation as Kyra observes Charlie. Then, in a throaty tone, Charlie hasn't heard Kyra use before, she says, "Slower."

Charlie feels a thrill ripple outward from the base of her spine. "Pardon me?"

"Go slower. I want to watch you peel that tangerine for me."

Charlie licks her lower lip, and Kyra watches her remove the peel, revealing the fruit underneath. Charlie pauses when the fruit is completely unpeeled.

"Good girl," Kyra says, "now take those thumbs and tear the fruit in half. Don't rush. Take your time."

The air seems to thicken as it passes through Charlie's nostrils, and her breath deepens. It satisfies her greatly to surrender to Kyra's commands, to give Kyra what she wants. Charlie runs her thumbs over the perimeter of the fruit and then slowly pulls the halves apart from north to south, waiting for Kyra's next directive when she's done.

Kyra leans forward and rests her chin on her palm, fingertips lightly resting on her cheekbone. "Pull off one segment, open your mouth, and put it on your tongue."

Charlie removes a segment of the tangerine, places it in her mouth, and bites down.

"Bad girl." Kyra's tone shifts an octave lower. "I didn't say you could bite it. Start again."

Charlie swallows the segment she bit and removes another section from the tangerine. She opens her mouth and lets her tongue rest on her lower lip. Wet. Exposed. She places the tangerine on her tongue and holds it in place with her top teeth, not breaking eye contact with Kyra. Charlie can feel her chest rise and fall with anticipation.

Kyra curls under the fingertips that graze her cheekbone and brushes her knuckles across her face and lips, mirroring Charlie's breath through the image on her screen.

"Bite," Kyra says, and Charlie obeys, the juice from the tangerine dripping rivers down her chin.

"Now get dressed and meet us at the park for John's game. Eleven o'clock sharp. I'll have a spot under the oak trees." Kyra abruptly hangs up, leaving Charlie breathless, hungry for more.

～

The park is brimming with people enjoying the sunny Sunday weather. Kyra has a red and white checkered blanket laid out under a shady tree, and a tote bag filled with snacks and water bottles. She is in white denim shorts, a fitted light blue tee shirt, and her hair is long and loose. John is in the tee shirt she picked out, with black running shorts and faded red running shoes.

Charlie approaches at eleven o'clock on the dot. "There she is!" John says when he sees her. Kyra turns to make eye contact, smiles, and waves hello. Charlie holds up a brown paper bag. "I brought chocolate chip cookies. Still warm."

"I'll save mine for after the game," John says as he stretches. "It's time for me to show 'em how it's done."

Kyra encourages him, "Go get 'em, tiger!"

Charlie chimes in, "We're rooting for you!"

With a quick smile and a kiss for Kyra, John takes off to join the game, leaving the two women behind.

"Chocolate chip cookies are my kryptonite," Kyra says, reaching for the bag and taking a bite out of a cookie. "These are delicious. Where are these from?"

Charlie watches Kyra lick the melted chocolate from the corners of her mouth and hands her a napkin. Neither of them mentions that morning's video call. "Shakery Bakery," Charlie says. "Their cookies were a major decision factor in my move back here."

Kyra laughs. "I can see why. What are some of your other faves?"

Charlie is quick to answer, "Sunshine market for ice

cream. Pistachio. Nico's for pepperoni pizza. Especially late at night. Taco Palace for…"

Kyra interrupts, "Tacos?"

"Arepas," Charlie says.

"I had no idea they made arepas!" Kyra says.

"You have to ask," Charlie explains, "nicely. I missed the old fashions from Pilar Bar the most, though."

"The place on 9th?" Kyra asks.

"That's the one," Charlie confirms.

"They have that old jukebox there. The one with actual records," Kyra muses.

"They do," Charlie says. "I love it. And their old fashions are the best in town."

"Noted," Kyra says, pausing to shift subjects. "So, what's your story? Are you dating? Looking for a relationship?"

"I'm open to it," Charlie responds. "I'm not sure I'm a one-woman gal, though."

Kyra nods her head yes, leaving room for Charlie to say more.

"I don't need to be the only one," Charlie continues, "but I want to be the most important one. When I was in grade school, Valentine's Day was a big deal. All the kids got those cheap paper valentines with chubby angels and kittens on them. Generic messages like 'Be mine' kind of thing. But if someone thought you were special, you got some candy with your valentine. A red lollipop. A box of those candy hearts. Some Hershey's Kisses. I loved that everyone got a valentine, but I wanted to be the one who got the candy."

"I see…" says Kyra, unsure how else to respond. After a few moments pass, she changes subjects. "How is the unpacking going? Almost done? Have you caught up with some of your other friends in town?"

"Almost. Just a few boxes left. It's so nice to be back. I didn't realize how much I missed it. I didn't realize how much I missed being around old friends."

Faking exasperation, Kyra says, "Who're you calling old!"

Charlie laughs. "Very funny," and then, with a more serious tone, Charlie adds, "I'm really enjoying getting to know you."

Locking eyes with Charlie, Kyra replies in somewhat of a dare, "Is that so?"

"Forgot my headband!" John calls out as he approaches before Charlie can say anything more. Quickly composing herself, Kyra says, "I have it. It's in my bag. Let me get it for you." She rummages through her tote and hands it to him. He puts it on, gives Kyra a wink and a smile, then jogs off to rejoin his teammates.

Charlie gathers her things. "Hey, I'd love to stay, but I should probably head out. I have a lot of work to catch up on today."

"Oh. Ok. Hey, Charlie?" Kyra calls out.

"Yes?" Charlie answers.

"I'm really enjoying getting to know you, too."

The afternoon sun sits lower in the bright blue sky as John and Kyra stroll back to John's house after his game, holding hands, footsteps in rhythm.

"I still got it!" John exclaims, happy with how he played.

Kyra laughs. "Yes, you do. You're good. It was fun watching you."

John grins. "I used to play all the time. I thought I was getting rusty. Must've been my cheering section."

Their conversation lulls into companionable silence as they continue their walk. "Thanks for being so nice to Charlie," John eventually says. "I'm sure it's a little weird for her to be back."

"She seems to be adjusting well," Kyra replies, "and I know she's glad to be closer to you."

John nods. "Yeah. I worry about her. She doesn't like to talk about it, but she came back because of a bad breakup. Really bad."

"She hasn't mentioned it," Kyra says, trying not to show her curiosity.

"I'm sure she hasn't." John shakes his head. "It was awful. The woman was married."

"Gosh."

"Yeah," John continues, "and Charlie was not part of the arrangement."

John replays the scene in his mind. His cell phone rang in the middle of the night, Charlie on the other end. She was crying hysterically. Terrified. Her lover's husband found out about Charlie and was livid. Threatening Charlie physically if she ever came near his wife again. The lover said nothing. Not even a goodbye. John had never heard Charlie sob like that.

"She always does this," John says.

"Does what?" Kyra asks.

"Gets attached to emotionally unavailable women. Then gets her heart crushed."

∽

The next morning starts the work week and Eric begins his in the coffee shop. Dressed in light grey jeans and a short-sleeved, burgundy button-down, Eric sits by himself at a corner table, an Americano in a plastic-lidded to-go cup in front of him. He is pouring over budget figures on his laptop, trying to come up with solutions for his situation with Vickie. He rests his forehead on his palm as he scrolls through the rows of numbers; the figures aren't looking good. Eric is so wrapped up in the budgeting that he doesn't notice the new guy from the gym standing in the order line, looking sharp in a freshly pressed tan suit, crisp white collared shirt underneath. The new guy notices Eric, though, and, once his coffee is ready, approaches.

"Good morning," he says.

Eric looks up with a slightly confused look on his face, trying to place him. *Ah, yes,* he remembers, *the hot guy from the locker room.*

"Good morning," Eric responds. "I recognize you from the gym. You look so different in clothes." Eric's cheeks immediately flush and grow hot. "I meant, I mean, I've only seen you in gym clothes. You, uh, look very different in work clothes. Gosh, how embarrassing."

The new guy's smile widens. "I know what you meant." He extends a hand towards Eric. "I don't think I've introduced myself. I'm Xavier."

Eric takes the offered hand. "Eric."

"I know," Xavier responds, a pause lingering between them before he asks, "May I join you?"

"Please do." Eric closes the lid to his laptop and gestures to the seat across from him. Xavier sits down.

"You're new to the gym," Eric starts. "Are you new in town?"

"I moved here recently. I just started a new job," Xavier explains.

"Congratulations," Eric continues, "what do you do for work?"

"I'm in finance."

"What does that mean exactly?"

Xavier smiles, "You know, no one ever asks me that. I raise capital that gets invested. I help make sure the investments make sense."

"Got it." Eric doesn't mention that his wife works in private equity.

"What about you?" Xavier asks.

"Social work," Eric replies.

"What does that mean exactly?"

Eric appreciates the reciprocity and interest. "I'm in elder care. I help people in later stages of life. It's always been my calling."

"That's really nice."

"Thanks. I love what I do. At least, most of the time."

Eric's phone screen lights up and dings, signaling the arrival of a new message. Xavier nods towards it. "Looks like someone is trying to get your attention."

Eric glances at his phone before tucking it into his bag, dismissing it. "It can wait."

They each take a few sips of coffee, and then Xavier asks, "Do you work around here?"

"A few blocks that way," Eric replies, indicating the direction with a head tilt.

"Me, too," Xavier says. "Want to walk together?"

"Sure. Let's go," Eric agrees with a smile he tries to hide.

The two stand up, exiting the coffee shop while chatting and laughing, an unexpected familiarity taking root between them. A short while later, Eric strides into his workplace, the smile he's been trying not to show firmly plastered on his face. It does not go unnoticed.

"If I didn't know any better," Sam teases, "I'd say you've got a crush."

"What was that?" Eric raises an eyebrow.

"Your cheeks are all red, and if your smile was any bigger, your face would crack."

Rolling his eyes, Eric dismisses Sam, but the older man persists. "Let me guess, sexting with Jules?" Sam prods.

"Sam!" Eric exclaims, half embarrassed, half amused. "What do you know about sexting?"

"I'm old," Sam retorts, "not an idiot."

"Touché," says Eric.

Switching to a more serious note, Sam asks, "So, things going well with you and the missus?"

"Yes, Sam. We're good."

"Last time we talked, you two were in the midst of a growing pain," Sam recalls.

"Is that what you call it?" Eric asks with an undertone of sarcasm.

"Among other things."

"I appreciate the concern, Sam. We're in a good place, and thanks for looking out for me. What about you? Any updates with you and Ms. Camilla?"

"She stopped letting me win at backgammon."

⁂

Jules starts her work week in the conference room with Peter, Hunter, Will, and Dylan. This is Dylan's first time presenting to the group, taking the team through his analysis. He is just a few slides in before Peter stops him. "How did you arrive at these figures, Dylan?"

"I used the model that we…"

Peter interrupts before Dylan can finish. "I can see that. But your numbers look off. What are your assumptions based on?"

Dylan falters, uncomfortable. "I, uh…" his voice trails off, the weight of the room's attention too heavy. Peter softens. "Julia can provide you with the revised assumption set we developed. Re-run your analysis with those figures and report back. That's all for today, everyone. Back to work."

Embarrassment paints Dylan's cheeks red as he swiftly gathers his laptop and exits. Hunter and Will follow. Jules stands to leave, but Peter calls her back. "Julia, could you stay for a moment?"

"Sure, Peter. What's up?"

Peter taps on a folder lying in front of him. It's the research Jules gathered about the new firm in town. "Great work, Julia. How did you manage to get this?"

A coy smile tugs at Jules' lips. "I never reveal my sources."

"This is exactly what I was hoping for. It's going to put us in a great position."

Jules nods in agreement. "I think so, too."

"Listen, I need another favor. I'd like you to take Dylan under your wing," Peter proposes.

"How do you mean?" Jules questions, hiding her reluctance under an even tone.

"No one understands this business better than you, Julia. I'd like Dylan to learn from you, develop better habits. Especially after today."

"Have you discussed this with Dylan?"

"I was hoping you could approach him, offer to mentor. I think it would carry more weight coming directly from you," Peter suggests.

"And not from Dad…"

"Exactly," Peter confirms.

Jules doesn't say no, but she doesn't say yes, either. "Let me think about it."

"Thank you, Julia. Join me and the guys for lunch later?" Peter asks.

"Thank you, but not today. I'm going to get a workout in."

Jules goes back to her office and takes a seat at her walnut-stained wooden desk, which contrasts against the white walls and light floor. In front of her desk are two contemporary, sapphire blue guest chairs, and on the corner of her desk is an oversized widescreen monitor. Her only personal item is a gold-framed photograph of Eric, covered in bubbles, giving Daisy a bath. Jules starts going through messages, trying to manage her reaction to Peter's request. Mentoring Dylan is the last thing in the world she wants to do.

As if he could read her thoughts, Dylan appears in her doorway. "Julia, about those assumption figures."

Without looking up, Jules replies, "I will send you a link to the correct data set." She continues to filter through messages, but Dylan doesn't leave. Instead, he asks, "Can I send you my spreadsheet and you just fix it?"

Jules looks up from her computer, finding his nonchalant and audacious expression. "What did you just say?"

"Can you just fix it? I mean, isn't that what you do here? Fix what my dad asks you to?"

Jules struggles to hide her exasperation. "What happened to 'I can hold my own'?"

"I can," Dylan says with a smirk. "I'm delegating."

Jules leans back in her seat. "That's cute. And not at all how this works."

"Isn't it?" Dylan steps into Jules' office, takes a seat in one of her guest chairs, and leans forward, putting his elbows on her desk.

"I didn't invite you to sit."

Dylan maintains eye contact and doesn't budge from his seat.

Jules' patience wears thin. "Look, I don't know what this is all about. But you need to figure out how to do your own work, and you need to leave my office." Jules rises and stands by her doorway, a clear signal for Dylan to leave.

Dylan stands, a smug grin on his face as he exits.

Jules closes her office door behind him, takes her

seat behind her desk, and looks out the window, fuming at Dylan's behavior and even angrier at Peter's request to mentor him. She can feel her stress levels rising and takes a deep breath to calm herself down. She would take it out on the spin bike, she decides. That almost always helps.

❧

Rage Against the Machine blares through the speakers of the darkened spin studio packed with the ambitious lunchtime crowd. From the front of the room, the instructor yells above the music, "Last song, riders! Crank up that tension for this last hill, and give me everything you got." Jules lifts out of her seat and leans over the handlebars as she turns the tension knob to the right and slows her cadence from a sprint to a climb. Claire, on the next bike over, does the same. They are both slicked with sweat, hearts pounding, pedals pushing and pulling in time with the music. As soon as the song comes to an end, they both release the tension on the flywheel, sit up, and towel off.

Jules and Claire meet once or twice a week for a lunchtime spin class, both appreciating the friendly face and accountability. Claire's office is only a few blocks away, where she works in employee benefits.

Claire had been going to the gym for years and frequently saw Jules there. As is often the case, the women would recognize each other's faces, nod, or say a polite hello but never actually introduce themselves. Nonetheless, Jules made a strong impression on Claire. She was always so put together. Her workout clothes were always the latest season's, her dark hair always neatly tied back. She had a great smile, which she usually only showed before or after class. During class, Jules was pure focus.

One day, before boxing class, Claire was standing near Jules and Beth and noticed that Jules wasn't smiling and was covering her mouth with her hand when she spoke. Beth kept asking what was going on until Jules moved her hand away and showed her. Her front tooth was badly chipped, and she hadn't yet gone to the dentist to fix it. This was during the "50 Shades" years, and couples, including Jules and Eric, were experimenting with all kinds of play in the bedroom. Just above a whisper, Jules admitted the broken tooth was from a ball gag incident gone wrong the night before.

Claire couldn't help but overhear and offer her input. Unsolicited, she tapped Jules on the shoulder and said her that her dental plan would probably cover it, considering it was an accident. Beth roared with laughter while Jules fought to hide her embarrassment. The three had been friends and frequent workout partners ever since.

"That was a tough class," Jules says, wiping the sweat from her forehead. "I really needed it."

Claire nods in agreement, her face bright pink from exertion. She takes a moment to catch her breath as the other riders file out. "I've been thinking a lot about our conversation the other day at the coffee shop... How are you, Jules?"

"Good. You?" Jules answers.

Claire clarifies, "I mean, how are you and Eric?"

Jules doesn't miss a beat. "Eric and I are great."

Claire pushes, her emotions getting the best of her. "But

are you? I mean, how can you be? Madelyn told me what happened, and I can't help but think that you're…"

Jules realizes the direction the conversation is taking, and her tone sharpens. "That what?"

"This 'seeing other people' business. That it's just covering up problems in your relationship," Claire finishes, her gaze steady on Jules.

"Is that what you think is happening?" Jules asks.

"Isn't it?" Claire's tone is now accusatory.

Jules pauses, her face hardening, "It's none of your business, Claire. But for the record, it's not about covering up issues in our relationship. Quite the opposite. And I wish you wouldn't make assumptions like that."

Claire's expression turns somber. "Madelyn gave me some of the details about the other night. I can't imagine how you're feeling, Jules. And then Eric was rude to Jerry at the gym…"

"Again, none of your business," Jules interrupts. "And Eric may be a lot of things, but rude isn't one of them."

"You're married, Jules. To Eric. What you're doing… It isn't right. I don't want to see you get hurt. Or Eric," Claire continues.

Jules holds her ground. "I'm not going to be judged by you, Claire. We can make decisions for ourselves."

"Can you?" Claire challenges, voice rising. "Because what you're doing doesn't make any sense. You should have gotten all of this out of your system before you got married."

"Gotten what out of our system?" Jules snaps. "Do you think this is a phase? That this is something you grow out of?"

"You made a choice, Jules. You chose Eric."

"I still choose Eric."

"Then why are you doing this? Putting your relationship at risk? I say this with love in my heart, Jules. It's wrong."

Jules dismounts her bike, facing Claire fully. "It doesn't matter what you think, Claire. I don't care if you understand. I don't care if you have love in your heart. I owe you no explanation. This conversation is over."

Jules turns her back to Claire and walks away.

৵

Evening falls over the home of Jules and Eric, the setting sun casting long shadows across the kitchen. They sit at the island, plates in front of them, oversized glasses of wine casting a warm, burgundy hue under the soft overhead light. Eric's plate is nearly empty. Jules' food is barely touched. Eric reaches over, taking Jules' hand in his.

"I'm sorry you had such a rough day," he says softly.

Jules sighs, gaze dropping to her untouched plate. "It was like college all over again. Being judged about who I am. By someone I thought was my friend."

"Awful," Eric agrees, squeezing her hand.

"I get it if she has questions," Jules begins, "especially if Jerry is reacting the way it sounds like he is. But to come at me like that…" Jules goes quiet for a moment. "She kept insisting something is wrong with us and our relationship," she continues, her frustration clear, "and that must be why we're doing this. It was so…"

"Insulting," Eric finishes for her.

"Exactly."

"I'm sure that's what it looks like to her," Eric reasons. "How she's rationalizing this. And she may be projecting onto you how she feels about Jerry's behavior. I have to imagine she's feeling pretty insecure."

"She's always been insecure," Jules replies. "It's like she didn't feel like a complete person until Jerry put a ring on her finger."

"We all have our labels," Eric explains. "Hers is 'Faithfully married to Jerry'."

"Yuck," Jules scoffs, "can you imagine?"

"Yuck, aside," Eric continues, "that's how she sees herself. 'Good marriage'—that's one of your labels."

"It is," Jules admits, her expression softening. "And when someone calls that into question, it hurts."

"It does," Eric agrees. "Don't let Claire's insecurity make you insecure. Not about who you are. Not about who we are. Not about our marriage. She doesn't have any secret magic decoder ring that allows her to see into our relationship. No matter how much love she has in her heart."

"That was the icing on the cake." Jules snorts, rolling her eyes and calming down. "I love you so much," she says, looking into Eric's eyes. "Thank you for talking this through with me."

"I love you," Eric responds, his voice warm. "That's what I'm here for."

The moment lingers before Eric changes the subject. "So, how are you going to handle Peter's request to mentor Dylan?"

Jules exhales deeply, and her brows knit together. "Honestly, I have no idea."

Eric can see the stress on Jules' face. He didn't mean to upset her. "Come here," Eric says softly as he takes Jules' hand and kisses the top of it, leading her toward the hallway. "Let's take your mind off all that."

Jules resists. "Babe, I'm not up for any playtime right now."

"I know," Eric replies, "just a little relax time."

Jules cracks a smile. "Relax time?"

Eric winks in return as he opens the door to their bedroom. He sits down at the foot of the bed and pats the area next to him. "Come. Lay down."

Jules shuffles over and lays face up on the bed as Eric takes her feet into his hands, cupping her heels and massaging them. She's rigid at first, but a short while later, her stress starts to release, and she sighs. "That feels great."

Eric continues, stroking her insteps with his thumbs. He runs his fingers between her toes and caresses the tops of her feet. Jules flutters her eyelids open to catch Eric watching her, eyes smoldering. Holding her gaze, he leans down and takes her big toe into his mouth, gently sucking. Jules squeals. Eric continues.

He glides his hands up her legs and moves to undo her button and zipper. Catching her eye for permission, Jules nods her head yes, recloses her eyes, and lifts her hips as Eric slides her pants down and off, leaving her underwear, noticeably damp, on.

Starting again at her ankles, Eric moves his hands up Jules' calves and lets his fingers tickle the back of her knees. Jules wriggles with delight.

Eric takes a seat between Jules' bent knees and moves

his hands up her thighs, light at first, just fingertips. Jules' responds with deepening breaths, and her legs start to quiver. They stay like this for a while, building Jules' energy and Eric's anticipation.

This side of Jules was a surprise to Eric. Her normally cool and collected exterior failed to give away her sensitivity underneath. Some of their most intimate encounters were in these states, Jules responding to the lightest of his touches. Eric felt deep love and power in these moments; Jules' surrender was like a beacon of trust in him, in their relationship.

Eric increases the pressure as he grips the front of Jules' thighs. Her hips roll in response, and her breath quickens. She widens her legs, and he moves his hands to her inner thighs, massaging, pulling.

Jules gasps and moans as the first wave of energy rolls through her. Eric pauses briefly as Jules catches her breath, and then he runs the top of his fingernails from the top of her knees over her thighs, starting the cycle all over again.

This time, her stomach and chest also quiver, and the pattern of her breathing changes. Eric runs his hands up Jules' centerline, caressing her neck and face. She turns her head to kiss the tops of his fingers before he slides them back down her body, over her breasts, and to her hips. He catches her eye once more to wordlessly ask for permission, and Jules once again nods her head yes.

Jules has gone from damp to drenched as Eric slides her panties to the side and puts first one and then two fingers inside of her. He can feel Jules' wanting, urgency building, the pressure inside of her body increasing. He smiles to himself as her hips arch to meet him. Her orgasm comes more quickly this time, the release of pressure only temporary, before his fingers are in her again, building toward her next orgasm and the one after. Her whole body shakes with pleasure. Eric feels it, too.

Jules sits up, reaching for Eric and the button of his jeans. He slides off his pants as he crawls on top of her, and when he enters her, a wave of energy runs from his stomach to the top of his head. He presses his chest against Jules', and they lie still for a moment, the wave of energy now coursing through both of them.

When he starts to move, his rhythm is slow and weighty. Deep. Jules' moans get louder, her breath more ragged, encouraging him to move faster. He feels the power of the universe in her as he peaks, body shuddering, electricity rolling through him. Jules wraps her arms and legs around him, kissing his sweaty brow, holding him close.

"I love you," Jules whispers in his ear.

"I love you more."

A few blocks away, at John's house, John and Kyra lounge on the couch, lost in the flickering glow of a television screen. A mostly eaten bowl of popcorn sits within reach. John's bare torso contrasts with his sweatpants, while Kyra's state of undress is reversed, legs bare, wearing the matching sweatshirt. Her head rests comfortably in John's lap. His fingers stroke her hair as they take in the story unfolding on-screen.

As the movie reaches its conclusion, Kyra sits up, stretching languidly. "I loved it," she declares.

"Great ending," John agrees.

"Really great," Kyra echoes, standing and shaking off the inertia of their movie-watching, a few errant popcorn kernels falling to the floor. "I have to head back to my place. I'm out of fresh clothes."

A pouty expression clouds John's face, "No."

"Yes," Kyra insists, her voice resolute, "I am meeting potential new clients for lunch tomorrow. I have to look fabulous."

"You always look fabulous," John replies, pulling her closer.

Kyra leans into his kiss before pulling away. "I'm glad you think so. But I really need to look sharp. If I land this account, it could make my year."

"I get it," John concedes, releasing his embrace and slumping back into the couch.

Kyra begins gathering her belongings as John watches her from across the room. "So, um…"

Kyra glances back at him. "Yeah?"

"I really hate it when you leave," John confesses, his eyes steady on her.

Kyra slows her movements but continues to collect her things. John rises and walks over to her. "And…I really love it when you're here." The tension builds as he carefully considers his next words. "Move in with me," he breathes. The words hang in the air between them.

Kyra breaks into a wide smile that lights up her face. She pulls her sweatshirt over her head and presses her bare chest against his, their lips meeting in a fervent kiss.

"Is that a yes?" John manages to ask.

"That's a yes."

❦

The next day, mid-day, outside of a downtown restaurant, Kyra stands among three middle-aged men in non-descript gray suits, a sharp contrast to Kyra's tailored brick-red suit. They are all smiling and shaking hands.

Charlie spots Kyra from the other side of the street and crosses as Kyra bids the men farewell. "Very productive session, gentlemen. I'm looking forward to working together." The men nod in agreement as the maître d' hails them a cab, leaving Kyra standing in front of the restaurant alone.

Charlie approaches Kyra from behind and observes, "That looked like it went well."

Kyra swivels to meet Charlie and can barely contain her excitement. "Better than I could have ever imagined. I closed the deal!"

"I'm sure you had it all along," Charlie says.

Kyra bats her eyelashes coyly. "Why, thank you for saying that."

Charlie takes Kyra's hand, planting a soft kiss on the back of it. "I mean it. You're smart. You're beautiful. You're the whole package, Kyra."

Kyra's smile falters, and Charlie notices the shift. "What's up?"

"Things are getting more serious with John. He asked me to move in."

"That's great. I'm excited for you," Charlie offers, her words sincere.

"Me, too. It's just that…" Kyra trails off, her expression apprehensive.

"Just that what?" Charlie prompts, her grip on Kyra's hand subtly tightening.

Kyra takes a deep breath. "Charlie, you're his best friend. And this. You and me. Things could get messy."

"I thought you had an arrangement," Charlie points out, her voice edged with a hint of bitterness.

"We did. We do. I mean…" Kyra stammers, her face paling slightly.

"I see. So, it's ok for you to see other women. Just not me," Charlie infers, her tone hardening.

"That's not what I mean," Kyra hurries to explain, but Charlie cuts her off.

"Kyra, I really like you. This chemistry, it's…" Charlie trails off, her eyes searching Kyra's.

"It is. I feel it, too. Which is why…"

Charlie interrupts, "You don't have to say it. I understand."

"Charlie, please…" Kyra pleads, reaching out to Charlie, who steps back, distancing herself physically and, as best she can, emotionally.

"I'm really happy for you both." Charlie's voice is steady despite the turmoil in her eyes. "I'm going to go."

"Charlie, wait. We can still be friends. We have game night tonight…" Kyra calls out.

"I'll see you around, Kyra," Charlie says and then turns away.

❧

"I don't think I've ever been this happy and this sad at the same time," Kyra confesses to Jules and Beth. Kyra is visibly upset, her usually vibrant demeanor muted. The low din of the bar bounces off the concrete walls and into the intimate corners of the softly lit area where the three women are gathered, drinks sitting on damp cocktail napkins on the high-top table in front of them.

Jules and Beth lean in closer, their hands reaching across the table to comfort her. "Oh, babe. Talk to us," Jules says.

"We're all ears," Beth adds.

Kyra takes a deep breath and begins. "John asked me to move in with him last night, and I said yes."

Beth looks confused. "Isn't that a good thing?"

"Well, kind of, yeah," Kyra says, then rethinks her words. "I mean, yes. Of course."

"Which is it? Kind of, or yes?" Jules asks.

"It's a yes," Kyra says.

"Ok," Jules acknowledges, "tell me why."

Kyra takes a deep breath and responds, "It's just so easy with John. I feel like he gets me. Gets all of me. He's playful, but he's also an adult. He's caring and a good person. He takes responsibility for himself and pays his bills. And when he asked me to move in, he was so sweet. For the first time ever, I feel like I want to share my life with someone." Her voice wavers, the reality of her words sinking in.

"And share a bathroom. It's a big step." Beth's sarcasm brings a slight smile to Kyra's lips.

"And while he seems okay with me seeing other women…" Kyra continues, then trails off.

Jules finishes Kyra's sentence. "Seeing Charlie is different."

Kyra nods her head yes and takes a big sip of her drink. "I ran into Charlie after my lunch meeting today. There she was with her sexy fucking haircut and those goddamn freckles. I am so freaking attracted to her. So, as I'm telling her about moving in with John, it's occurring to me that it means ending things with her, romantically, at least, if I want things to go well with John. Which I do. So, I told her that we couldn't see each other like that anymore."

"Oh boy," says Beth.

"Yeah. I thought I had this under control. I feel good about the decision to move in with John. I'm crazy about him. I don't want anything to mess it up," Kyra goes on.

Jules nods, "I get it. Dating his best friend would definitely mess things up."

"But Charlie looked so hurt," Kyra continues, "and then I felt hurt, and it's making me question whether I'm doing the right thing. I didn't realize I was…"

"Catching feelings?" Beth asks.

"Big time," Kyra confirms. "I hope I'm doing the right thing. I'm so bad at monogamy." Kyra takes the last swallow of her drink and signals the waitstaff for another one.

"For what it's worth," Jules adds, "I'm not so good at it, either."

"What do you mean?" asks Beth.

"I got ambushed. By Claire. At spin class this week. Madelyn told her what happened, and Claire is convinced our ENM is because Eric and I are having marital problems."

After an awkward short pause, Kyra adds, "That's not all Madelyn's been saying."

"What're you talking about?" asks Jules.

"I'm not the only one with the feels," Kyra replies. "Madelyn has them, too. For Eric. She thinks she felt something special that night. And that's why you're so pissed."

"I'm sure she did feel something special," snaps Jules. "Eric's cock in her throat."

"Ouch," says Kyra.

"Yikes," says Beth.

"Exactly," states Jules.

Kyra shakes her head in apology. "I shouldn't have said anything. I hate breaking news like this. I'm sorry. Are you mad?"

Jules raises her hand, "No. No apologies. I need to know. And, yes, I am mad. At myself. For letting that ridiculous night happen. Madelyn can feel however she wants. I trust Eric. What happened, happened. We've moved on." Jules takes a breath to settle down and then raises her glass. "To moving on."

Beth and Kyra raise their glasses. "To moving on."

Kyra shifts topics. "So, what's happening with the couple you went on a date with?"

"We're going on another one," Jules replies.

Beth's eyes widen, "Really? When?"

"Next week," says Jules. "I'm really looking forward to it. It was so nice to be around another couple where we could just be ourselves."

Kyra smiles. "What are they like?"

"She's around our age. Really beautiful and quite charming. She takes good care of herself. He's a little older. And straight. He doesn't seem to have an issue with Eric being bi, but I'm not sure how it will go." Jules takes another sip of her drink. "I'm just happy we found another couple."

"I'm happy for you," Kyra says.

"Me, too," Jules replies.

Kyra checks the time on her phone and downs her drink. "You two are the best. Thanks for meeting me out and listening. I've got to head to John's. It's game night, and I'm already late."

Beth also chimes in, "I've got to run, too. Jules, see you and Eric tonight for Kevin's graduation cake? Bring Daisy?"

"We wouldn't miss it. I'll get the bill, and we'll be over shortly." Jules reaches for her purse.

Kyra and Beth stand to leave, each hugging Jules and leaving kisses on her cheek. "Talk soon. Love you," says Kyra.

"Love you," says Beth.

"Love both of you," says Jules as she watches her friends leave and waves for the check.

"Husband, are we boring?" Beth asks Alex as she walks through the door that leads from their garage into their kitchen. Alex is standing at the counter, icing Kevin's cake, and placing the 'Congratulations, Graduate!' decorations on top.

"What do you mean?" Alex asks.

Beth elaborates, comparing their life with the recent escapades of their friends. To her surprise, Alex chuckles. "I was wondering the same thing the other day when I was talking to Eric." Alex takes Beth's hand and faces her. "I don't know if we're boring or not. And, honestly, I don't care. What I do know is this. You are the woman of my dreams."

Beth's heart flutters, warmth spreading throughout every part of her. "You are the best man I know. But still. Would you ever want to…?" she presses, leaving the question hovering between them.

Alex's response is immediate, unwavering, "You are all I need."

"Me, too," Beth murmurs, returning the sentiment.

Beth's phone lights up with a text from Jules.

We're getting ready to leave the house. Do you need us to bring anything?

Beth responds: Just yourselves. Mason can't wait to see Daisy.

Beth calls out to the boys from the kitchen, "Eric, Jules, and Daisy are on their way. They should be here soon."

"Outside is all set up," Alex reassures. "I just need to grab the napkins." Beth can already hear the tremble in his voice. "You going to be ok today?" she asks, leaning into him.

"I make no promises," Alex responds with a soft smile.

Beth has always found Alex's depth of emotions endearing, particularly his feelings for Kevin. Their closeness was one of the things Beth found most attractive about Alex when they first met. Kevin was just 11 and had already endured so much loss with the passing of his mother. Alex and Kevin were a team, the bond of trust so strong between them. It was that trust that allowed Kevin to welcome Beth and Mason into their lives. While Beth has always been 'Beth' and not 'Mom' to Kevin, she always loved him as her own, and Kevin quickly took on the role of big brother to Mason. It wasn't just Alex managing his emotions; Beth's heart also ached at the thought of Kevin graduating high school and leaving for college at the end of the summer.

As if on cue, Mason runs into the kitchen, "I'm ready for cake!" He is just a little older than Kevin was when they became a blended family.

Kevin strolls into the kitchen, suddenly looking and sounding so mature. "Not yet, kiddo. Have a snack," he says to Mason. Alex and Beth both wonder to themselves how time has passed so quickly.

The front door chimes as Jules, Eric, and Daisy arrive and let themselves in. Daisy charges into the kitchen, heading straight for Mason.

"Daisy!" Mason exclaims, grabbing a tennis ball and leading Daisy out back to play fetch.

"Hello, hello!" Eric and Jules greet Alex, Beth, and Kevin. Jules kisses Beth and Alex on the cheek and gives Kevin a big hug. Eric opens his arms. "Get over here, graduate," he says to Kevin.

"Uncle Eric!" Kevin replies as he goes in for the hug.

"Alright, everyone," Beth announces, holding back tears, "out of my kitchen. The drinks are outside. I'll be out in a minute."

Everyone files outside except for Jules, who smirks at Beth. "You're not the boss of me." Beth laughs in return. "How are you two holding up?" Jules asks.

"So far, so good, maybe? I don't know. This is so hard. I need to keep it together for Alex. That much I know," Beth replies. "I caught him watching Kevin sleeping the other night like he did when Kevin was a little boy. He was teary, and it was all I could do to not ugly cry."

"Oh, babe," Jules remarks.

"Yeah." Beth continues, "Thank goodness Mason is still in grade school. I don't know what we're going to do when it's his turn."

"Good thing we don't have to think about that quite yet," Jules replies, and her mind wanders back to the beginning of her friendship with Beth and when she first met Mason.

Jules and Beth shared a mutual respect before they shared a friendship. Their paths crossed as first-year students in their MBA program under the harsh fluorescent lights of a lecture hall. Jules was meticulous in the projects she presented in business school. She was polished, professional, and her analyses were well substantiated. No fluff. No hype. Solid. While reserved in demeanor, when Jules spoke, she resonated with confidence. Beth took notice and was impressed.

Beth was older than many of the other students in the cohort, with significantly more work experience, even more than Jules. Beth's class participation was well-informed, practical, and tuned to how things work in the real world, not just academia. Students would take notes when Beth asked questions, Jules included.

It was a surprise when Beth showed up to class one day with Mason in tow. First year, first semester, and the cohort was still getting to know each other. Mason was just a toddler, and Beth's stress was obvious. Working groups were presenting that day, and attendance was mandatory. Typically calm and cool, Beth was struggling to get Mason settled before the session began, laying out coloring books, crayons, and snacks on the desk. Jules was in the row behind and overheard Beth say to the boy, "Ok, Mase. We can do this. I just need you to stay focused, and then I will take you for ice cream. Deal?" Mason's eyes lit up when he heard Beth mention ice cream. Up until this point, Jules was unaware that Beth was also a mom.

The professor was an older woman, a career academic, and tough. She was tough on the students, tough as a grader, and generally difficult in personality. Taking her place at the front of the room, she scanned the rows of students and fixed her eyes on Mason and then Beth. Beth offered a small smile as an apology, but before she could get any words out, the professor said, "I didn't realize we were running a daycare today."

Beth stammered, "I, um, I'm sorry. My childcare arrangements fell through at the last minute, and I didn't want to miss the presentations."

The professor shook her head slowly no. "This is a distraction."

Jules, without a second thought, stood and said, "I'm not distracted."

The professor shifted her focus from Beth to Jules and said, "Excuse me?"

The entire class turned to watch Jules as she continued. "He's quiet as a mouse and keeping himself busy. I'm not distracted at all."

The professor turned her focus back to Beth. "Will you be able to keep him quiet?"

Beth nodded her head yes.

The professor took a moment and then announced,

"Alright. Let's get started. Group 1, please come to the front for your presentation." One by one, the groups moved to the front of the room, presented their projects, and then took their seats. Other than a little shifting in his seat, Mason hardly made a noise.

When it was Beth's group's turn to present, Jules leaned over to Beth and whispered, "I'll sit with him."

Beth took Jules' hand, squeezed it, and said, "Thank you," as she stood to join her group in the front of the room. Jules took the seat next to Mason and said, "That's your mom up there." Mason just smiled at Jules and reached for his crayons, more interested in his coloring book than anything else.

Beth took the lead on the presentation and quickly found her rhythm when the slides came up. She was a natural presenter, easily guiding the class through the materials and fielding questions.

When she concluded, she thanked the class for their attention, and as she made her way back to her seat, Mason looked up from his coloring and yelled, "You did it, Mom!" The class broke out into applause and cheers, and even the professor turned up the corners of her mouth in a reluctant smile.

Beth planted a kiss on Mason's cheek and whispered in his ear, "You're getting two scoops today," and Mason wrapped his arms around his mom's neck.

When the final groups finished their presentations, Beth gathered Mason's things. Jules lingered, and when she caught Beth's eye, she said, "You hit it out of the park today. On several fronts."

Beth smiled, but there was a weariness in her eyes. "You like ice cream?" she asked Jules.

"Who doesn't?" Jules responded.

"My treat," Beth said, and she, Mason, and Jules left the lecture hall for the ice cream shop.

The sound of a glass breaking interrupts Jules' train of thought.

"My bad," they hear Mason mutter as Alex walks into the kitchen, looking for the paper towels, a broom, and a dustpan. "Not a big deal," Alex reports. "Mason knocked over a glass."

Outside, Eric sits across the picnic table from Kevin while Daisy chases Mason around the yard. "Kev, quick, while it's just us, want a sip of my beer?"

Kevin laughs and takes a small sip from Eric's bottle. "Thanks, Uncle Eric." Kevin's face is identical to Alex's when he was Kevin's age. As he looks at the young man, he can't help but feel emotional and nostalgic. His mind quickly floods with memories of him and Alex back in the day.

Eric and Alex met in kindergarten but became friends in the third grade when they were each targeted by the same bully. Eric hadn't yet gotten his height, and Alex hadn't yet gotten his girth when the run-ins started to occur. It began with stolen lunches and escalated to teasing and threats of fighting on the bus. Eric and Alex found themselves sticking together, consoling one another when the incidents occurred, and celebrating when the bully changed schools at the end of the school year. They have been best friends ever since. Eric came out to Alex in high school and, for a long time, Alex was the only other person in Eric's life besides Eric's father who knew.

Alex's reaction was pretty plain. "What does that mean

for you exactly?" he inquired after Eric told him about his sexuality. "It means I'm attracted to people romantically, sexually, because of who they are, not based on gender," was Eric's response. Alex thought about it for a minute and simply thanked Eric for telling him, for trusting him. Alex assured Eric his secret was safe with him, and they didn't really speak much of it after that.

Alex was just as tender as Eric and led with his heart. He was always falling for this girl or that girl, and if they weren't interested, he took it very hard. In his high school years, Alex went from being scrawny to filling out nicely, and when he made it to college, the girls he noticed started noticing him back. When Alex laid eyes on his first wife for the first time, he was hypnotized. His attraction was instant. And while she wasn't the settling down type, she cared for Alex, loved him in return. They dated through college and for years thereafter, taking the occasional break when she would inevitably see other people. This was torture for Alex, and each time they broke up, he swore it would be the last; that he would move on. But after she got pregnant following one of their reconciliations, they made the commitment to make it work. When Kevin came, it filled both of their worlds for a long time. Before she got sick. Before things changed.

It was a complicated loss. Alex and his first wife had a deep love for one another. Her illness came quickly and by surprise. Shortly after her death, Alex was contacted by one of her lovers, who was highly distraught after receiving news of her passing. As the details of the affair came to light, a mix of grief and rage rose within Alex. It took years before he was ready to date again, before he could contemplate trust.

Eric and Jules introduced Alex to Beth once they were both ready to date. Beth and Alex connected instantly and were married within a year. Eric was the best man, and Jules was the maid of honor at their wedding.

"So, tell me what you've been up to. What's your plan for the summer?" Eric asks Kevin, bringing his focus back to the present.

"Beth got me a job as an office clerk so I can save up for school. Most of my friends are working as well."

"You still seeing that girl?" Eric asks.

"Yeah. Kind of. We still hang out."

"What's going to happen this fall?"

"I don't know," Kevin replies. "I haven't really given it much thought. She'd like to keep things going, but I'm not sure yet."

"Keeping your options open?" Eric asked with a raised brow.

"I guess you can call it that, yes." A nervous smile crosses Kevin's lips. While he and Eric have always been close, Eric can tell this topic still makes him uncomfortable.

"Do you need to have the 'big talk' from Uncle Eric?"

"Gross."

Eric laughs. "I deserved that." There's a moment of silence as Kevin takes another sip from Eric's beer. He takes a deep breath and locks eyes with Eric, who can sense a question lingering.

"Hey, while my dad is inside, I was hoping I could ask you about my mom." He asks it so casually, but Eric knows the struggle he must be feeling, having all these question marks surrounding who he is.

"Of course, Kev. What do you want to know?"

"She wasn't much older than me when she and Dad started dating. You knew them both. Dad doesn't really like talking about her, and this is already a tough time for him. I guess I'm just wondering what she was like around this age."

Eric nods, thinking about what he should say. "Your mom was like a ray of sunshine. She was tall, which is where you got your height from, and had these piercing blue eyes. Your dad couldn't stop staring at her. No one could when she was around. She was like a magnet—people were just drawn to her. She and your dad dated on and off during college, and after graduation, they got pregnant with you. When you came along, you were the center of their world. They poured every drop of love they had into you. I know she would be so proud of you right now. With what you have ahead of you."

Beth, Alex, and Jules come outside from the kitchen and take a seat at the table with Eric and Kevin, signaling the end of their exchange.

"Thanks, Uncle Eric," Kevin says with a grateful smile.

"Anytime, Kev."

"Dad got me a guitar for graduation," Kevin announces. "I'm taking lessons online, and some friends and I are thinking of starting a band." Kevin strikes a dramatic air guitar pose for full effect.

"How fun," Jules says, "I'm sure you will be great."

"And just in case," Beth adds, "it came with a speaker and some headphones…"

"You know," Eric says coyly, "Your dad and I had a band."

"What?! You and Alex? Jules, did you know about this?" Beth asks.

"This is news to me," Jules replies, leaning in.

Alex shoots Eric a look. "There is a reason we don't talk about it. We were awful."

Eric nods in agreement, adding, "Yes. True. But what we lacked in talent, we made up for with enthusiasm."

Alex rolls his eyes. "We were in high school and had a set of four songs. Total. We did emo ABBA covers and thought we were so clever. I sang and played a banged-up keyboard that I found in someone's trashcan. Six of the keys didn't work, and it sounded like a stomach cramp when you pressed them. Eric had an electric drum kit. Whatever happened to that drum kit, Eric?" Eric just shrugs, and Alex continues, "We gelled our hair into spikes and practiced at my house after school. Good god, it was embarrassing."

"I have a thousand questions," Jules says, unable to hide her widening grin. "Did you ever play any gigs? Any groupies or fan clubs we should know about? Is there any merch? T-shirts? Secret tattoos?"

"We talked about playing at the school talent show," Eric replies, taking a sip of his drink. "But I couldn't get Alex to do it."

"Thank goodness," Alex adds. "I would still be regretting it. And before you ask, I've destroyed all evidence. Photographic, audio, and otherwise."

"No!" says Beth.

Eric holds his hands up. "I tried to stop him. I thought it was gold."

"What was the name of your band, Dad?" Kevin asks.

Alex shakes his head no, but Eric can't resist. "Meatish Sweetballs."

Jules, Beth, and Kevin nearly choke on their laughter. Even Alex softens and laughs, raising his glass to Eric.

Just as their laughter settles down, the backyard fills with the sound of Mason's muffled giggles. Daisy has him pinned to the ground while sitting on his chest as she licks his face. "Argh!" Mason yells. "She's tea bagging me!"

All ears perk up, and all eyes widen. Beth has the nerve to ask, "Mase—did you just say tea bagging?"

"Yeah," replies Mason from under Daisy's kisses. Jules covers her mouth with her hand to muffle a giggle.

"Ok," Beth continues, "what do you think that means?"

"It's when you put your butt on someone," Mason responds with authority.

"More like 'flea bagging' when Daisy's doing it," Kevin adds, and another round of laughter erupts from the table.

Beth just shakes her head. "You can't make this stuff up."

"On that note..." Kevin reaches for the cake cutter, "Happy graduation to me."

"Hey, hey, hey, easy there," Beth says. "You're the one being celebrated. I'll cut the cake." As Beth slices the cake, Alex hands her the dessert plates.

"Let's have a toast," Jules says as she refills everyone's drinks.

Once everyone's cup is full and they each have a piece

of cake in front of them, Alex stands. "Congratulations, my beautiful, handsome, kind, brilliant son. You make me so, so proud. I can't wait to see what the future has in store for you. To Kevin!"

Cups are raised, "To Kevin!"

"This is for you," Eric says to Kevin, sliding a wrapped gift and card across the table. "We're so proud of you."

Kevin opens the card, smiles at Eric and Jules, then tears the wrapping paper from the gift. It's a framed Polaroid picture of Kevin and Alex when Kevin was about seven years old. Kevin was in his baseball uniform, and he and Alex were grinning wide at the camera, Kevin with no front teeth. The sky was bright blue behind them, contrasting sharply against the orange dirt of the baseball diamond, and they were each squinting a little from the sunlight. Eric had gone to the game to cheer them on and took the picture right after Kevin's team won.

"I love it!" Kevin says. "I'm taking it with me to school."

Eric nods in acknowledgment, both to Kevin and to Alex.

The gathering winds down with Beth, Jules, and Eric shuttling used plates and glasses to the kitchen while Alex loads the dishwasher.

"That was great," Jules says.

"Cake was delicious," Eric adds. "Thank you for having us."

"Thank you for coming," Alex says. "New milestone, new chapter. He's going to do amazing things, that kid."

"Yes, he is," Beth agrees, planting a kiss on Alex's cheek.

"I'm going to say goodbye to the kids and get Daisy,"

says Jules, picking up Daisy's leash from the counter and stepping back out into the yard.

"I'll join you," says Eric. Kevin and Mason are playing tag, and Daisy is busy herding them.

"Alright, you two. We're heading home," Jules announces as she approaches and clips the leash on Daisy's collar.

"Noooo!" cries Mason, hugging Daisy around her neck. Daisy licks Mason up the side of his face, from jawline to forehead, and gives Jules a big dog grin. Jules laughs as she pulls Mason into a hug. "I love you, Mase."

"I love you, too, Aunt Jules."

"You be good, Mase," says Eric.

"No way, Uncle Eric," Mason responds, prompting another laugh from Jules.

Kevin walks over with arms wide, and Jules and Eric both go in for a hug.

"Thank you for the present," Kevin says.

"Our pleasure," Eric and Jules reply in unison. "We love you."

Eric and Jules go back inside to wish Beth and Alex good night before making their way to their car to start the short drive home.

"My goodness, time flies," Jules says as they pull out of the driveway.

"Tell me about it," Eric agrees. "That was harder than I thought it would be."

"It's crazy," Jules says. "When I look at the boys, I still see them as little kids. That picture of Kevin—that's how I think of him. Now, he's so tall he can rest his chin on the top of my head."

Eric nods in agreement. "He's so grown. It was really something to look through those old pictures. That one of him and Alex is one of my favorites."

"Those pictures are treasures," Jules adds. "I remember when I got you that Polaroid camera. We had just started dating and took that first trip right before graduation." Jules smiled at the memory.

"I remember being so in love with you and so afraid of suggesting the trip," Eric admits with a laugh.

"What do you mean?" Jules asks in surprise.

"Oh, come on, you were so focused on school, you had your dream job lined up, we were all set on our path forward. I didn't want anything to get in the way of that or deter your hustle."

"But?" Jules prompts, waiting for Eric to say more.

"But, I also remember feeling like we needed to do something, just the two of us, to mark the occasion. Live in the moment, you know? Enjoy a little slice of life before it passed us by." Jules and Eric smile at each other, and Jules' heart fills with gratitude, feeling lucky to have Eric by her side through so many of life's milestones.

"It was one of the best trips we ever went on..."

A few days after Eric suggested the pre-graduation trip, Eric and Jules loaded up Eric's car with their backpacks, hiking boots, several bags of salt and vinegar chips, red vines, a cooler with two 6-packs of beer, and iced coffees.

Closing the hatchback, Eric announced, "All set. Let's do this."

Jules hopped into the passenger seat and turned, grinning at Eric. "Let's go."

She put on a mix she had arranged for the trip, and music filled the car. The busy highways turned to tree-lined back roads as they made their way out of the city, and they rolled down the windows, letting the fresh air in. Out of the corner of his eye, Eric watched Jules catch her windblown hair into a ponytail and put sunglasses on. Jules considered asking Eric about which job offer he was leaning toward taking, but decided against it. She wasn't prepared for the answer if it meant him moving to another city. Instead, they drove in comfortable silence, holding hands, Eric's eyes on the road, Jules watching the scenery go by.

The road wound along meadows teeming with wildflowers. Purples, yellows, and reds set off against the backdrop of the deep blue, cloudless sky. They passed fenced-in pastures with grazing horses and wooden farm stands with hand-painted sandwich boards offering buckets of fresh produce for sale.

Hours went by as they climbed up into the mountains, and the sky turned golden as the sun began to drop below the horizon. The air became noticeably cooler, and fireflies twinkled in the trees on the sides of the road.

"This is it," Eric said as they slowed their approach to a set of rustic cabins. He parked in front of the building with the office sign hanging over the door. Jules couldn't hide her delight as she stepped out of the car and stretched her arms over her head, filling her lungs with fresh mountain air.

"Just beautiful," she said.

"Like you," Eric replied.

They got the key to their cabin and unlocked the door to find a double bed with clean linens flanked by two-night tables with pull chain lights, an oval braided rug on a swept but still dusty, wide-planked floor, and a postage stamp-sized bathroom with a shower, no tub.

On the opposite side of the room was a windowed door that opened to a screened-in porch with two woven chairs and a small table in between. The porch looked out over the mountains, which were dark blue against the orange, golden, and pink tones of the setting sun. The air was crisp with a piney smell, and, for Eric and Jules, each breath melted away a layer of stress from the graduate programs they had just completed.

They exchanged excited glances, popped out back to the car to grab their bags, and settled in on the porch with their cooler and snacks. Eric opened two cans of beer, handed one to Jules, and they toasted. "To mountain roads and fire-flies," Eric said.

"To fresh air and sunsets," Jules replied as they clinked cans and took their first sips.

"I didn't know how badly I needed this," Jules continued, "thank you."

Eric smiled in return. "So, now that I have you all to myself, no books or spreadsheets to distract you, and we've decompressed from the drive over here, tell me... What's your favorite color?"

"Depends on the day," Jules replied, "but usually green."

"Green?" Eric nodded. "I wouldn't have guessed that."

"What about you?"

"Gray."

Jules nodded back. "I can see that."

"Favorite song?" Eric continued.

"Oohh…that's a tough one. Probably *We Got The Beat* by the Go-Go's."

"That was a great album."

"It was. And you? What's your favorite song?"

"Anything off the Purple Rain album."

"Prince! I love Prince!"

"That makes two of us," Eric responded.

They finished their beers and cracked open two more. This time, Jules asked a question. "Can you remember your dreams?"

"Not usually," Eric replied, "but sometimes. You?"

"Only the crazy ones. And then I can't remember them for long. Plus, the more I try to remember, the more the details slip away. Why is that?"

"I don't know." Eric shrugged. "Chips Ahoy or Oreos?"

"Oreos."

"Wow," Eric laughed, "You didn't even have to think about that one. Checkers or Chess?"

"Checkers."

"Really. I would have put money on you being a Chess girl."

"Favorite food?" Jules asked.

"All of them."

Jules laughed. "I can see that."

Slowly, the sun faded, the sky darkened, and the stars

came out—what felt like millions of them. "So many stars," Jules observed, "we never get to see this in the city."

Eric watched Jules watch the sky.

"When was your first kiss?" Eric asked.

"Like real kiss?" Jules clarified.

"Yes."

"Sixth grade."

"Sixth grade!"

"Yep. Chris Nelson. We were at a birthday party, and he kissed me in the hallway. I didn't know what I was doing, so I opened my mouth and stuck my tongue out a little. He did, too. His breath tasted like warm milk. I liked it."

"I got kissed when I was a kid at summer camp, but it happened so quickly I didn't get a chance to kiss back," Eric said.

"Sniped!" Jules said.

"Exactly!" Eric replied. "My first real kiss was sophomore year in high school. Debbie Haverty. She had pretty hair and braces. I kissed her under the bleachers at a basketball game. I tried to touch her boob over her shirt, but she wasn't having it."

Jules laughed. "Debbie Haverty, huh? My competition?"

"You have nothing to worry about."

They leaned back in their chairs, finished their second beers, and opened thirds, taking in the night sky. The sound of crickets chirping seemed to get louder.

Eric stood. "I'll be right back."

Jules heard Eric step into the bathroom, lift the lid, urinate, flush, and wash his hands. It felt oddly intimate to her to hear him in this way. She took a few more sips of beer and realized how tipsy she was feeling, but it felt good.

The windowed door creaked, and Eric stepped back out onto the porch. Instead of settling back into his chair, he walked around to the front of Jules, took her hand, and asked, "Dance with me?"

Jules replied by standing and wrapping her arms around Eric's shoulders while his arms encircled her waist. They swayed, slowly and a little clumsily, to the rhythm playing in Eric's head, and Jules leaned into Eric's chest. He smelled like beer and dryer sheets. Eric rubbed his face in Jules' hair. She smelled like flowers.

Jules tilted up her face to find Eric looking at her. She swept his hair off his face with her fingers and pulled him into a kiss. His arms tightened around her waist.

"I want you closer," he whispered against her lips. Jules responded by grabbing his hand and moving it to her breast. When he kissed Jules again, it was rougher, more urgent, and slowly, he guided them back into the room, and they tumbled onto the bed. Jules pulled Eric's shirt over his head and took off her own, followed by her bra. They pressed their bodies together, delighting in the skin-on-skin, and Eric undid the button and zipper of Jules' jeans, then stood at the edge of the bed to pull them off her. He paused to take in the sight of her naked body. She smiled, parting her legs teasingly; she wanted him to see her.

Lust and desire washed over Eric, and he put his face between her legs. His tongue found a sweet spot quickly, and Jules lifted her hips to meet every stroke. She was already panting and on the edge when he put two fingers inside of her. Jules' thighs locked, keeping him right where she needed him. His fingers and mouth moved together, beckoning, sucking, and he felt her tighten around him. Her face flushed, a stream of hot liquid shot out of her, and she bolted upright, "Oh god. I'm so sorry. It's not pee. I promise."

Eric, caught off guard, wiped his face. "It's ok."

Jules pulled the blanket over her lap. "Oh no. I made a mess. I'm… I'm so embarrassed."

"No, no," Eric comforted, "talk to me. What just happened? Did you…"

"Yes. When I get a little drunk and let my guard down. The first time it happened, I was in high school. I was with this guy, and we were doing shots in his basement. Neither of us knew what it was or that my body would do that. He gagged."

"Oh, Jules. That's awful. I'm so sorry." Eric sat up and tilted Jules' chin up to look at him. "You have nothing to be ashamed about. That was beautiful. I loved it."

"You're just being nice."

"No, really. I love making you feel good, and, well, now I know it was working."

Jules turned her head away and laughed a little.

"I'm serious," Eric said. "Look at me." Jules turned to face him.

"You are the most beautiful and intelligent woman I have ever met, and, damn, if you're not also the sexiest. I cannot stop thinking about you. Your body drives me crazy. I am not a squeamish guy. In fact, I'm the opposite. What happened just now, with me between your legs, I want more of it. I want all of it."

Tears welled in Jules' eyes. "You mean it?"

"I wouldn't say it if I didn't." Eric leaned over and kissed the tears rolling down Jules' cheeks. "Now, salt and vinegar chip crumbs in the bed… That's another story."

Jules let out a half-cry, half-laugh and hugged Eric close. "Thank you," she whispered. "Let me go clean up." Jules stood, and Eric watched her walk naked into the bathroom, closing the door behind her. She turned on the shower, and steam quickly filled the small room. She stepped into the hot water and let it run down her body. She knew she was developing feelings for Eric from the night of their very first date. But these were real feelings. Love. And also fear. Again, she suppressed her worries over where Eric would accept a position, if he would take a job out of state, wondering if they could make a long-distance relationship work.

She heard the bathroom door open, and Eric peeked his face through the shower curtain. "Want company?"

She smiled at him. "I'm not sure two of us will fit."

Eric waggled his eyebrows. "Let's try."

Jules rolled her eyes and made room for Eric to squeeze in. They were chest to chest, arms straight down, unable to move much. "Our first shower together," Eric announced.

"Yes," Jules acknowledged, water pelting their faces.

"Not as romantic as I thought it would be," Eric observed. "I'll hop out."

Jules laughed and nodded in agreement.

Eric dried off with the too small towel, coarse from too many bleach cycles, and tucked back into bed. A few minutes later, Jules came out wrapped in the other towel and took out a gift from the bottom of her bag. She handed it to Eric.

"A Polaroid?" he asked excitedly as he unwrapped the paper.

"Yes. Already loaded with instant film. I thought you might like it."

"I love it! I've always wanted one of these. Thank you. Wait. I have an idea."

He put on the tee shirt that Jules wore and handed her his. They sat up in bed, wearing each other's shirts, and Eric held the camera facing them. "Look at the lens," he said as he pushed the red button, and the flash went off. Eric took the picture from the feed and shook it while it developed. The image reflected Jules smiling wide, wet hair tucked behind her ears, and Eric planting a kiss on her cheek.

"My eyes are all red!" Jules exclaimed when she saw the picture.

"Don't care. You look adorable," Eric replied.

"Alright, your turn." Jules extended her arms, holding the camera facing them. With a mischievous grin, she took Eric's earlobe between her teeth and tugged as she pressed the red button. Each of them giggled when the image developed into a wide-eyed, shocked-but-smiling Eric. He placed both polaroids on the bedside table and stood to get two more beers.

"Tell me about where you grew up," Jules said, reaching for hers. They lay reclined, facing each other on the bed.

"Suburbia," Eric responded. "Good public school system. Sleep away camp during the summer. Just me—no siblings. My folks are teachers. They're getting ready to retire in a few years and move to a golf community in Florida."

"The one where all the old people drive around on golf carts and have venereal diseases?" Jules asked.

"No. Not that one."

"That's too bad."

"Is it?" Eric asked sarcastically. "What about your parents?"

"My parents split up when I was finishing high school," Jules replied. "No sibs for me, either. Well, technically, that's not correct. My dad went on to have a second family, but I've never met his kids. I'm not that close with him."

"I'm sorry for that."

"Don't be. They really weren't happy together, and everyone just moved on. I grew up in suburbia, too. My schools were ok, but I had a really great math teacher who was very influential on me."

"Is that why you're into finance?"

"Pretty much, yeah. Numbers are fun for me. Like a puzzle."

"Why red vines?" Eric asked, reaching for the licorice package.

"Because they are versatile and delicious," Jules responded.

"Versatile?"

"You can use them as straws."

"Fair enough," Eric acknowledged with a laugh.

"Why social work?" Jules asked.

"It fits me. I like helping people, being of service. Especially for people who really need it."

"Acts of service is your love language."

"One of them, yeah. Favorite Stevie Wonder song?"

"Ooh, that's a tough one." Jules thinks for a second. "Probably a tie between *Superstition* and *Master Blaster*. Least favorite Stevie Wonder song?"

"*Part-time Lover*," Eric replied.

"Agreed. Not my fave. Who is your celebrity crush?"

"Selma Hayek. Yours?"

"Selma Hayek." They each giggled.

"Tell me about Alex."

"He's my best friend. Has been since we were kids. He's always had my back. I've always had his. He's honest and loyal. I'm lucky to have him."

"Sounds like it."

"Yeah. Like a brother. And Kevin is hilarious. I love that kid. I remember the day he was born. We were barely out of college. I was in the waiting room with Alex's and his first wife's families. That kid was in no rush to come out, and labor was taking forever. Finally, Alex comes out in this paper surgical smock holding Kev—who was so freaking tiny with this smushed little head—and Alex was smiling, crying, and terrified, all at the same time. I remember asking him if he was alright while the grandparents were passing the baby around, and his answer was, 'Hell fucking no—I have no idea what I'm doing. But I love this kid so much already. I'll figure it out.' That's Alex. He figures things out with his heart." Eric paused to take a sip of beer and shifted subjects. "Now that you won't be studying all the time, what do you like to do on weekends?"

"I will probably be working," Jules said flatly. "This job is intense."

"No fun." Eric pouted. "Here. Give me your hand." Eric took Jules' palm and ran his fingers over the lines. "I don't know, Jules. This line right here, this is your fun line."

"Yeah? What's it say?"

Eric grew serious, slowly shaking his head no, then looked up at Jules playfully. "It says you're going to have lots of fun!"

"That's great news." Jules laughed and started chewing on a red vine. She then asked, "Have you ever been arrested?"

"No, but I used to shoplift gum," Eric confessed. "You?"

"Shoplift gum? No." Jules smirked.

"Get arrested?" Eric clarified.

"No," Jules confirmed.

"Have you ever done drugs?" Eric asked.

"Recreationally. In college," Jules replied. "Not so much since then."

"Same. What do you look for in a partner?" Eric asked.

"Gosh… I mean, the table stakes stuff—honesty, loyalty, respect, kindness. But also being loved and supported for who I am. I'd like to be with someone who is secure in themselves. Has a good sense of humor. Someone who is up for adventure. You asked about my parents before. Their marriage was pretty awful. I know they stuck it out the last few years thinking it was for me, but really, it was brutal. Loveless. They just gave up. I want the opposite of that." Jules took another sip of beer. "What about you? What's important to you?"

"Everything is important to me," Eric said. "All the things you said, plus I want to be with someone who is willing to put the work in. Feed the relationship so that it evolves and grows. Work through the hard stuff. I want to be one of those couples that makes it to their 50th wedding anniversary and is still madly in love."

"This romantic in you...it's quite endearing," Jules complimented.

"Thank you," Eric acknowledged. "I don't often get to show it."

"It suits you," Jules affirmed.

"What about kids?" Eric continued.

"What about them?"

"Do you want them?"

"I don't think I do. It's not that I don't like kids, I just don't see myself as a mom. What about you?"

"I could go either way. It's not a dealbreaker for me one way or the other."

Jules took the information in and grew quiet for a moment. She couldn't keep the question to herself any longer. "So... We haven't really talked about your plans after graduation. I know you have a bunch of offers on the table. Have you made a decision on where you want to be?"

Eric took a second before responding. "As a matter of fact, I have."

"Are you willing to share? I don't mean to pry if you're not ready to talk about it." Jules felt a lump rise in her throat and was unsure of what she would do if he said he was moving to another city.

"I'm taking the job in town. It's the right one for me." Eric broke into a wide grin as he saw the relief wash over Jules' face. Jules wrapped her arms around Eric and hugged him close.

"I'm so glad you said that," she said. "I'm not ready for this to end."

"That makes two of us," Eric replied, returning Jules' hug.

⊷

Eric and Jules pull into their driveway, step through the front door, and stop to look at the Polaroid pictures they took on that very first trip together, now framed and hung in their entryway. Jules smiles, kisses Eric on the cheek, and lets Daisy off the leash. Eric lingers in front of the photos, still remembering. Jules will never know that he'd actually taken the job out of state, but that night with her changed everything. He'd decided then and there to be wherever she was, and not a day goes by when he regrets that choice.

⊷

Kyra strides through the front door laden with a grocery bag of snacks and a 6-pack of beer, the plastic rustling against her side as she steps inside. "Hi. Sorry I'm a little late. I had drinks with Jules and Beth and stopped at the store for some snacks."

John sits on the couch and looks up from his phone, his face cloudy. "No game night tonight. Charlie didn't show. I called and texted. No answer."

Kyra frowns slightly, her heart aching for Charlie. And for herself. She starts to wonder if she should tell John what happened, but John changes the subject before she can get any words out. "So, um, how did the lunch meeting go?"

Kyra's face lights up. "I won the deal!" she says, brimming with excitement.

"Yeah you did! You're incredible," John replies, grinning. He helps Kyra unload the grocery bags and put everything away.

"So, um, I have something for you..." he says, voice tinged with excitement and a little nervousness.

"You do?" Kyra tilts her head, curious.

"Yes. A little surprise."

Kyra's lips curl into a playful smile. "I like surprises."

John takes her by the hand, grip firm but warm, and leads her down the hallway into the bedroom, and then to the door of his walk-in closet. He pauses for a moment and, with a small smile, he pushes the door open and gestures her inside. Kyra steps forward as her eyes adjust to the softly lit space. The racks that once held John's clothes are bare, the hangers gone. To the left and right are empty sections waiting to be filled. At the back, a sleek built-in dresser topped with a glowing vanity mirror and flanked by pristine shoe cubbies.

"For you," John announces, his eyes never leaving Kyra's face.

A gasp escapes her lips as she takes in the sight. "All for me?" she asks, as she opens her arms wide and slowly twirls.

John's smile grows. "All for you."

The moment feels suspended in time as Kyra steps closer to John.

"Hold my gaze," she says in a tone that doesn't leave it up for discussion. John locks eyes and feels his whole body light up with anticipation. Kyra lifts his hands to one of the clothes hanging bars, and their lips meet in a fiery kiss, an early preview of what is to come. Kyra pulls away slightly, and he reaches his face toward her, mouth hungry for more. "Do not let go," Kyra says. "Do you understand?" John nods his head in agreement. Without breaking eye contact, Kyra slowly sinks to her knees, unbuckles his belt, and takes him into her mouth. A low groan escapes his lips as she smiles up at him.

"Not so fast," John's tone is heavy with breath, "you're mine." In the blink of an eye, John has Kyra upright, his hands expertly undoing her belt. He pulls off her pants, lifting her to sit on top of the built-in dresser. As he leans her back against the mirror, he bends forward, kissing down the midline of her chest, then her belly, his intent clear. He stands upright, pushes himself into her, and they move in synchrony.

"I love you," John whispers in between breaths.

"I love you," Kyra echoes back.

John's body trembles with pleasure before tumbling into Kyra's arms.

A few minutes later, fresh from a shower, Kyra hangs up her suit in her new closet. She joins John, who is lying on the bed, draped in a towel. "So, um, I'm really glad you're here," he says as he tucks a strand of Kyra's wet hair behind her ear.

"Me, too," Kyra replies with a warm smile.

"How was the rest of your day?" he asks.

Kyra again considers whether to tell John what happened with Charlie. Clear the slate. Let him know she chooses him and the relationship they are building. But a little voice in her head screams, *What good would that do? It might really upset him.* She keeps it to herself instead.

"I got to catch up with Jules and Beth."

"Are Jules and Eric recovering from the threesome gone wrong?" John asks.

"I hope so. Though Madelyn seems to have gone off the deep end. She's developed feelings for Eric."

"What a mess." John shakes his head.

"Seriously," Kyra agrees, a small sigh escaping her lips. "I'm all for people expressing themselves, but sometimes it's best to keep it at a safe distance. On the plus side, Jules and Eric found another couple to spend time with. More experienced."

"That sounds promising," John says.

"Yeah. They are going on a second date," Kyra continues.

"Second date, huh…" John says.

"Yeah. This should be interesting."

CHAPTER 4

MEET MY GOOD FRIEND MOLLY

Jules stands naked in Miles' and Elena's guest bathroom. Her bare skin glistens in the soft overhead light. Turning on the faucet, she cools her flushed face with a splash of water. In the mirror, her pupils are dilated with wild intensity, and the beads of sweat dotting her hairline reflect the sensations coursing through her body. Her breathing pattern is erratic; her jaw is clenched.

Eric steps into the bathroom behind her, shirtless and wrapped loosely in a hot pink fleece blanket. His pupils, too, are dilated, and his body temperature vacillates between sweating and freezing. "How are you doing?" he asks.

"I'm rolling my fucking face off. I haven't felt like this since college."

Eric cracks a smile and nuzzles into Jules' neck, lips pressing against her heated skin. "No kidding. Everything is tingling."

Jules pulls away to lean over the sink again, soaking a washcloth with cold water. "I'm burning up."

"I'll get you some ice water when we go back out there," Eric offers.

"Thank you," Jules breathes out, placing the washcloth against the back of her neck.

A moment passes, and Eric speaks back up with a tentative undertone. "It looks like you're having a lot of fun out there."

Jules fixes on Eric's gaze in the mirror. "I've never come so hard in my life."

Jules turns and exits the bathroom, leaving Eric alone with his reflection. His expression falls and tears well up in his eyes.

⁓

"Oh, Eric. I'm so sorry. I can see how much that hurt you," Dr. Layton says. A few days have passed since his exchange with Jules in Miles' and Elena's bathroom, and Eric is seated, crestfallen, in Dr. Layton's office. "Begin at the beginning," Dr. Layton encourages. "How did it get there?"

Eric takes a deep breath and reluctantly dives back into the events of that evening.

⁓

The din of ambient conversation and clinking glasses surrounds them in an off-the-beaten-path bar as Miles and Elena sit opposite Jules and Eric in a secluded corner booth. Each of them is nursing a drink. Miles, Elena, and Jules are smiling. Eric is not. Even though Eric agreed to come, he's having trouble hiding his apprehension and restlessly fidgets with his cocktail napkin. His residual guilt from the encounter with Madelyn continues to make it difficult for him to express to Jules how he really feels. He doesn't want to disappoint her or be perceived as standing in her way or holding her back. *Get it together*, he thinks to himself. *We're here. Maybe Jules is right. I just need to keep an open mind.*

"How is your…"

"It's really good to…"

Jules and Miles speak over each other to start the conversation, and Jules smiles politely, deferring to Miles. "We're so glad you decided to see us again," he says. "You look especially pretty tonight, Jules."

Elena is quick to follow. "Just radiant."

Jules blushes, murmuring her thanks. Eric shifts in his seat, trying to let go of his resistance. "So, how have both of you been?"

"Really good," Elena responds, turning her focus to Eric. "We've been excited to see you again."

Jules jumps in, "Us, too. Our last visit was so…" She trails off, searching for the right word.

Miles provides it, "Refreshing."

"Yes," Jules agrees. "Refreshing. It was so nice to feel so open."

The conversation ebbs for a moment, and Eric asks, "What are your days like? What keeps you busy?"

Miles and Elena share bits and pieces of their lives—working downtown, Pilates for Elena, competitive tennis for Miles—painting a picture of their regular routine. They have an anniversary trip coming up, celebrating 14 years of marriage. Elena kisses Miles on the cheek, and he puts his arm around her as they speak about their upcoming plans. Miles explains that it's the second time around for him, his first marriage lasting only a year, but that it worked out perfectly since it prepared him for his beautiful life with Elena. Miles is Elena's first husband, but she has had numerous long-term relationships. Elena refers to Miles as her home base, her ride-or-die. It is clear to both Jules and Eric that Miles and Elena care for and respect each other deeply, and the trust and love between them is obvious. A spark of hope ignites in Eric. Miles and Elena seem to have figured out how to do non-monogamy, and it piques curiosity in Eric.

"So, is it ok if I ask? How does this work for you two? This. When you two…"

"When we date?" Elena offers.

"Yes! Thank you," Eric says with a shy laugh.

In response, Miles and Elena open up about their relationship, about dating separately and together. Elena starts, "It depends. We don't often date together. Miles has some lady friends he sees on occasion. Some I've met. Some I haven't. It really just depends on how well Miles intends to get to know them. If it looks like it will be more of an ongoing connection, I like to meet them."

"What's that like?" Jules asks.

"It can vary. For the most part, it's friendly. I've learned some lessons along the way. Public places are a must. I trust Miles to establish boundaries, but it's important to me to know they are understood."

"You don't get jealous?" Eric asks.

"Of course I do. But it's fleeting. Meeting them helps me see them as people and not mythical beasts of competition," Elena responds with some levity.

"I get jealous, too," Miles adds. "Elena has her

relationships as well. I typically don't meet the people Elena is involved with. We manage our emotions differently."

Eric faces Elena. "Do you see men and women?"

"I have relationships with both men and women, yes," Elena clarifies. "I also enjoy being another couple's third. You know, unicorning. Despite your last experience, it can be quite pleasurable for all involved."

"I'm sure under the right circumstances…" Jules adds.

"How do you meet people? How do they meet you?" Eric asks.

"Mostly the apps," Miles responds. "Sometimes there are events or parties."

"Ok," Eric says, feeling more confident. "Practical question. How do you manage scheduling? What happens when one of you has plans, but the other doesn't?"

Miles answers, "For some people, lifestyle is all they do. They are on the apps constantly, always looking for new connections. New experiences. We get into phases where it feels like that, but then it settles down. We find that we are generally aligned when it's getting to be too much, when it's interfering with our relationship. Every now and again, one of us finds ourselves in a relationship with someone who wants more than we can give. That causes a lot of stress all around."

"We've learned how to prioritize each other and make sure things feel somewhat balanced," Elena adds. "And we try to schedule at a time when we can both be…otherwise occupied."

"How often do you get to go on dates together? With another couple?" Jules asks.

Elena responds, "It's always fun for us to engage with another couple. That doesn't happen often. It can be hard to get the chemistry right."

Seeing an on-ramp, Miles begins, "Um, speaking of chemistry…"

∽

Jules, Kyra, and Beth are huddled together at a high-top table, the surrounding bar noise offering a comfortable backdrop to their conversation. With a mischievous smile, Jules announces, "We saw Miles and Elena again over the weekend."

"The couple you met last time?" Beth asks.

"Mmmm hmmmm," Jules responds coyly.

"Did you guys have fun?" asks Kyra.

Jules nods her head, and Kyra raises an eyebrow.

"Like a lot of fun?" Kyra continues.

Jules makes eye contact with Kyra and can barely contain her excitement. "Like, all the fun."

"Whaaaat!" Kyra leans forward in her seat. "I want all the details!"

"Don't leave a single thing out!" Beth adds, eyes wide with anticipation.

Jules just smiles at them over her glass, eyes twinkling. She takes a leisurely sip of her drink, letting the suspense build.

∽

The energy in the bar shifts as Elena casually picks up where Miles left off, "How do you two feel about molly? MDMA? We have some. From a reliable source."

Jules collects herself enough to respond. "It's been years since I've done molly. Not since college."

Eric, nodding in agreement, adds, "Same."

"I'm game," Jules states, which takes Eric by surprise. He feels caught off guard, pressured, rushed, excited, and nervous, all at the same time. Turning to Jules, he says, "Don't you think we should talk about this first?"

Jules looks back at Eric with a patient but determined expression. "You're right. We should. Would you like to do this?"

Eric recognizes what is happening. He knows she's made up her mind. He inhales to calm himself, get a hold of his feelings. It doesn't feel right, but it doesn't feel completely wrong, either. "If you're good with it," he capitulates, "then I guess I am, too."

"It's settled, then." Miles smiles, leans back, and signals for the check. "Let's go back to our place. We're going to have a great night."

"We can follow you over." Jules stands to excuse herself. "I just need to use the restroom first."

Elena rises. "I'll join you."

⤺

Jules emerges from a bathroom stall and washes her hands under the cool rush of water. Elena appears from another stall and makes her way to the sinks.

Reflected in the mirror, Elena locks eyes with Jules. "This is going to be fun," she says with a smile.

Jules meets her reflection and smiles in return. "I think so, too."

"So," Elena turns her body to face Jules, "what are the ground rules?"

Jules pauses, thinking. "We're new to this, as you know. And our last experience didn't go so well. Is it okay if we take it slow?"

Elena nods, her expression gentle. "Absolutely. No pressure. You set the pace."

Relief washes over Jules, "Thank you."

"Of course. Just one thing…" Without another word, Elena presses her lips to Jules'. Jules leans into the kiss, enjoying Elena's softness, her pulse quickening with excitement. Elena's hands come up to cup Jules' face, and her lips part slightly, allowing Jules to taste the alcohol on her tongue. When they pull apart, Jules is breathless, eyes wide.

Smiling, Elena gives her one last look before exiting the restroom, "See you at our place."

⁂

Eric is in the driver's seat, and Jules is beside him on the short drive to Miles' and Elena's. Jules can feel Eric's nervousness. "How did it go with Miles when Elena and I were in the restroom? Did you guys talk?" Jules asks.

"He's a nice enough guy, I guess. We really didn't talk about anything. Just waited for you two to come back." Eric says.

"Awkward?"

"Who, me? Always."

Jules laughs, easing some of the tension. "Thank you for agreeing to do this," she continues. "Elena and I spoke in the restroom—she promised we could take it slow. No pressure." Eric nods in acknowledgment but says nothing as Miles pulls into the driveway and Eric pulls in behind him. Before exiting the car, Jules takes Eric's hand, and he looks at her.

"I love you," she says.

"I love you, too," Eric replies. They open their doors and follow Miles and Elena inside.

Shortly afterward, the four of them stand gathered around the kitchen island in the inviting warmth of Miles' and Elena's home. On the smooth, polished surface of the stone counter, four capsules of MDMA lay in a small, neat line.

Miles and Elena each reach for a capsule, their movements familiar and practiced. Elena lifts her gaze and locks eyes with Eric. "Here's to new friends," she declares as she and Miles take the capsules and swallow.

Reaching for a second capsule, Elena brings it to Eric's mouth, slipping it past his lips. She doesn't pull back immediately. Instead, she lets her finger linger by his lips and leans in, initiating a deep kiss that has Eric surrendering to her touch.

Miles mirrors Elena's actions with Jules, placing the capsule into her mouth before he, too, follows it with a kiss. The room falls quiet but for the sounds of breath.

"And now," Miles announces, "we wait."

Beth and Kyra hang onto every one of Jules' words as the story unfolds.

"Good god, that's sexy," Beth breathes out, gulping down her drink.

"No joke. Keep going," Kyra urges, motioning to the waitstaff for another round.

∽

"30-40 minutes for the come-up," Elena informs Jules and Eric. "Jules, please come upstairs with me. I have something I'd like to show you." Jules nods and follows Elena's lead.

Ascending the staircase and down the hallway, Elena and Jules arrive at a closed door. "Ready?" Elena asks with a playful grin, pausing with her hand on the doorknob. Jules nods her head yes again. As Elena opens the door, a well-appointed adult playroom unfolds before Jules' eyes. It is the size of a large master bedroom and furnished beautifully. Textured wallpaper in deep, muted tones. Plush scatter rugs over wide plank flooring. Perfect soft lighting and lush, velvety draperies.

Jules gasps, eyes wide as she takes in the sight. "Holy shit."

A laugh emerges from Elena. "Welcome."

Jules navigates the room's perimeter, her fingertips grazing the lingerie hanging neatly on hangers and the extensive assortment of floggers, paddles, and crops adorning the wall. By the time Eric and Miles join them, Jules is giddy with what the night now has in store.

"Holy shit," Eric echoes Jules' sentiment as he, too, takes in the surroundings.

Jules giggles. "That's what I said."

The room shivers with anticipation as Elena picks up a feathery boa from a hanger and wraps it around Jules, pulling her close. Their lips meet just as the men begin closing the distance.

Elena disentangles herself from Jules, picking up a

second boa and draping it around her own shoulders before moving closer to Eric. She pulls him in for a kiss, this one a little more eager. Her fingers tangle in his hair, shooting electricity through his body. Her lips feel foreign but good. When she pulls back, Elena leads him to the sofa where Eric finds himself seated, Elena straddling his lap, their bodies pressed against each other.

A delighted squeal from Jules slices through the heated air as Miles lifts her off the ground, carrying her toward the sofa next to Elena and Eric. Both men are seated, the women on top. In this close-knit formation, Elena leans across the divide, her lips first finding Miles', then Jules.' The exchange of kisses marks the next stage of the night's adventures.

Elena's hands expertly work the buttons of Jules' blouse and then the rest of her clothes before she undresses herself, leaving them both completely naked. She takes her time, making sure her audience enjoys the view. Returning her attention to Eric, she draws him into another kiss, pressing his hands against her bare chest, giving him permission to stroke and squeeze. Miles follows suit, removing his own shirt before pulling Jules closer, his mouth tracing kisses down her collarbone.

The scene intensifies when Elena rejoins Miles and Jules rejoins Eric. Elena is enthroned on the top of the back-rest of the sofa, Miles' head bowed in worship between her thighs. Her sighs and murmurs grow louder as her pleasure increases.

Eric is seated against the backrest, Jules standing on the sofa, her feet on each side of Eric's lap. His face is buried between her legs as she clutches his hair. The charge running through both of their bodies intensifies by an order of magnitude as the molly takes hold. Their temperatures rise, and every nerve ending in their bodies comes alive. Jules gasps, and Eric moans, grinning wide as he drinks her in. Miles looks up at Elena and winks as he reaches over and wraps his hand around Jules' thigh. Elena catches Jules' gaze, and a silent communication passes between them. Elena extends her hand, and Jules, trembling with anticipation, takes it. Hand in hand, Elena leads Jules across the room.

Jules, Kyra, and Beth are almost finished with their second drink. Kyra and Beth are rapt with attention.

Jules paints a vivid image. "Elena is now completely naked. And gorgeous. Leading me to another area of the playroom. Every breath I took was lighting me up. She takes me over to this mechanical thing, kind of half barrel-shaped, low to the ground."

"A Sybian?" Kyra interjects.

"A what?" Beth asks.

"Yes," Jules confirms to Kyra. "You know what that is?"

Kyra nods wide-eyed in acknowledgment. "Yes. But I've never been on one. Are you telling me..." Kyra's voice trails off, leaving the question hanging in the air.

Jules confirms with a simple, "Yes."

"Jules..." Kyra whispers.

"Wait," Beth pauses to get clarification, "What is a Sybian?"

Kyra responds, "It's like a saddle that sits on the ground.

You can straddle it or squat on it, and it has a motor in it. Not like a vibrator motor. Like a lawnmower motor."

Beth is confused. "So, you sit on it, and it vibrates?"

"There are different attachments. You put those on and then sit on it," Kyra clarifies, waiting for it to click for Beth.

Beth nods her yes head slowly as she starts to get the picture, and then she shakes her head no. "I don't think my knees could handle it."

"Are you serious?" Kyra asks Beth. "You would miss an opportunity like that because of your creaky old lady knees?"

"Hey!" Beth replies. "Don't talk like that about my knees! We can't all be as fuck fit as you!"

Kyra feigns defensiveness. "What's wrong with being fuck fit? I work hard to be fuck fit. I wish there were fuck fit classes at the gym."

"Like what?" Beth snaps. "Juicy joints and 'ginas?"

Jules nearly spits out her drink from laughing.

"You win, Beth," Kyra responds. "Jules. Keep going."

✦

The exploration continues within the sanctum of Miles' and Elena's playroom. Elena picks up an attachment from the array of accessories in the room, fitting it to the Sybian with ease. With well-practiced hands, Elena applies lubrication to herself, luxuriating in the sensation. She passes the device's controller, resembling a remote, to Jules.

Miles and Eric are still seated on the sofa. They maintain a generous distance, becoming spectators to the intimate performance unfolding before them. For a second, Eric considers moving closer to Miles. *Sure, he's straight,* Eric thinks to himself, *but he seems open to all kinds of pleasure.* He also knows that Eric is bi. Eric wonders if, maybe, there's an opportunity now to explore a little, touch, connect. He glances over at Miles, who is completely locked in on Elena and Jules, and the thought quickly disappears. Too risky. It doesn't feel right. Instead, he returns his attention to the women.

"I'll go first," Elena offers, her voice pitched with excitement. She mounts the Sybian with confidence, positioning herself to fully experience its potential. She turns to Jules, giving her a nod of readiness.

Jules, controller in hand, turns the machine on. The room fills with the hum of the Sybian's motor, momentarily startling Jules. Elena encourages Jules with a reassuring wink, and Jules responds by slowly adjusting the dials. Elena's body moves in rhythm with the machine, her smile growing wider as the sensation increases. Jules adapts quickly, her uncertainty replaced with the desire to please Elena. She watches Elena in awe as her eyes close, and she gets lost in the rhythm. Her lips part, and her moans, soft at first, gradually intensify into wild screams of pleasure. Jules' fingers deftly manage the controls, pushing Elena towards an orgasm that shakes the whole room.

Breathless and flushed, Jules watches Elena's climax, her words barely a whisper, "That was…beautiful."

Elena slowly dismounts from the Sybian, eyes shining as she turns to Jules and says, "Your turn."

Jules, trembling with anticipation, selects an attachment for the Sybian from the collection before her. She lubricates herself and tentatively gets in position. Elena turns to her husband, blowing him a kiss before she takes a seat facing Jules, controller in hand. Eric's eyes search Jules' face, waiting for her to turn and do the same or, at least, acknowledge him. But her focus is only on Elena. He feels a wave of insecurity rise in him, and he pushes it down, telling himself he is overreacting.

"Ready?" Elena asks.

Jules takes a deep breath and nods her head, her lips parting slightly as excitement courses through her. Elena activates the controller, and the buzz of the Sybian reverberates through the room. Elena holds Jules' gaze, letting the tension build before adjusting the dials. Elena's face splits into a grin as her fingertips adjust the settings on the controller. Jules' eyes widen as the sensation intensifies, a surprised "Whoa!" escaping her lips.

"Just wait…" Elena teases. *Love to Love You, Baby* by Donna Summer comes streaming through the speaker, and the last words Jules utters before Elena revs the engine up are, "I fucking love this song." The Sybian's vibrations amplify, and Jules begins to rock, her body moving in sync with the device between her legs. A moan escapes her, a sound so raw, so potent, that it leaves Eric stunned.

Emboldened by Jules' reaction, Elena adjusts the dials on the controller again. The intensity of the Sybian ramps up, and Jules' body reacts accordingly, her head arching back as waves of pleasure roll through her. The climax hits with a force that leaves Jules breathless, falling forward as a rush of satisfaction overtakes her.

Catching her breath, Elena leans in, her fingers gently

brushing against Jules' flushed cheek. Jules tilts her eyes upward, meeting Elena's gaze, and, with her voice a low grunt, says, "Again."

❦

Beth and Kyra are slack-jawed and at the edge of their seats, not wanting to miss a single word of Jules' story. "I just kept going and going. I don't know if it was the Syb, the drugs…" Jules muses.

"I'm sure it was all of it," Beth adds, fanning herself with her napkin.

"No joke," Kyra adds in agreement, leaning back in her seat.

Jules nods. "It was. And having Eric there made it so special. I felt so loved. So cared for. So connected to him. I've never come like that in my life."

❦

"I've never seen her come like that," Eric says to Dr. Layton as he winds down his version of the night with Miles and Elena. Dr. Layton makes a note of the struggle in his tone and waits for him to continue. "It's not like I don't want her to feel like that. It was spectacular. I could feel her energy from across the room." The statement hangs in the air for a moment before he adds, "But that's the whole point. I was across the room. I might as well have been a million miles away—that's how distant I felt from her. And when she said what she said in the bathroom… That she'd never come that hard in her life," Eric pauses, "it broke my fucking heart."

⚜

Beth saunters through the front door, still a little tipsy from her evening with Jules and Kyra. Alex is relaxed on the couch, the glow of the TV illuminating his face.

"Well, hello there, husband," Beth singsongs with an undercurrent of mischief in her voice. "I didn't see Kevin's car outside. Is Mason asleep?"

Alex's lips curl in an intrigued smile. "Hello, wife. Yes. Kevin is out with his friends. Mason's out like a light. Good time with the girls?"

"Mmmm hmmmm," Beth hums out a long, low confirmation.

Alex grins wider. "I see you've had a few drinks."

Beth's smile widens as she slowly starts to unbutton her blouse, her movements deliberate and teasing. "What makes you say that?" she replies playfully.

Alex flicks off the TV and sits up, his posture now alert. Quiet fills the room. "It's not date night," he ventures cautiously, a spark of anticipation in his eyes.

With a coy tilt of her head, Beth confirms, "It is definitely not date night." She moves to unhook her bra, a suggestion of something thrilling about to happen.

Alex stops her. "Leave it on."

Beth's hands fall to her sides, her stance in front of him bold and confident. Alex leans forward, his hands gliding up her thighs, disappearing under her skirt. He maintains eye contact as he slips off her underwear.

Alex takes off his t-shirt, unbuttons his jeans, and pulls Beth onto him. Their mouths crash together urgently as his fingers move between her legs; he is excited to find his wife wet and ready. Her teeth sink into his shoulder, muffling a cry of pleasure as he enters her, and she begins to ride him. Their breathing is ragged, their movements synchronized. When they finish, Beth takes a seat on the couch next to Alex, facing him, smiling.

"Well, Sexy Babs," Alex murmurs, "that was a pleasant surprise."

Beth's eyes twinkle back at him. "You're so sexy."

"So, what did the girls have to say?" Alex asks.

"Jules and Eric went on another couple date. They had a night," Beth replies.

Alex shakes his head. "Those two. Did you realize we have such kinky friends?"

Beth laughs and runs her fingers across Alex's shoulders and back. "It appears we do. Oh, come closer, you silverback! I found another one. It's attached!" Alex recently started sprouting the occasional long, gray hair on the back of his shoulders and it had become a game whenever Beth discovered one.

"Pluck it!" Alex says.

"You sure?" Beth asks, already pinching it between her fingers.

"Get it out!" he says, and Beth yanks.

"You know," she says, "in our younger days, hair pulling might've been our kink… But now, in mid-life, it appears that hair plucking is way more satisfying."

Alex giggles. "Oh yeah, baby."

Beth winks and segues back to Eric and Jules, "Yeah. They went out again with the couple they met on the app, and things got pretty crazy. Jules said she had the best orgasms of her life."

"Really?" Alex says. A wave of concern for Eric swells in him.

⁊

Among the rows of beers and wines at the package store, John navigates a sea of colorful labels and detailed tasting notes. He scrutinizes a six-pack of craft beer, eventually adding it to his basket. The chill from the refrigerated cases contrasts with the warm overhead lighting of the store.

A burst of familiar laughter echoes, catching his attention. There, further down the aisle, stands Charlie. She's animatedly conversing with another attractive woman, their body language indicating something more than just friends.

As the woman steps away, John approaches, trying to fight the sudden wave of awkwardness overcoming him, "So, um. Hi."

Charlie recognizes John's voice and swallows hard before turning to face him. She still hasn't recovered emotionally from how things went with Kyra, but she knows none of that matters now. Kyra's decision is made. Charlie has to move on. She extends her arms, pulling John into a friendly hug. "Hi!"

"What happened the other night? I texted you, like, a hundred times to see if you were ok," John says.

A flicker of regret washes over Charlie's face as she responds, hands fidgeting. "My fault. I was busy and lost track of time." John has known Charlie a long time and knows there's something she's not being honest about.

"I've been worried about you. You went radio silent."

Charlie rubs the nape of her neck. "I know. I owe you an apology. I guess I've had a lot on my plate, getting settled and everything."

John's features soften. "That's ok. I'm just glad you're alright. How's everything going with work?"

Charlie's face brightens. "Work is good. I have my office set up in my new place. It's coming together."

"That's great," John says. His eyes shift subtly, landing on the spot where the woman Charlie was talking to was standing. "So, um, who was that?"

Charlie follows John's gaze, her lips curling into a smile. "What about her?"

"New friend?" John asks.

Charlie shrugs. "Early friend, yes."

John raises an eyebrow, a light tease in his tone. "Attractive."

Charlie grins, leaning against her cart casually. "Very."

"So, um," John says, "I have some news. Kyra is moving in."

Charlie hides her reaction with a hard swallow. "Yeah. She mentioned that was happening. Sounds like things are getting serious."

"They are. I really care for her, Charlie."

Charlie nods, using every ounce of self-control to hide her feelings. "She's pretty special."

"She is," John gushes. "I'm glad you see it, too. So come hang out with us! We miss you! We can do movie night. Game night. Whatever you like."

Charlie notes the "we" in John's invitation and simply nods in return, not really giving an answer.

"Glad I ran into you," John says.

"Yeah," replies Charlie. "See you around."

The two part ways, with Charlie heading one way down the aisle and John heading in the opposite direction. His phone vibrates with an incoming call from Kyra.

"Hey, I'm in the car on my way home. Are you home yet?" she asks.

"Not yet. Running errands. Probably another hour or so," John responds.

"Frick," Kyra sighs, her disappointment evident. "Jules and Eric had a sexy night with that couple. Jules gave us the full download on how it went, and now…"

"You have a boner…" John smiles.

"A huge, juicy boner."

John breaks into a laugh. "Sorry…"

"Sorry for me," laments Kyra. "I'm going to need a cold shower."

"Don't cool off too much," John teases.

"I'll try to keep it up until you get home," Kyra says.

"So, um," John shifts subjects, "I was thinking…"

"What's up?" Kyra asks.

"How do you feel about a cookout at the house? Getting everyone together. I'd like to actually meet Jules and Eric and Beth and…"

Kyra replies before John can finish, "I love that idea. I want to meet more of your friends, too."

"Yeah?" John asks hopefully.

"Absolutely," Kyra says.

"Good. We will make it official."

There's an unspoken sense of excitement for what the

cookout represents. Meeting each other's friends is a big step for both of them.

"Oh, and guess who I just ran into." John mentions running into Charlie, dropping the news that she might be seeing someone new.

There is a brief pause as Kyra takes in the information, an involuntary frown forming on her face. "That's terrific. I'm really happy for her," she replies, masking her disappointment. Kyra ends the call with a soft, "See you soon," her frown deepening after she disconnects from the call.

～⑤

At work the next day, Jules sits in her office, lost in thought, staring out the window. Her reflection bounces back at her from the glass, and the corners of her lips reveal a private, self-satisfied smile, thinking of the evening she and Eric shared with Miles and Elena. A soft knock at her door interrupts her reminiscing.

"Julia. Have a minute?" Peter asks.

She turns away from the view, giving Peter her full attention. "Of course, Peter. What's up?"

Peter fills her in on an upcoming event where the management team from the new firm she researched will be in attendance. It's an important occasion, he tells her, one that requires Jules' seasoned expertise. "Of course I'll attend. Just get me the details," she agrees. Peter lingers at her doorway, his fingers fidgeting with her door frame.

"Anything else?" Jules asks.

"Yes. I'd like Dylan to attend with you."

Jules blinks but maintains her composure and speaks

before she's had a chance to fully think things through. "Sure, Peter. It will be good to have a second set of boots on the ground."

Peter lightly taps his knuckles on the doorjamb, thanks her, and walks away. As Peter retreats, Jules' phone buzzes on her desk. It's a message from Beth.

I'm so fucking proud of you. I love you so much.

A warmth spreads through Jules at her friend's supportive words, reigniting her smile. She leans back in her chair, gaze returning to the view outside her window, happy to be alone again with her thoughts and putting Peter's request completely out of her mind.

That following Saturday, late in the afternoon, Jules and Beth are surrounded by half-empty boxes at Kyra's apartment while helping her pack in preparation for her move to John's. Kyra has been in her place for over a decade. Each closet, drawer, and cabinet are like a treasure trove of memories for Kyra. Some fresh, some long forgotten. According to some plan of organization only existing in Kyra's mind, Jules and Beth each hold up items, and Kyra points to their appropriate box.

They find little keepsake boxes filled with concert ticket stubs. Old yearbooks with messages scribbled on the inside covers—grayscale photos of Kyra with braces, Kyra without braces, Kyra with short hair, doing sports, arms slung around the shoulders of teammates. Kyra's cheeks were plumper back then. She still has her youthfulness, but her cheeks are more angular now. More grown up.

Beth continues emptying out shelves and comes across an old wig of Kyra's. Long, straight, jet-black hair—part of an old Halloween costume. Beth puts it on over her medium brown bob and turns to Kyra and Jules. "How do I look?"

"Pretty hot," Jules replies.

"Agreed," adds Kyra. "You should take it home."

Beth checks herself out in the mirror. "I think I will. Thanks." Beth puts the wig in her tote bag and continues emptying shelves.

They find a shoebox full of birthday and holiday cards from over the years, many of which are from Kyra's past relationships. "Gosh," Beth says as she flips through them, "some of these go way back. Oh, my goodness. This one is from Michael. I remember when you dated him. Whatever happened to that guy?"

A smile rises on Kyra's face. "That was forever ago. I'm surprised you remember him. He used to love it when I fed him jellybeans. Especially the red ones. He's married now. I think he has a few kids."

"Oohh, I want to look." Jules takes a few cards from Beth's pile and starts flipping through them. "These are from Christy. The lifeguard. I remember when you were seeing her. She was gorgeous, super fit. And if I'm remembering correctly, she was a wild one."

Kyra chuckles. "Unconventional, yes. She was a lot of fun."

"You two were on and off for years," Jules recalls.

"We were," confirms Kyra. "I had a hard time keeping up with her physicality."

"What do you mean?" asks Beth.

"She was really into grappling. You know, like wrestling. And she was so fucking strong. Having two older brothers, I thought I could keep up. I was working out, in good shape. I thought I could hold my own." Kyra takes a breath and shakes her head. "Boy, was I wrong. She was so fast and so powerful. I'd be pinned almost immediately."

"Kind of hot," Jules observes.

"Yes," Kyra says. "Till she leg swept me and sat on my face. Almost broke my nose."

Beth cackles.

"She muff-stomped you!" Jules exclaims.

Kyra takes a moment to consider Jules' words. "Yes," Kyra deadpans, "yes, she did."

Beth is giggling so hard she can hardly get the words out. "Is that a thing?" she asks, "Like ham slap? From that Jimmy Fallon skit?" All three women are now holding their ribs, uncontrollably laughing.

"No, Beth," Jules says when she finally catches her breath. "Just no."

The Chinese food Kyra ordered for her, Beth, and Jules arrives, and they sit on the floor around Kyra's coffee table, eating from the folded, white paper containers, taking a break from packing.

"So," Jules begins with a more serious tone, "do you think John just might be the one?"

Kyra tucks her chopsticks into a container of noodles and considers Jules' question. "I'm crazy about him, if that's what you're asking."

"You wouldn't be moving in with him if you weren't. But that's not what I'm asking," Jules replies.

"Are you asking Kyra if she's going to marry John?" Beth clarifies between bites.

"Marriage?" Kyra ponders out loud. "I don't know. It's just such a big commitment."

"It is if you take it seriously," Beth says.

Kyra turns to Jules. "How did you know Eric was, you know…"

"My person?" Jules says.

"Yes," Kyra says. "Your person."

Jules props her elbow onto the coffee table and rests her chin on her fist. "We did everything backward and all at once. We finished grad school and moved in together downtown. We weren't having kids, so there was no real pressure to make things official, and I was working all the goddamn time." Jules' mind wanders back in time as she relays the story.

"Hey babe, let's take a ride," Jules said to Eric on one of her rare Saturday mornings not at the office or traveling for work. Jules' workload was as intense as she anticipated out of business school, working late most nights, one or both weekend days, often away for three to four days at a time on deals. Eric was building his own career, which was intense emotionally but not nearly as demanding on his time. He was supportive of Jules and her climb up the corporate ladder, but he did miss her. And she missed him.

Jules drove with Eric in the passenger seat as they headed out of the city and into the suburbs. Apartment buildings gave way to residential streets and single-family homes. They passed a park with big, shady oak trees and baseball diamonds with cheering families and kids rounding the plate in little league jerseys.

"Where are you taking me?" Eric asked.

"You'll see," Jules said. A short while later, Jules pulled in front of a beautifully updated mid-century modern with clerestory windows framed in dark bronze aluminum. The facade was dark gray painted brick with warm wood accents. There was a concrete landing and a heavy, wood-grained, teak front door flanked with updated contemporary light fixtures. A paved driveway ran along the left side of the house, a patch of garden planted in front. A bright red sign hung from a post announcing: *For Sale*.

Eric raised an eyebrow at Jules and asked, "What have you done?"

A realtor pulled up and waved as she stepped out of her car. "Hi, Jules. You must be Eric. Let's take a look. This one won't be on the market for long."

Jules broke into a smile and got out of the car. She took Eric's hand as they followed the realtor up the walkway. The realtor opened the front door and said, "Go on in. Take a look. I'll wait for you out here."

Jules and Eric stepped inside. The house was empty of furniture but full of warm, bright light. The main entry led to an open floor plan with a generous living area, an updated kitchen with stainless steel appliances, and a large island. The floors were hardwood and the walls freshly painted. There were patio doors in the kitchen that led to a small deck and a well-manicured backyard. Off the kitchen was a dining room, which led to a hallway, off of which was a guest bathroom, two bedrooms, and closets for storage. On the other side of the living area was another hallway that led to the master bedroom and a small office. The master bedroom had an en suite with an oversized glass walk-in shower, double sinks, and a large tub.

"Ok, Jules. What's going on?" Eric said after they had done an initial walkthrough.

"Do you like it?" Jules asked.

"What's not to like?" Eric responded suspiciously. "This place is great."

"Does it feel like home?"

"Wherever you are is home."

"I'm being serious," Jules said.

"So am I," Eric responded, maintaining eye contact with her. "This is pretty far out of the city, and with your work schedule, I don't know if I'd want to be all the way out here. I think I'd get lonely."

"So that's the thing…" Jules began, a smile creeping across her lips.

"What do you mean?"

"I think it's time for a change," Jules continued. "I don't like being away from you so much, either. I have another offer on the table at a boutique private equity firm. It will still be intense, but not like it is now. The hours will be much more manageable. And way less travel. You've heard me talk about Peter before—the position is with his firm, and I think it's a fit."

"You're going to leave the bank?"

"I think so, yes."

Eric's face lit up. "This means more time together?"

"Absolutely."

Eric's face broke into a smile, and he hugged Jules tightly. "Yes!"

"Yes, what?" Jules asked.

"Yes to all of it. Yes to more time together. Yes to this house. Yes!"

"Really?" Jules said.

"Really," Eric confirmed. Jules and Eric spent more time walking around the house, making early plans for what pieces of furniture would go where, what colors they may want to paint the walls, where they were going to hang their pictures. When they emerged back out the front door, the realtor asked, "So what do you think?"

Eric and Jules both nodded at the realtor eagerly, and the three sat on the front porch to discuss the offer. When the realtor called the next day to report that the sellers accepted, tears rolled down both Jules' and Eric's cheeks. Jules took the position with Peter's firm, gave notice at the bank, and Eric and Jules used the next few weeks to pack, order a few new pieces of furniture, and prepare to start the next chapter of their life.

Moving day arrived, and Beth and Alex showed up early, with coffees, to help load and unload the truck. After the last box was unloaded, Eric announced that he and Alex were going to pick up some pizza and beer, and Jules and Beth flopped onto the sofa, thankful for the rest.

"Jules, this place is fantastic. I love it," Beth said.

"It's going to be a big change, but I love it, too."

"It feels so…" Beth trailed off.

"Domestic?" Jules offered.

"That's one way to put it, yes," Beth said. "I guess I never thought you'd leave the city. I'm going to miss having you so close."

"It's not that far. And, besides, maybe if things get serious with Alex, you can start looking out here as well."

"If things get serious?" Beth said.

"You know what I mean," Jules replied.

"It's more complicated with kids involved," Beth said. "But, yes, you've given us a lot to think about with this move of yours."

Jules rubbed her palms together. "My evil plan is working."

It took Eric and Alex longer than expected, and when the front door finally opened, Alex was balancing two pizza boxes and a twelve-pack. Eric was holding an 8-week-old border collie. She had soft, black fur with a white blaze on her head, chocolate brown eyes, and fit in the palm of Eric's hand. Eric could barely contain his excitement.

Jules stood looking confused at Eric. "What's this?"

"She," Eric said, holding up his hands for Jules to see, "is our new puppy." Jules' expression was hard to read, and Eric's enthusiasm momentarily wavered.

"We never talked about a dog," Jules said. Beth and Alex looked on, saying nothing. Jules walked toward Eric and took the puppy into her arms. The puppy snuggled up onto Jules' shoulder and, after a few frantic licks, curled her head into Jules' neck with an audible sigh. Jules' heart melted. She looked up at Eric, making eye contact, and said, "I love her."

That night, after Beth and Alex left to drive back to the

city, Jules and Eric were lying in bed in their new master bedroom. Unpacked boxes were piled high in the corners, one with a lamp on it, the only light in the room. The new puppy pancaked on Jules' belly while she stroked her ears. "The cuteness is unbearable," Jules said, unable to take her eyes off her. Eric smiled in agreement, endeared by this soft side of Jules.

"So, what should we name her?" Eric asked.

"I'm not sure," Jules said. "Have any ideas?"

"Puppers?"

Jules rolled her eyes. "That's terrible."

"Gertrude?" Eric offered. "We can call her Gerty."

"Not feeling it," Jules said after giving it some thought.

"Do you have any ideas?" Eric asked.

Jules carefully studied the puppy's face and said, "Daisy. I'd like to call her Daisy."

"Daisy it is," Eric agreed. "Welcome to the family, Daisy."

Jules smiled. "Welcome to the family, Daisy."

Eric took a deep breath. "There's one more thing I'd like to talk about since we're a family of three now."

Jules looked at Eric. "What's up?" Eric eased off the bed and kneeled on the floor. Jules sat up with Daisy in her lap, a puzzled look on her face.

"I, uh, was wondering…" Eric began.

Jules gave Eric her full attention, her heart pounding in her chest.

"I was wondering how you might feel about making things official." Eric reached into his pocket and took out a blue velvet box. He opened it and showed the ring to Jules.

"This was my grandmother's. My mom has been saving it for me. For when I found my 'one'." Jules' bottom lip quivered, and she covered her mouth while Eric continued. "It was her mother's, and it's been in my family for generations. It belongs on your finger, Jules. Please, will you marry me?" Jules looked at the antique setting of the ring, the sparkle of the diamonds in platinum, then looked up to meet Eric's gaze. Too overwhelmed with emotion to make words, she nodded her head yes.

"Yes?" Eric confirms. Jules nodded her head yes more enthusiastically, and soon, the word tumbled out in a joyful sob.

Eric took Jules into his arms. "Best day ever. I love you so much."

Jules hugged Eric tightly back. "I love you more."

Beth teases and reaches for an egg roll. "Eric had to make an honest woman out of Jules once he made her a dog mom."

Kyra laughs and turns to Beth. "What about you and Alex? Was there a specific moment that you knew?"

"It was different for us," Beth replies. "We were both married before and had kids. It wasn't just us—we were combining a family. Plus, the marriages we came out of… They left some marks. We both had some baggage, or, as I like to say, matching luggage."

Both Jules and Kyra laugh. Beth continues. "The heart wants what the heart wants. I know it's cliche, but it's true. Maybe it's because we came to each other having experienced such hurt and heartbreak, but once we were ready, we knew. And we were healed enough to know that we could trust again. Trust each other, at least." Beth wraps her fingers around the A, K, and M charms on her necklace, holds them in the palm of her hand, and rubs her thumb against her clavicle. "I wouldn't change a thing."

⁊

Madelyn stares out of her window at nothing in particular. Another Saturday night loomed ahead of her, vast and empty. She pours herself her third glass of wine and settles on the couch in her one-bedroom apartment, folding her long legs underneath her. This place was all she could afford after her last relationship fell apart, and she had to scramble to get her own space. *Don't they all fall apart*, she muses. *Even the great ones—the ones that look so solid from the outside. There are always cracks.* She exhales a smug sigh. *The foundations are never as solid as they seem.*

She flips her phone over and checks her messages. Again. Still no response from Eric. She knew she felt something that night. There was a connection. She was sure of it.

Wouldn't it make things messy with Jules? she wonders. *Of course it would. But isn't it already messy? Wasn't it Jules who invited the mess?*

She clicks on the television for some background noise and replays that night in her mind. Eric's flirting. His response to her. His arousal. The way he gasped when she put him in her mouth. He could barely contain himself. Madelyn smiles to herself, remembering.

She drums her fingers on the couch cushion. Surely, he is thinking about her, too. One more message just to remind him that he's on her mind. That she'll be there when he's ready.

No. She doesn't want to appear too desperate. Too needy. Both are labels she'd been called before by former boyfriends as they were ending things. Citing the litany of reasons why it wouldn't—why it couldn't possibly—work out with her. Why she wasn't the one. Not marrying material.

She takes another gulp of wine and flips channels, looking for something to distract her. Anything to distract her. Saturday nights were always the toughest reminder of her loneliness. The only thing worse was sitting alone at a bar somewhere, waiting to see if anyone would pay attention to her, or endlessly swiping on the apps, trying not to be disgusted at the messages that came through. Trying not to be hopeless.

She looks around her cramped apartment. She had to get rid of most of her furniture when her last relationship failed. It wouldn't fit here. Nowhere to put everything. Some of it wouldn't even fit through the narrow front door. She told herself it felt good to let go of those things. Make room for the new. Turn the page. This was what she said when asked how she was handling the breakup, moving into a place on her own. But it was all a veneer. She hated having to say goodbye to her things. One more reminder of what she couldn't have, of the unfair hand she was dealt. Why couldn't she have a nice house with a man that she loved? One that loved her back? One that also cooked delicious meals for her? That she would do anything to please?

She flips her phone back over and unlocks the screen. Before she can reason herself out of it, she starts typing.

The rhythmic pounding of running shoes on pavement echoes as Alex and Eric jog side by side on an after-work run. Eric's usual calm and even demeanor is replaced with a restless agitation, his brow furrowed and jaw set. Eric's body occupies the physical space next to Alex, but Eric's mind is a million miles away.

"Hey, man. Everything ok?" Alex asks. He's always been able to read Eric, and after Beth informed him of the events of the other night, Alex suspected that Eric may need an outlet.

"I'd rather not talk about it," Eric says, his words clipped.

Alex simply replies, "Ok. Alright."

Silence envelops them again, punctuated only by their steady breaths and the sound of their footfalls. But the quiet feels too heavy for Alex, too full of Eric's unspoken consternation.

Alex breaks the silence again, his voice soft. "It's me, Eric. You can talk to me. I can tell something's up. What's going on with you?"

Eric slows to a walk. "I know. I'm sorry. It's just that… We went out again with Miles and Elena the other night," Eric confesses, the strain evident in his voice.

Alex nods. "Yeah. Beth came home supercharged after getting the download from Jules."

"Goddammit," Eric curses, his fists clenching.

"I'm sorry," Alex says. "We know the girls talk. Did I say something wrong?"

"It's not you. I just wish Jules wouldn't talk about it," Eric mutters.

"According to Beth…" Alex starts, but Eric cuts him off.

"Yeah, Jules had the best fucking night of her life," Eric says bitterly.

"Whoa. I thought this was what you guys wanted?"

Eric grinds to a halt, his chest heaving. He collapses onto a nearby bench, his head in his hands. "I don't know what we wanted. We had a shitty threesome that I'm still feeling guilty about. We then promise each other we'll take things slow. Next thing I know, we're doing drugs with strangers, and her body does things I've never seen it do before while I watch from across the room, not even touching her. It's a lot to fucking process."

Alex pauses for a moment, considering his next words carefully. "That is a lot to process, man. Do you need to stop doing this? Go back to how you were?"

"I don't know if that's even possible." Eric's voice is barely a whisper. "The thing is, I want this for her. I want her to feel these things and grow and not be inhibited. I really do. I'm the last one in the world who wants to hold her back, and I feel like that's what I'm doing. I never thought I would feel like this."

Alex places a comforting hand on Eric's shoulder. With a heavy sigh, Eric drops his head back into his hands, the emotionality of his situation crashing down around him.

"And I don't want to be held back, either," Eric continues. "There are things I want to do and experience in all of this. But I don't want to lose her, lose us."

Standing at the kitchen island, Jules watches as Eric pushes open the front door after his run with Alex. Daisy's ears prick up at Eric's return, and she bounds over to greet him in the entryway. Jules beams at the sight of it; the two loves of her life. Eric drops his running jacket on the floor; his phone lands with a thump on top of it.

"You're home early," Eric observes.

"I couldn't sit in my office anymore. I thought maybe we could go out for a drink. Have a night," Jules suggests, her voice hopeful, flirty.

Eric responds gruffly. "Have a night, huh?"

Jules frowns in response to his heavy, unreadable tone as Eric starts to walk off.

"Hey, what's going on?" Jules calls after him.

"I think I need a break from our 'nights'," Eric replies over his shoulder.

Jules reels, stung by his words. "I meant just us. Hey, look at me."

Eric turns to face her. "What do you want from me, Jules?"

"I want you to talk to me," Jules says. "What is this? What is going on here?"

"I don't know if I'm ready to talk about this," Eric replies. "I don't have everything sorted out in my head."

"Let's sort it out together. I mean, we have this amazing night the other night, and…"

Eric cuts her off. "*We* didn't have an amazing night. *You* did."

"But I thought…" Jules starts.

"I know what you thought," Eric interrupts. "I didn't want to say anything. I didn't want to get in the way of you…"

Jules cuts him off this time. "You are never in the way."

"With this, I am. And I don't know how to handle it. I'm happy for you, but I'm also…"

"Are you saying that you are mad at me?"

Eric shakes his head. "Not mad, exactly. But jealous? Envious?"

"Of what? We're doing this together," Jules argues.

"We've been in these situations together. But we're not together in this. For fuck's sake, I was across the room from you having to watch you…"

"You mean like I had to watch you with Madelyn?" Jules counters, her voice rising with each word.

Eric takes a step back from her, turning his back to compose himself. When he faces Jules again, his eyes are a storm of emotions. "Jules, we have a great sex life. Better than I could have ever imagined. My fucking life's purpose is to give you pleasure. And in two minutes on that thing, I watched your goddamn head explode. How am I supposed to compete with that?"

Jules' retort is quick. "You're not competing with that."

"Aren't I?" Eric fires back.

"I can't believe you're doing this." Jules shakes her head in disbelief and frustration.

"Doing what, exactly?" Eric challenges.

"Taking that experience and making it about you. Not about me. Not about us. About you," Jules says, her anger seeping through her calm exterior. Eric remains silent, waiting for Jules to continue. She does. "So, what is this, Eric? Is the outer limit of my pleasure what's achievable with your cock?"

"I'm not saying that," he replies. "I just felt so far away from you."

"And I never felt closer to you," Jules' tone escalates. "Look. I get it. We weren't expecting that. And it went really fast."

"And there was nothing there for me," Eric snaps.

"What do you mean by that?" Jules questions.

"Miles is as straight as an arrow. You know that. Elena indulged me, but they were both into you." Eric's tone is accusatory.

"You act like I don't know what that feels like," Jules counters, a note of defiance in her voice.

"I know you know what that feels like. I'm agonizing over the guilt from that night. Trust me." Eric paces and then turns to face Jules, "I want you to have these experiences. But I want to have them, too. Seeing you like that. Seeing what your body is capable of—when I thought I knew what it was capable of. I'm working through a lot."

"I can see that." Jules softens, her anger dissipating. "Eric, you are the love of my life. And I never, ever want to hurt you. But please, please...do not shut me down on this." Her voice wavers as tears prick at her eyes. "I will try to explain this to you as best I can. My whole life, I've held back. Sometimes, because I let what other people think over-influence me. Sometimes, out of fear. What I've realized is that my body is capable of more. I am capable of more. And I don't even know what that is. But I want to know."

"And I want you to know," Eric concedes.

"Then support me. Love me. I'm not moving further away from you in those moments. I'm moving closer. And I will do the same for you," Jules says, stepping closer to him.

"Promise?" Eric asks, voice barely above a whisper.

"Promise," Jules says.

Eric steps forward, gently wiping the tears from Jules' cheeks. He pulls her closer, their lips meeting in a tender kiss of reconciliation. Eric's phone, unnoticed, lights up in the hallway with incoming texts.

CHAPTER 5

BAD, BAD, BOYS

It is late in the afternoon, toward the end of the workday. Jules' phone vibrates on her desk, signaling a group text to her and Beth from Kyra.

> Kyra: Drumroll, please!
> Beth: You have my attention.
> Jules: Mine, too. What's up?
> Kyra: It's time for you to meet John!
> Beth: Wow!
> Jules: Yes!
> Beth: Are you sure, meeting the friends is a big step... :)
> Kyra: We're having a cookout this weekend so we can meet each other's people. Can you make it? And bring Eric and Alex so they can meet him?
> Beth: Absolutely!
> Jules: Same! I can't wait for us to meet him. What should we bring?

Kyra: Just bring yourselves. I'm actually heading to shop now.
Jules: Are you downtown?
Kyra: Yep. Wine store.
Jules: I'll come meet you. I have an event tonight, so I have a little time.
Kyra: Great. See you in a few.
Beth: I'm still at work. You girls have fun. See you this weekend. I'M SO EXCITED TO MEET HIM!
Kyra: Xoxoxo

∽

A few minutes later, Jules is maneuvering a shopping cart through the aisles of the wine store as Kyra picks out an assortment of bottles. Jules is dressed in all black for her evening work event. She wears a form-fitting shift, leather belted at the waist, a structured blazer, and heels.

"I think I'm really falling for this guy," Kyra confesses, her tone a blend of giddy excitement and deep seriousness.

Jules flashes her a teasing smile. "It appears so. We almost never meet your '*lovahs*'."

"It never gets this serious," Kyra says.

"Kyra and John sitting in a tree, k-i-s-s-i-n-g…" Jules pauses for dramatic effect, "…first comes love, then comes…"

Kyra laughs and playfully shoves Jules, trying to hide the blush creeping up her cheeks. "It's a cookout, Jules. Get a grip."

"I'm teasing. Well, kind of," Jules retorts, her grin growing wider. "I mean, you are living together."

"I know, right?" Kyra concurs.

"The sweet but un-glamorous side of love. Laundry. Electric bills. Mowing the lawn."

Kyra rolls her eyes. "Tell me about it. I'm a little stressed about someone other than me washing my underwear."

Jules chuckles. "Wait till you wash his."

"Ha!" Kyra bursts out. "You stop that crazy talk right now."

The pair meander down the aisles, and Kyra's tone shifts, turning serious as she says, "Charlie will be there."

Jules raises an eyebrow. "Yeah?"

"With her new girlfriend." Kyra adds flatly.

"Ouch," Jules says. "How do you feel about that?"

Kyra shrugs. "I'm kind of glad she's with someone. I think it's for the best."

"You're probably right," Jules agrees.

Kyra swallows hard. "It still fucking hurts, though."

"Then you're definitely right." Jules' tone is firm as she pulls Kyra into a hug. "At least if you want things to keep progressing with John."

Kyra nods. "Which I do."

"There you go," Jules confirms.

Kyra pulls herself together and shifts topics. "So, what's your event tonight?"

"Work. I told Peter I would go. There is a new firm in town that we would like to get to know. Some of the management team will be there, and this is a good opportunity to meet them," Jules explains. "And... I'm supposed to be showing Dylan the ropes."

"Peter's son?" Kyra says. "Isn't he, like, 10 years old?"

Jules snorts. "He just graduated from college. But, yes, that's the one."

"You're too good to Peter," Kyra says, shaking her head.

"I really am. Dylan is awful. Next level awful. I'm not really sure what I'm going to do about it yet."

Kyra grimaces. "I can only imagine. Why are you doing it?"

"Because I told Peter I would," Jules responds. Saying it out loud floods Jules with resentment. *This is not what I signed up for,* she thinks to herself. *Maybe it's time to consider a change.*

Jules glances at her phone, noting the time. "Speaking of which, it's time for me to go babysit."

"Thanks for keeping me company." Kyra blows Jules a kiss.

"See you this weekend," Jules bids, preparing herself to face the rest of her evening.

Shoes already starting to pinch, Jules stops at the pharmacy on her way up to the event. The store is empty but for the young sales clerk who is half in, half out of the stockroom, talking on his phone. Jules quickly finds the ibuprofen she's looking for and waits at the register. She can hear the sales clerk laughing on his phone, informally joking on what clearly sounds like a personal call. Leaning over the counter to make eye contact and signal she is ready to check out, the clerk simply gestures for her to wait a minute. Jules shakes her head to herself. *When did this become acceptable behavior,* she wonders, just like she found herself wondering when the associates at work behaved this way. *Why can't everyone just do their goddamn job?*

Another minute passes, and he is still on his call, back facing Jules, with no indication of wrapping up. Jules exhales a heavy sigh, pops the ibuprofen into her bag without paying, and leaves the store. She knows it's stealing, and stealing is wrong. Just as wrong as the clerk making her wait. She'd stop back into the pharmacy on another day to make it right, but for now, her focus is on the event. She shakes off her annoyance while riding up the elevator, checking her makeup in the mirrored doors along the way.

There is an audible rhythm typical of these networking events. A rhythm Jules knows well. Groups of two to four engage in predictable, superficial conversations about recent deals, golf games, and family events. There is a long line at the bar that moves slowly due, in part, to bored bartenders and, in another part, to attendees attempting to meet and connect with other attendees. Heavy hors d'oeuvres are passed, mini beef wellingtons, tuna wantons, mini crabcakes. Contact information is exchanged, and polite, subdued laughter bounces through the crowd.

Against this backdrop, Jules finds herself in discussion with three partners, including the head of finance, of the new firm in town. The partners are quite savvy, and their track record lines up with Jules' research. Solid performers. Manageable temperaments. There is also an immediate rapport between Jules and the head of finance. They have several contacts in common and have worked on some of the same transactions. It came as a surprise to both of them that they didn't already know one another.

There is something already familiar about him, a feeling reminiscent of when she first met Beth. He is easy. A straight shooter. No guile. While their paths have not yet crossed directly, the contacts they have in common bring a certain social proof—validation that he can hold his own professionally. This, too, Jules finds interesting. The potential to work with someone new, someone who can carry their weight, excites her.

"So, tell me," Jules says, warming to his personality, "what do you like to do when you're not working?"

"How do you know I don't work all the time?"

Jules smiles. "I don't."

"Well, since you asked, I'm really into music. I'm taking DJ lessons."

"Really?" Jules responds, pulling her hands up to her ears like she has headphones on. "Like two turntables and a microphone?"

"Exactly like two turntables and a microphone. Except it's pretty much all digital now. I was a mixtape kid."

Jules beams. "Me too! I loved making mix tapes. I would pour my heart into them. Some mixes…" Jules pauses, thinking back to the days when she would lie on her twin bed, stare at the ceiling, and listen to her favorite songs for hours. "Some mixes felt so personal. Like an audible diary."

"Yes," he nods in agreement. "I feel the same way. Some of my mixes were just for me. I would feel way too exposed if anyone else heard. But some were just for fun. I would theme them."

"Theme them?" Jules asks.

"Yeah. I know people make mixes for working out or road trips. I get a little nerdier."

Jules' smile widens. "I'm listening."

"Give me a theme."

"Hmmm…" Jules thinks for a moment. "Fire."

"That's an easy one. *Light My Fire* by the Doors, *Burning Down the House* by Talking Heads, and, one of my all-time favorites, *I'm on Fire* by Bruce Springsteen."

"Oohhh," Jules replies. "I think I love this."

"Challenge me," he says with a cheeky smile. "Or should I say… *Hit Me with Your Best Shot*."

Jules smiles broadly, bites her lip, and thinks for a few seconds. "Private equity themed, by deal stage."

"Wow, respect," he replies, nodding his head and taking a moment to think. "Ok, here we go. *You're the One that I Want*, John Travolta and Olivia Newton-John, target identification. *Who Are You* by The Who, diligence. *The Gambler* by Kenny Rogers, deal terms and negotiation. *Under Pressure*, Queen, closing. Bonus track: *Welcome to the Jungle*, Guns and Roses, post-close integration."

Jules' eyes grow wider as he lists each song, and then she laughs with delight when he's done. "You have a real talent for this," she says, raising her glass.

"Why thank you," he responds, clinking his glass to hers.

Dylan stands on the periphery and yawns audibly, not bothering to cover his mouth. Eyes shift from Jules to Dylan, and the head of finance asks, "Are we boring you?"

A mix of amusement, embarrassment, and damage control rushes through Jules, and her brain goes into overdrive.

"Pardon us for just a moment. We'll be right back." Jules excuses herself and Dylan, gesturing for him to follow her over to the bar area. He follows reluctantly, and when barely out of earshot, he says, "This is boring. I hate these things."

"It's part of the job," Jules points out, her tone firm.

"I'm sick of hearing about people's golf game and economic outlooks," he complains.

"Also part of the job," Jules states, not missing a beat. "That yawn just now—incredibly rude. You need to get it together and stop embarrassing yourself and the firm."

"What are you, my fucking mother?" His tone is aggressive, his face uncomfortably close to Jules.

Something snaps in Jules. All of the anger and frustration that's been bubbling inside her crystalizes into rage. She takes a step back, straightens her blazer, then steps back into Dylan's space. "Absolutely not. But you definitely need a lesson on who's boss here."

"Oh. Is that what this is about?"

"That's exactly what this is about. You will wait. For me. In the conference room downstairs. Kneel at the head of the table. Do not make a sound. Do you understand?"

Dylan chuffs, both unsure and curious. "Are you fucking serious right now?"

"Do you understand?" Jules repeats, her gaze unyielding.

Dylan huffs but finally nods. "Yes."

Jules turns to walk away, and Dylan says, "So I'm just supposed to…"

"You don't get to speak," Jules cuts him off.

Dylan exits. Jules orders a club soda with lime and takes her time finishing her drink before taking the elevator downstairs. Her breath is measured, her face expressionless. When she enters the conference room, Dylan is not as she instructed. He sits at the head of the table, not kneeling, his fingers idly drumming a rhythm of defiance on the table's surface. Without any change of expression, Jules turns to leave.

"Wait! I wasn't sure you were coming," Dylan protests, a note of insecurity in his voice.

Slowly, begrudgingly, he kneels at the head of the table.

"Head down," Jules says.

He drops his head down, a cocky smirk on his face.

The silence in the room roars, the tension growing thicker with every passing second. Jules walks around the conference table, stepping directly behind Dylan. She can hear his breath. Dylan makes a move to touch her, but she steps back out of his reach, her expression and tone of voice stern.

"Do not," she warns, "touch me."

Dylan raises his hands in a placating gesture, then drops them by his sides.

Jules resumes her position directly behind him and lets the anticipation build. A few moments pass, and she reaches around Dylan's throat from behind, pulling the knot of his tie loose, making the loop slightly larger. She raises the loop to his mouth and pushes it between his lips, gagging him with the silk fabric and securing it behind his head. "Look at me," she demands. He cranes his neck up and to the side to meet her gaze, his expression revealing his surprise and a little fear. Exactly what Jules is looking for. With a forceful tug of the gag, she pulls him up and bends him face down over the table. Dylan squirms but acquiesces.

"Are you really fucking doing this?" Dylan's words come out muffled.

Jules responds by pushing Dylan's torso flat on the conference table. "Do not move. Do not speak." She almost doesn't recognize her own voice. Something inside her has changed, taken over.

Jules undoes her leather belt, pulling it slowly out of the loops. She drags it across the floor, making a swishing sound as she paces back and forth behind him. Dylan's breath is ragged, and his muscles twitch as he braces for the first blow.

The first lash lands with a soft thud across Dylan's back, the intensity lighter than Dylan was expecting but still stinging. She leaves the strap there, watching him quake underneath. With a swift movement, Jules lifts the strap off Dylan, doubles it, and strikes him again. And again. And again; each lash landing with more force than the last, the pauses in between uneven, unpredictable. With each strike, Dylan exhales sharply.

As the intensity builds, the room fills with the sound of Dylan's moans and whimpers. His whimpers turn to cries, his breath catching, pleading. When Jules finally removes the gag, Dylan sinks to the floor at her feet, a heap of breathless surrender.

Stepping over Dylan, Jules leaves the conference room; the click of her heels against the marble floor echoes in the hallway.

"Julia?" Dylan's sharp but confused tone cuts through surrounding chatter of the networking event.

Jules blinks hard, maintaining her composure, as her consciousness returns from the depths of her imagination back to reality, where Dylan, red faced, is staring at her. The firm partners are still off to the side, waiting for Jules and Dylan to rejoin their conversation. Jules' imagination frequently ran wild, but this took her breath away. *What the fuck did my brain just do? Where the fuck did my mind just go?* Jules pushes her thoughts aside, steadies herself, and looks Dylan directly in the eyes.

"Stop embarrassing yourself and the firm, Dylan. I'm sure daddy wouldn't like it." Jules turns and walks back to the group, Dylan trailing behind. All eyes are on him as they approach, and he stammers, cheeks hot, "Excuse me. I didn't mean to be impolite."

Jules is quick to redirect and smooth things over, "Let's continue our conversation offline," she says to the head of finance. "I'll have our office reach out to schedule."

"That sounds good," he replies before moving on to network with others. Once they've gone, Dylan mutters under his breath, "What an asshole."

Jules doesn't bother with a response. She picks up her bag and leaves.

Jules slips into the front seat of her car, and the music blares as she starts the engine. She immediately shuts the music off, leaving her alone with just the sound of her breath. She takes a moment and sits, arms straight, both hands on the steering wheel, inhaling and exhaling through her nose. Her breaths shift from shallow to deep, and the expansion and contraction of her lungs and diaphragm cause a soft undulation in her spine. She is very aware of the energy building inside of her. She does not try to constrain it.

She leans forward to put the music back on, *Wildfires* by Sault, and hits the button to retract her sunroof. She backs out of her spot, exits the parking lot, and starts the drive home. As she picks up speed, the wind gently tousles her hair and caresses her face. She presses down on the accelerator, feeling the hum of the engine coursing through her body, and puts her mind on autopilot, letting the sensations take over. While she moves quickly through physical space, her experience of time fluctuates. The entirety of the scene with Dylan transpired in a matter of seconds in her mind; the drive home stretches like rubber.

Jules arrives home from the event, leaving her bag and blazer at the front door, still clad in her sleek, belted, black dress. The house is mostly dark, save for the soft light filtering from the bedroom, where Eric is reclined against the headboard in pajama bottoms, engrossed in his phone.

"Hi, gorgeous. How was…" he begins, looking up from his screen and turning it face down on his night table.

Before he can finish, Jules advances on him. She climbs onto Eric, facing him, silencing his words with a hand over his mouth. Eric's eyes widen in pleasant surprise as he goes still underneath her, his question left incomplete.

Jules raises a finger to her lips, signaling that he should remain silent. She pulls his arms up over his head, guiding him to grasp the headboard. Eric leans in to kiss her, but she leans back, just out of his reach.

"Be still," she commands, her voice low but firm.

For a moment, Eric obeys, settling down beneath her. But then he leans in again, trying to capture a kiss. Jules pulls his head back by his hair, a move that only excites him more. She hikes up her dress, pulls down his pajama bottoms, and straddles him. Jules is soaking wet; he can feel it even before she slides onto him. He leans in once more, and this time, she meets him, their kiss raw and passionate, filled with grunts and moans. She begins to ride him. Slowly at first, teasing them both. He can already feel her tightening around him.

"Come for me," Eric manages to gasp into her mouth as he pushes deep into her.

Jules throws her head back in response, grinding harder against him. She leans up, giving in to her pleasure as she splashes all over him. Eric grins widely and pushes back inside of her. "More," he commands, which brings a smile to her face. Jules puts her hands on his shoulders, gripping hard, and rides him again, letting her pleasure build, and then she lifts up and peaks again. Her cries fill the room, and it's all Eric needs as he pushes back inside of her once more, this time finding his own release. They are both breathless, the room charged with their spent passion.

Eric, grinning, tries to catch his breath. "Good event, I take it?"

"It was fine," Jules replies, her voice nonchalant as she dismounts, unzips her dress, and heads to the bathroom. Over her shoulder, she says, "Kyra and John are having a cookout this weekend. We finally get to meet this guy."

She says nothing of Dylan's behavior at the event or where her mind went in response, but alone again and under the hot water of the shower, Jules tries to sort out what happened, even if it was just a fantasy. Something about the power dynamic of it mixed with the unprofessionalism excited her. It's all completely out of character and, for Jules, very confusing. She's used to her imagination running wild, but not like this. And the turn-on she experienced from it only stoked this internal conflict. This unchartered territory existing in her own private thoughts makes her uncomfortable and also thrills her. She shakes her head to collect herself, wondering what she may have inadvertently unleashed. One thing she knows for sure—she won't resolve it tonight. She turns off the faucet, dries herself off, and gets ready for bed.

A few blocks away, Beth snuggles with Mason before bedtime, reading a chapter book out loud as his eyelids grow heavy. His walls are painted a medium shade of blue and are covered with posters of his favorite baseball players. His sheets are navy blue cotton printed with colorful planets and stars, worn soft from years of washing. His bookshelves overflow with books and toys, and his desk is messy with art supplies and science kits. Beth loves being in here with Mason. Being close.

Beth started reading to Mason when he was still in her belly. It is their nighttime ritual, as much for her as it is for him. She feels lucky that he hasn't yet outgrown it, that he still lets her be so close to him at age 11. When she hears the steady rhythm of his breathing, she kisses the top of his head, careful not to wake him, as she tucks the blanket in around him, shuts off the light, and closes his door.

Kevin is out with friends, so just she and Alex are up. Alex is in the family room on the sofa, watching sports, and she can hear the nightly commentators spar over which team played better, which players played worse. A sense of anticipation builds inside of her as she slips into her bathroom and takes out the long, jet-black wig she got from Kyra. Excitedly, she pins her hair up, bows her head forward, and slips on the wig. When she flips her head back up, she likes what she sees in the mirror. *This is going to be fun*, she thinks to herself.

With a wide-toothed comb, she smooths out the fly aways and brings out a little shine. She's careful to adjust the bangs so they make a pretty frame for her face; she hasn't had bangs in decades. Then she chooses an eye shadow with a little sparkle and adds eyeliner with some thick mascara, brushes on a little blush, and finishes with a deep red, glossy lip. She hums as she approaches her closet, trying to decide between a black dress or her red one, the one with the tags still on. *Decisions, decisions...* She slips the red one over her good bra and panties and takes in the sight of herself in the mirror. "Yes—definitely the red one," she says softly and takes off the tags. The dress has hung in her closet for years, and it still fits her well, hugging her body, flattering her curves. She slides each foot into a nude pump and does one last mirror check. Alex will be completely surprised.

Beth is careful to keep her steps quiet as she walks down the hallway, and when she turns the corner into the family room, she says, heavy with breath, "Pardon me. I think I might be a little lost. Do you think you might be able to help me...find my way?"

Alex peels his eyes from the TV screen and does a double

take when he sees Beth adorned in her wig and red dress. He sits up straight and clicks off the television. She has his full attention, but his expression is hard to read.

She walks toward him slowly, sexily, and just before she reaches him, his expression changes again. She knows that face. He's uncomfortable. "Talk to me," she says in her normal voice, dropping the role play. "What's going on?"

Alex looks to the side, fidgets, and then meets her gaze. "It's not that you don't look great. You look good enough to eat."

"So, what's the problem?" Beth asks, starting to feel self-conscious and a little defensive.

"There's no problem, it's just that…"

"Just what?"

"I don't like it when you don't look like you. I don't like what this represents. I know you are playing, and, trust me, you are killing it in that dress, but the hair, the makeup… It's not you." He reaches for her hands and guides her to sit facing him on the couch. "I'm attracted to you, Beth. Just you."

"I thought you'd like mixing things up a little," Beth says.

Alex shakes his head. "I don't think I do. Maybe it's because of my history. But really, it's because of you. I just want to be with you."

Tears well up in the corners of Beth's eyes, and she smiles as she takes off the wig. He reaches over and takes a bobby pin out of her hair. Then another. And another. Her everyday bob is now loose and falling around her shoulders. "There you are," he says.

"Here I am," Beth responds, leaning in for a kiss. She pulls her head a few inches back. "The dress is staying."

Alex nods his head excitedly in response, "Absofuckinglutely."

⚜

The weekend rolls around, and it's the heat of the afternoon. John and Kyra are bustling around the house, finalizing last-minute preparations for the cookout. Only a few minutes remain before guests start arriving.

Kyra pauses, approaching John with a small, neatly wrapped gift box cradled in her hands.

"Is that for me?" John inquires, an intrigued smile on his face.

"It is. Open it." Kyra hands over the box to him. Inside the box is an apron that boasts, "Hot and Spicy – the food's good, too!" The corners of his mouth smile wider as he holds it up to his chest. Laughing, he leans in for a kiss. "I love it. Thank you."

Kyra matches his smile, kisses him back, and reaches over to tie the apron around his waist. Her eyes meet his. "I love you."

"I love you," he replies.

She likes the sounds of those words in her mouth. He does, too. The intimate moment is interrupted by the ring of the doorbell. The first guests are here.

"Here we go!" John announces, heading towards the entryway with Kyra in tow. They open the door to find Beth and Alex, both with big smiles on their faces.

"We're right on time!" Beth exclaims, brandishing the beer as if it's a trophy.

Kyra laughs at her friend's punctuality. "Yes. Come on in."

Alex extends a hand to John, greeting him warmly. "Hey, man. I'm Alex. Nice apron."

"Thanks. I'm John. Let's head out back," John replies, leading the way towards the backyard. More guests arrive, including Claire, Jerry, and Madelyn. Beth approaches Kyra. "You invited Madelyn?"

Kyra shakes her head. "I didn't invite her. But I didn't *not* invite her. Claire must've mentioned it." Glancing around the yard, Kyra adds, "I need to grab a few more things from inside. Be right back."

Beth watches as Kyra disappears into the house, saying softly to herself, "This should be interesting."

Inside, Kyra gathers condiments and napkins to bring outside when Jules enters. Going in for a hug, Jules says, "I hope it's okay. We let ourselves in."

Kyra returns the squeeze, "Of course! Welcome! I'm so glad you're here."

Jules scans the house. "This place is great. Tour later?"

"Don't let these front rooms fool you. I'm still unpacking, and there are boxes everywhere back there. I still can't believe I live here."

"My baby is all grown up," Jules teases.

"How was your event the other night?" Kyra asks.

Jules shrugs. "It was fine."

"And Dylan?"

"Dreadful. As expected."

Kyra responds by rolling her eyes, and Jules quickly shifts the conversation. "Where's John? I want to meet him."

"He's out back. I'll introduce you. I just need to grab a few more things." Kyra opens the pantry door to gather a few more items from the shelves and, when she closes it, Charlie is standing there.

"Charlie." Kyra freezes.

Charlie, holding a bottle of wine, greets her. "Hi."

"I wasn't sure you were coming."

Charlie simply nods in response.

"John mentioned you're with somebody new," Kyra says. "Did you bring her?"

Charlie shakes her head no. "Not sure that's working out."

"I see…" Kyra acknowledges, not sure what else to say.

"Charlie!" Jules says. "I'm Jules. It's so nice to meet you." Jules offers a smile, extending her hand to shake.

"Pleasure's mine." Charlie returns the handshake, her eyes shifting from Kyra to Jules.

"Kyra's told me all about you," Jules addresses Charlie.

"Has she?" Charlie asks.

"Yes. I know you're new in town."

"Newly back in town, yes," Charlie replies, setting down the bottle of wine she brought on the counter, signaling the close of the conversation. "I'll leave this here for you, Kyra. I'm going to head out back to catch John."

As she exits, Charlie adds, "Jules, it was really nice to meet you."

Jules replies, "You, too, Charlie."

When Charlie is out of hearing range, Jules exhales a heavy sigh. "Wow," is all she can manage.

"Yeah," Kyra agrees.

"Whatever went on with you two…" Jules trails off, searching for the right words.

"I know. You felt it?"

"Impossible not to."

"Fuck," Kyra mutters.

Meanwhile, in the backyard, the cookout is in full swing. Eric makes his way towards the grill area where Alex is standing with John and Jerry. Madelyn's eyes track Eric as he crosses the yard, hoping he will notice her. He doesn't. A mix of anger and rejection rises in her as she reaches for her phone.

"Eric!" Alex calls out. "Hey, man. This is John."

"John! Great to finally meet you. I'm Eric, Jules' husband."

"Of course! Welcome. So, um, help yourself to a beer," John says. His hands are busy flipping burgers, flames licking upwards through the grates of the grill.

"Great setup you have here, John," Jerry says, looking around. "Ever do a movie night with just the guys?"

Eric and Alex exchange glances. Eric takes a beer from the cooler, and his gaze wanders across the yard until it lands on Miles, who is walking his way. As their eyes meet, Miles offers a wink, sending a small wave of terror through Eric.

"Miles!" John exclaims.

"John! Perfect day for a cookout," Miles responds as he approaches.

"So glad you could make it. Miles, um, this is Alex, Eric, and Jerry. Some of Kyra's friends. Everyone, this is Miles," John introduces them.

"Hey, man. Nice to meet you," Alex greets Miles with a nod.

"You, too," Miles responds, his eyes shifting back to Eric.

"Elena with you?" John inquires.

"She's here. Wouldn't miss it. She couldn't wait to meet the one that settled you down," Miles informs them, causing John to chuckle.

Alex's eyes widen as he realizes that Miles and Elena are the same pair that had the encounter with Eric and Jules. He makes eye contact with Eric, who confirms his suspicion with a slight nod.

"Hello, Miles. Nice to meet you. How do you know John?" Eric asks, masking his anxiety.

"We work together. We've known each other for years," Miles says.

"Is that so?" Eric replies.

John interjects, "It is. Miles took me under his wing and showed me the ropes when I was getting started. I call it the tough love part of our relationship."

"John was a natural," Miles adds. "Quick learner."

"You're too kind, sir," John replies and returns his focus to the grill.

Across the backyard, Elena approaches Jules, Beth, and Kyra. With a gentle tap on Jules' shoulder, she draws her attention. Jules turns, surprised to find herself face-to-face with Elena. The recognition in Jules' voice catches Beth's and Kyra's attention. "Elena!"

Elena steps forward and wraps Jules in a warm embrace. The two share a moment of intimate familiarity.

"Hello again," Elena says, a fond smile on her face as she brushes some loose strands of hair off Jules' forehead.

"It's so nice to see you," Jules replies, taking a step back but keeping her arm around Elena's waist. "Please, meet my friends Beth and Kyra."

Maintaining her arm around Jules, Elena reaches her free hand towards Beth.

"Hi, Beth," Elena greets, her voice friendly and inviting. Beth shakes Elena's outstretched hand. Turning her attention to Kyra, Elena extends her hand once more. "Kyra? John's Kyra? I've heard so much about you!"

"That's me," Kyra replies, returning Elena's handshake with a small smile.

"We've known John for ages," Elena continues. "What an absolute delight to meet you. We weren't sure he'd ever settle down. You must be very special."

"Thank you." Kyra's eyes shift towards John. "It's a big step for both of us."

"I'm going to say hi to John and tell him I've had the pleasure of meeting you," Elena announces, her gaze lingering on Jules. "Jules, really great running into you." She plants a soft kiss on Jules' cheek before stepping away.

"You, too," Jules calls after her, watching as Elena crosses the yard. Jules' face flushes pink, and her breath quickens.

As soon as Elena is out of earshot, Beth turns to Jules. "Holy shit. Was that…?"

"Yes," Jules confirms.

"She's fucking gorgeous," Kyra says, still staring after Elena.

"I told you," Jules replies, a smug grin on her face. "I wasn't expecting to run into them…"

"In public?" Beth finishes Jules' sentence.

"Yes. In public." Jules fans herself, eyes darting around

the party. "I'm a little overheated. I'm going inside to splash some water on my face."

"I bet," Kyra teases.

"You're one to talk," Jules retorts. As she begins to make her way back into the house, Claire approaches her.

"Jules!" Claire calls out.

"Claire," Jules responds.

"Jules, about the other day, what I said…" Claire begins, faltering slightly.

"What about it?"

"I'm just trying to look out for you. I didn't mean for it to go like that," Claire explains.

Jules doesn't respond, her expression guarded as she takes in Claire's words.

"I guess what I'm trying to say is that I'm sorry if I offended you. Truly. I'm sorry."

Jules remains silent for a moment, considering Claire's apology, and quickly concludes there is no point in holding a grudge. "Apology accepted. Water under the bridge."

"Great!" Claire exhales. "Thank you. I have been so nervous thinking about this. Can I give you a hug?" Claire asks.

"Sure," Jules says, accepting the awkward hug. She pulls away, glancing towards the house. "I'll be right out. I need to go freshen up."

Jules walks through the screen door, across the kitchen, to a short hallway with doors on both sides. "Nope, not that one," Jules says out loud when she opens the door to a linen closet. She turns to open and step into the opposite doorway and finds Kyra and Charlie pressed up against the sink, kissing. Jules swiftly exits the room, pulling the door shut behind her. Taking a deep breath to compose herself, she opens the door again and steps back inside, securing the lock behind her.

"What the hell is the matter with you two?" Jules hisses, her voice a low whisper.

Kyra and Charlie are wide-eyed, both flustered and guilty.

"I, uh…" Kyra stammers, struggling to find words.

"We, uh…" Charlie echoes.

Jules holds up a hand to stop them. "Get your shit together and get out of here," she orders.

"But, Jules, I…" Kyra starts.

"Go!" Jules insists, cutting her off.

Kyra and Charlie straighten their clothes and wipe their mouths. Charlie sticks her head out of the doorway and peeks left and then right to ensure no one is nearby.

"Coast is clear," she announces before she exits, Kyra directly behind. Alone, Jules splashes water on her face, shaking her head at what she just witnessed.

Back at the grill, Elena strides up to John and beams. "Guess who I just met!"

John's face lights up at the sight of her, and he wraps her in a warm hug and lifts her off the ground. "What do you think? Isn't she amazing?"

"I think you might have met your match!" Elena responds as John puts her down. She takes her place beside Miles, tucking in under his arm.

John, laughing, addresses the group. "Everyone, this is Elena. Miles' much better half."

"Hey, now!" Miles protests, feigning offense as Elena chuckles at his side.

Alex extends a hand towards Elena. "Hi. I'm Alex. Beth is my better half."

"Hello, Alex," Elena greets, shaking his hand.

Eric steps forward next, also extending his hand, "And I'm Eric. Pleased to meet you."

Elena accepts his handshake, a sly smile tugging at her lips. "Eric... You look familiar. Is it possible we've met?"

As Elena's words hang in the air, a flush rises in Eric's cheeks. Before he can stammer out a reply, Jerry steps forward. "I'm Jerry," he announces, taking Elena's hand and raising it to his lips. "You are a stunning woman."

"Oh, man," Alex groans, "C'mon, Jerry."

"What?!" Jerry feigns innocence.

Eric shakes his head. "You're grossing everyone out."

John wipes his hands on his apron. "You guys don't go anywhere. I'll be right back." He heads towards the house and finds Kyra and Charlie in the kitchen. "There you both are. My two favorite people. Come on outside. I, um, want to say a few words," he tells them.

"Just grabbing some more ice," Kyra responds. "We'll be right out."

John steps forward and takes Kyra by the hand. "That can wait. C'mon."

He leads Kyra outside, leaving Charlie alone in the kitchen just as Claire enters.

"Well, hi. I'm Claire. Friend of Kyra's," she introduces herself.

Charlie extends her hand. "Nice to meet you. I'm Charlie."

Claire's eyes light up with recognition. "John's Charlie?!"

Charlie nods. "That's me."

"Gosh, Kyra told us all about you. So nice to meet you!" Claire says.

Charlie raises an eyebrow. "I didn't realize Kyra spoke about me."

"She sure did. It's real nice to put a face to the name."

Charlie gestures towards the screen door leading to the backyard. "Well, I think they want us to head outside."

Claire nods, "Yes. Of course. I'll be out in just a minute. I need to use the little girl's room. So nice to meet you. I'll see you out there."

In the backyard, John guides Kyra to the center of the party, standing tall as he clears his throat. He clinks a beer bottle with a fork, the sound ringing out, silencing the group. Jules merges back into the crowd next to Eric, her hand finding his. Beth and Alex join them, standing close. Charlie manages to find a spot among the sea of faces, all looking toward John and Kyra with anticipation.

"So, um, I'd like to start by thanking everyone for coming out," John begins, his voice carrying across the yard.

Jules nudges Eric with her elbow. "Hand me your phone. I want to get this on video," she whispers. Eric unlocks his phone and passes it to Jules, who begins recording. As she does, others among the guests follow suit, their phones held up high to capture the moment. Panning across the crowd, Jules spots Madelyn. Madelyn's eyes are locked on Jules and Eric, and when Jules catches Madelyn's eye, Madelyn holds her gaze before looking—and then backing—away. *This is turning into quite the event,* Jules thinks to herself, bringing her focus back to the screen.

"For those of you who haven't had a chance to meet Kyra yet, this is Kyra," John continues, turning towards her with a warm smile. The crowd breaks out into cheers, prompting Kyra to blush a deep shade of red.

"And this is John," she says, her voice carrying over the applause.

The crowd responds with another round of cheers.

"You are all here today because you're important," John continues. "You're here because you're important to me. Or you're here because you're important to Kyra. So, I want to say in front of all of you…"

His eyes find Kyra's, his words taking on a deeper, more intimate tone. "If you're an important person to Kyra, you are now an important person to me." He takes a deep breath. "Because, Kyra, I love you. And I'm excited to share this next chapter with you."

John sweeps Kyra off her feet in a theatrical dip, and the crowd erupts. Charlie, crushed, backs away and out the side gate.

As Jules zooms in to capture the celebration, a text notification pops up on Eric's phone from a sender she doesn't recognize—someone saved in Eric's phone as "X." She taps to open it, and her body stiffens. On the screen, she finds hundreds of texts between Eric and this person, exchanging pictures of each other. Torsos in form-fitting workout gear progress to shots of bare, toned abs. Bathroom mirror shots of muscled backs taken from behind. Belly buttons and well-defined thighs, and then skin-tight boxer briefs, Jules recognizes some as Eric's, revealing various states of excitement underneath.

Jules' breath hitches, and her eyes widen like saucers. Eric, noticing her reaction, realizes what she is seeing. "Jules! It's not what you think!"

Jules pulls away from him and heads directly towards the house. Beth, noticing the sudden change, follows after her, concern etched on her face. Alex, left standing beside Eric, raises an eyebrow in silent question. Eric shakes his head as he turns to follow Jules and Beth into the house, Alex trailing behind.

Inside, Eric's fists pound against a locked bedroom door, his voice strained with desperation. "Jules, please! Let me in."

A few feet behind him, Alex watches, unsure of what's just happened but very worried about his friend. The door opens slightly, and Beth steps out, closing it swiftly behind her.

"Can you give us a few minutes? She's really upset," Beth tells Eric, her voice gentle but firm.

"It's not what she thinks. I just need to explain," Eric counters, eyes pleading.

"Just a few minutes."

Beth reenters the room, locking the door behind her before sitting next to Jules. She wraps an arm around her and looks over her shoulder as Jules continues scrolling through the texts on Eric's phone, tears falling faster as the images become increasingly raunchy.

"I'm such a fucking idiot," she mumbles through sobs.

Beth grimaces. "Not going to sugarcoat this. It is a lot."

"I had no idea. I don't even know who this person is. The face is cut off in all these photos," Jules whispers, her voice barely audible. She expands the images on the screen, searching for any indication of who this person might be. The only thing that comes close is a watch, a Patek Phillipe with a blue face and a silver metal band, that is in one of the photos.

"I'm so sorry, Jules," Beth says, her hand rubbing soothing circles on Jules' back. Another knock echoes from the door.

"I don't think I can talk to Eric right now," Jules says, voice shaky.

"He says he can explain," Beth offers.

"I don't know how you explain this," Jules replies, her eyes never leaving the phone screen.

Eric's pleas continue to stream through the door, and Beth turns to Jules, "What do you need?"

"I need to not see him right now." Jules' voice is choked with tears.

Beth's hand tightens on Jules' shoulder, "Ok. What else?"

"I need some space. I've got to… I've got to get myself sorted. Figure this out." Jules can barely get the words out.

"Do you want to come stay with us for a few days?" Beth asks.

Jules nods her head.

"Ok. I've got you," Beth reassures her. "Stay put. I'll talk to him." She squeezes Jules' hand before standing to face Eric again.

When she steps out, Eric looks at her with desperation. "Can I go in now? I need to talk to her."

Beth meets his gaze. "She's having a hard time right now."

"I know. I'm so stupid. It's not what it looks like. I can explain," Eric insists, his voice urgent.

Beth shakes her head. "Not now."

"What do you mean?" Eric says, his confusion evident.

Beth takes a deep breath and maintains eye contact with him. "Eric, we love you. Both of you. But Jules is going to come home with us for a little while. Till things calm down."

Eric shakes his head. "What? No. I just need to talk to her."

"She's not in a position to talk to you right now," Beth tells him, placing a gentle but warning hand on his chest.

"What is that supposed to mean?" Eric's tone sharpens, his confusion turning into anger.

Beth repeats, "Eric, she doesn't want to talk to you right now."

Eric's face crumples at her words, his shoulders slumping in defeat. "Beth, please!?"

Beth sighs, placing a comforting hand on his shoulder. "Just give it a little time, Eric. Let her cool off."

Beth turns to Alex. "Can you please pull the car around?"

Alex nods, offering Eric a supportive pat on the shoulder before stepping away to retrieve the car. Beth turns back to Eric. "I'll come by later to grab a few of Jules' things. She just needs a little space."

As Eric steps back, defeated, Kyra enters the hallway. "Hey. What's going on? Anyone see Charlie?"

"I think I saw her leave a little earlier," Beth replies, glancing at the door.

"Oh," Kyra says, her brow furrowing as she notices the tension in the room. "What's going on? Everything ok?"

"I'll get you up to speed a little later," Beth says. "We need to head out."

As Eric retreats, Beth knocks on the door, signaling to Jules that it is time to leave. Kyra watches as Jules emerges from the room, her eyes swollen and red.

"Let's get you out of here," Beth says softly, taking Jules by the arm. She guides her along the hallway, mouthing, "I'll call you" to Kyra before leaving.

Outside, Eric watches from a distance as Jules climbs into the backseat of Beth's and Alex's car. Catching sight of him, Beth walks over and hands him his phone before returning to the passenger seat. He watches in silence as the car pulls away, leaving him alone in the side yard.

✍

At Beth's and Alex's, Beth prepares the guest room for Jules, stuffing pillows into pillowcases, making up the bed with fresh sheets. "Take all the time and space you need."

Jules turns toward her. "Thank you. I don't know what I'd do without you."

"I'm going to check on Alex. Need anything else?"

"Just some time to myself," Jules responds.

A gentle kiss on Jules' forehead marks Beth's departure. The door clicks softly shut, leaving Jules alone with her thoughts.

Beth joins Alex in the living room. "She ok?" he asks.

Beth eases down next to him on the sofa, her eyes clouded with worry. "For now, yes. Those texts… I'm kind of in shock."

"That bad?" he asks.

Beth nods her head.

"What the hell was he thinking?" Alex says.

Beth drops her shoulders in resignation. "I have no idea. I've never seen her like this. They've had their issues like everyone else, but nothing like this."

Alex's eyebrows knit together, and the corners of his mouth turn down. "Why wouldn't he tell me?"

"Oh, babe." Beth shifts to put her arms around him. "This isn't on you. What if he had told you? What would you have been able to do about it?"

"I don't know. Something? Anything?"

"We need to let things settle down a bit," Beth says. "Give them some space to get things sorted."

"Do you think they'll make it through this?" Alex's question hangs heavy in the room.

"I really don't know."

Eric sits alone at his kitchen island, the ghostly glow of his phone the only light in the room. Jules won't answer his calls, so he taps out another text.

Jules, please. I know what this looks like. Just let me explain.

Jules wraps herself up in a blanket and pours muffled sobs into the pillow. The chime of Eric's text arriving is the only other sound in the room. She wipes her eyes and reaches for the phone, taking in Eric's words. The hurt is unbearable. Jules starts to type out a response and then stops herself. Time after time, she deletes her words, then starts over. Everything she writes seems wrong. Like she's communicating with a stranger. Eric stares at the pulsating dots, anxiously waiting for her text to arrive. The dots vanish with no response as Jules reaches for the light switch and tries to find sleep.

Hours pass, and Jules is still awake. She can't settle down. Sleep can't catch her. She sits up, walks to the guest bathroom, and turns on the shower as hot as it will go. Steam billows up above the shower curtain, and Jules steps in, the heat of the water turning her skin bright red on contact. It takes her a minute or two to adjust, and the sting of the hot water feels good. Her lungs open up, and her breath deepens. She closes her eyes, turning her focus inward.

What the fuck just happened? she thinks to herself. Eric, the person she loves and trusts more than anyone in the whole world, kept this, whatever this is, from her. Eric's attraction to men is no secret in their relationship. It's encouraged. *But why would he keep it from me? Why wouldn't he tell me he met someone who interested him? That they were starting a conversation? That things appeared to be escalating? When did I become an outsider? What else isn't he telling me?*

OK, Jules counsels herself. *Keep it together. Stay calm. Just stay calm.* She takes a few deep breaths before her mind starts spinning again.

What the hell have they done, and at what cost? Very little, if any of this, has gone according to plan. But what, exactly, is the plan? Jules takes a moment to reground, regroup. Personal growth. Self-expression. Expansion. She thought the container of their relationship was big enough, strong enough, to hold all these things. Hold all sides of them. Instead, she can feel the doubt lodge itself deep inside her gut, sending a shockwave of exhaustion through her entire body. She leans against the shower wall, bends her knees, and crumples to the tub floor.

No, Jules shakes her head. *No*. She isn't ready for this.

⁕

Alone in the house with Daisy, Eric is also unable to sleep. The lights are on above the kitchen island, and he paces, checking his phone every few minutes to see if there is something, anything, by way of a response from Jules. He mulls over the events of the afternoon in his mind. What was he thinking? Why did he let Jules find out that way?

Goddamnit, he thinks. This is nothing compared to what he had to witness between Jules and Elena. The feelings of jealousy and insecurity resurface, flushing his face hot. No matter how many times he replays the conversation with Jules afterward, he still can't find peace with what happened that night at Miles' and Elena's. He's still hurting, and it's making him defensive, clouding his perspective.

Still, he can only imagine what she must be thinking, what it all must look like to her. It started out innocently enough. He was the new guy at the gym, new friend material. Like Eric, he took good care of himself. Was proud of the effort he put in to stay fit. The pictures, the flirting, the feelings… It never crossed into anything actually physical. But to look at that thread, especially through Jules' eyes, Eric knows that isn't how it appeared. If only Jules could let him explain.

He checks his phone again. Nothing.

How will Jules ever trust him again?

CHAPTER 6

EVERYBODY'S GOT A PLAN

THE SHRILL SOUND of the alarm clock slices through the quiet morning in John and Kyra's bedroom. It's early, dawn barely breaking. Kyra rises softly, leaving John tucked in and undisturbed. She showers, dresses for work, and stands at the kitchen sink, faucet running. Her eyelids are heavy. She is still getting used to not living alone, the sounds of this new place, sharing a bed every night, and how different her sleep is. Kyra lets out a big yawn, fighting the urge to crawl back under the covers, her mind still dancing on the lines of consciousness. As she fills the coffee pot with water, she feels the sensation of arms wrapping around her, hugging her from behind. Warmth washes over her, her breath deepens, and her eyes close. Fingers find the buttons of her blouse and undo them, one at a time, from the top toward the bottom. Leaning back into the embrace, Kyra surrenders to the moment, a low moan echoing through the room. A hand reaches into her hair, pulling her head back. Lips nuzzle her neck. Kyra's eyes slowly open, her head tilting slightly sideways, and the face she sees kissing her is not John's. It's Charlie's.

John softly shuffles into the kitchen, sees Kyra alone at the sink, and, from behind, plants a light, good morning kiss on her cheek. Kyra, pulled away from her fantasy, flinches, startling them both.

"You caught me off guard," Kyra says, putting a hand on her chest.

"I can, um, see that. Everything ok? You were pretty deep in thought over there."

"Yeah. Yes. Of course..." she assures him. Her racing heartbeat says otherwise.

∽

The same morning, in Eric's and Jules' bedroom, the drawn curtains barely hold back the morning light. Two figures are asleep under the covers. One starts to stir, restless. It is Eric. He sits up, reaches over, and immediately checks his phone. There are messages from Xavier, but no response from Jules. His head hangs with disappointment. He pulls back the sheets to find Daisy still heavy with sleep and whimpering.

"I know," Eric scratches Daisy behind her ears, "I miss her, too. Come on. Time to get up." Eric stands and begins the day with a heaviness to his movements. He dresses, puts food and water down for Daisy, and barely touches his own breakfast. He locks the front door behind him and leaves for his appointment with Dr. Layton.

There are dark circles under Eric's eyes from poor sleep, and he can't stop picking at his cuticles. It takes a few minutes before he can settle down enough to get words out. Dr. Layton sits in her chair across from him and waits patiently, encouraging him to take as much time as he needs. "Whenever you're ready," she says, "tell me where you'd like to start."

"I..." Eric begins, "I, uh... I met this guy at the gym. He's new in town. Very attractive. And there's chemistry. Or there was chemistry. I stopped responding to his messages. We ran into each other at the coffee shop a few weeks ago and started chatting, exchanged numbers. It started with sharing workout pics, but those turned into body pics. Suggestive body pics. It was flirty and fun and, at least at the beginning, seemed innocent enough..." Eric stops himself, not wanting to admit to the next part, but Dr. Layton's expression prompts him to keep going.

"I didn't tell Jules about it. Or him. I kept it all to myself. Which is stupid because I actually think she would have been okay with it. If I had been honest. But I wasn't. We were at a cookout for one of her friends last weekend, and Jules was using my phone to take videos. A text came through, and she saw it. Saw them. The pictures. The messages. I can only imagine what it must've looked like to her. What I must look like to her."

"How bad?"

"Really bad."

"Did anything physical happen between you and this person?" Dr. Layton asks.

"No. Just the texting. But I'm sure that's not what it looks like to Jules."

"I see," responds Dr. Layton.

"Jules has been staying with Beth and Alex since she found out. She hasn't answered any of my calls or responded to any of my texts."

"So, no communication?"

"None. And it's driving me nuts. I can't lose her, Dr. Layton." Eric's voice breaks at the thought of the possible consequences of his actions.

Dr. Layton thinks for a moment and then proceeds. "Before we talk about Jules, let's talk about you. You've told me what happened. You haven't yet told me why."

Eric takes a few breaths before he responds. "I've had a lot of time to myself to think about that question. I wish I had better answers." He looks down, avoiding eye contact with Dr. Layton. "I liked the attention. I liked the flirting. It felt sexy. I felt sexy."

"What else?" Dr. Layton asks.

"I liked keeping a secret from Jules."

"Did you want to get caught?"

"I don't know. Maybe? Not like that."

"Did you want to hurt her?"

Eric considers Dr. Layton's question. "I think part of this was retaliation, yes. For how things went with Madelyn. For what happened at Miles' and Elena's."

"You said part of it might be retaliation. What are the other parts?"

"I liked feeling dirty in a way that I don't get to with Jules. That's just not how we are with each other."

"Do you and Jules ever exchange texts or photos like that?"

"We don't. It's not Jules' thing. She doesn't want

anything like that showing up on her phone while she's at work."

"But you'd be into it if she was?"

"I would, yes."

"Not just the photos part. The secret-keeping? Feeling dirty?"

"I don't know, Dr. Layton. I don't recognize myself, and I don't understand my own behavior. Urges, sure. We're all human. But this… I don't know how I'm ever going to be able to make things right. I don't know how we get past this."

Later that afternoon, Beth, Kyra, Jules, and Claire throw punches and jab their way through boxing class. Jules and Kyra both hit harder than usual. When the class ends, they walk together towards the locker room, dripping with sweat.

Post shower, Claire clears her throat. "Y'all, Jerry and I are coming up on our one-year anniversary, and we're getting some friends together this weekend to celebrate. We will be at that cute little spot, Pilar Bar. Casual. No gifts. Are y'all free? Do you think you can make it?"

Beth responds first. "How sweet. Congratulations. I'm sure Alex and I can stop by."

"Same for me and John," Kyra adds.

"Jules," Claire says, "full disclosure, Madelyn will be there, and Jerry is inviting Eric. I hope that's ok and that you'll still think about coming."

"I'll definitely think about it," Jules says.

Claire nods her thanks to Jules and continues. "Can you believe it's been a year? I remember when I first met

Jerry. He was such a sad, lost little puppy. He just needed a good woman to take charge. Give him direction. You know, train him. And now look at us. Mr. and Mrs.," Claire says, glancing at her rings and checking her appearance in the mirror. "First anniversary is paper. I'm having something special made. You'll see it at the party. Anywho, I've got to run. I've got to get supper ready. See you ladies later."

Kyra waits for the locker room door to close and whispers, "You know, she has this whole southern belle thing going on, but I bet she and Jerry are freaks."

"What do you mean?" Beth asks.

"I bet they are kinky ass freaks in the bedroom," Kyra responds.

"Please stop," Beth says. "I don't want those images in my head."

Jules interrupts, unable to hold back tears. "What if Eric shows up? What if I'm not ready to talk to him?"

"Oh, babe, it'll all be okay," Beth says, taking a seat next to Jules.

"I'm so sorry," Kyra says, sitting on Jules' other side. "If it helps, you're not the only one struggling." Kyra goes on to tell Jules and Beth about her lingering feelings for Charlie, that she can't stop thinking about her, but that she's committed to making things work with John. Kyra looks to Beth and says, "Seriously. How do you and Alex do it? You lead such a drama-free existence."

Beth looks at Jules and feigns exasperation. "Did Kyra just call me boring? I think she just…"

"I think she did…" Jules giggles through her tears.

"That's not what I meant!" Kyra defends herself.

Beth folds her arms across her chest. "Then what did you mean?"

Jules can't resist piling on. "Yeah, Kyra. What did you mean?"

"I mean, you and Alex are so solid. So connected… like…"

"Like Eric and I used to be," Jules finishes Kyra's statement, deflated.

"Oh, no. Jules, that's not where I was going," Kyra pleads.

Beth puts her arm around Jules' shoulder and rocks her gently from side to side. "Just give it a little more time. You're all set up at our house, anyway. You stay as long as you need."

"Wait," says Kyra, "Are you guys a throuple now?"

Beth snorts, and Jules rolls her eyes. "Shut up, Kyra."

∼

Xavier scans the gym, hoping to see Eric. He isn't in the free weights section, on the treadmill, or in the locker room. Disappointed, Xavier puts on his headphones, pulls up the hood of his sweatshirt, and starts his workout.

Something is amiss. For the past few weeks, the frequency of his messages with Eric has been increasing, and Xavier found himself checking his phone often, over the moon when Eric's messages came through.

The photos were an easy place to start. Both of them take good care of themselves, and it felt like a natural progression to move from mirror shots taken in the weights section to shirtless shots taken from the changing room and then shots taken pre and post-shower. Like a visual call and response.

Xavier worried he was getting too attached when he started making playlists for Eric. Secret messages in the lyrics, in the song order. Like a kid in grade school passing a note with checkboxes: *Do you like me, yes or no?*

For all of his outward confidence, Xavier found himself uncomfortably insecure when it came to Eric. It's not like he hadn't seen the wedding band on Eric's finger. It was there in plain sight. It's that he chose to ignore it, assuming there was some sort of arrangement in place. The radio silence from Eric these past few days was evidence to the contrary.

How did I let this happen? Xavier thinks to himself. He'd heard all about the heartbreak stories of friends getting involved with married men. Falling hard. Getting hurt. But there is something so endearing about Eric. He's sincere and sexy all at the same time, and their interactions had started innocently enough. It felt so natural with Eric, so easy.

Xavier turns up the volume on his headphones and starts his run on the treadmill. By the end of his last sprint, he's covered with sweat and clear on what he wants to communicate. It may be over, but he wouldn't be ignored.

Alone in her office at work the next day, Jules is lost in thought. Peter knocks on her door and takes a seat in Jules' guest chair. "Tell me how the event went the other night. What were your takeaways?" he asks.

"The new firm was there, including their new head of finance. Two of the partners started in venture and moved into private equity. They all have strong track records of delivering impressive results."

Peter raises his eyebrows in pleasant surprise.

"Yes. I thought so, too," Jules agrees. "The head of finance, though, came out of banking. Like me. I like him a lot, and we know a lot of the same people. In fact, it's a little odd that our paths haven't already crossed. From what I can tell, he works like we do. He can think strategically, but he's not afraid to dig into the figures. He seems very smart and, based on initial impressions, I think we'd work well together. They have a lot of dry powder and are looking for deals. I think we could be quite useful for one another."

"You sound excited."

"I am. I always enjoy working with smart people."

"Dylan didn't seem to take to him," Peter says, the disappointment clear in his voice.

"I'm not sure Dylan knows what to look for quite yet." Jules doesn't mention Dylan's unprofessional behavior.

The receptionist's voice comes through on Jules' speaker phone, "Julia, call for you."

Jules responds, "Ok. I'll pick up." Peter nods and leaves as Jules reaches for the phone. "Hello?" she says.

"Are we living in a material world, and is this the material girl?" says the voice on the other side of the line. Jules recognizes the voice, remembering the exchange at the event.

"Indeed," Jules responds with her bright, bold laugh.

"I won't keep you long. Just wanted you to know that the numbers look good. The lawyers are finishing up the paperwork, and we will get the green light to go."

"Yeah?" Jules says.

"Yeah," he confirms. "I think we are going to make a great team."

"Me, too," Jules replies. "I think we are going to hit it out of the park."

"Great. Well, I'll let you get back to it. And, Julia?"

"Yes?" she says.

"If you ever think of making a change, your talent would be most welcome here."

Jules smiles to herself. She hasn't felt this appreciated professionally in a long time. "You really know how to make a material girl feel special. Thank you," she replies and then ends the call.

Jules stands and walks the hallway down to Peter's office. "Looks like we're moving forward," she says to Peter, grinning.

"Really? Was that them?"

"Yes. Documents should be coming our way soon."

"Terrific work, Julia. I couldn't be happier. Come. Let's grab a bite downstairs and talk about next steps," Peter says.

As they walk down the hallway, Peter discloses, "I'd like to keep the team small. Surgical."

"Can you be more specific?" Jules asks.

"I'd like you to work directly with Dylan on this," Peter replies.

Jules blinks, taken aback, "Peter, I…"

Peter anticipates her objection. "I know. I know. He's a brand-new associate and has a lot to learn. This would be a great opportunity for him to have some one-on-one time with you without the peer pressure of some of the others."

Jules attempts to keep her reaction in check and manages to deflect. "This one is going to require some special skill sets. Before we make a final decision on staffing, let me give it some thought."

Peter nods. "Yes. Please. Give it some thought."

Peter and Jules approach the elevator, the doors slide open, and they step inside. As they turn, facing the closing elevator doors, Dylan rushes around the corner. "Hold the…" he begins, but he's too late. Jules locks eyes with Dylan and lets the elevator doors close before he reaches them.

Eric sits alone at a table in the coffee shop, a lukewarm coffee sitting half-empty in front of him, along with Vickie's letter of resignation. He was unable to come up with a solution that would give Vickie the additional staff she needed at Avendale. The conversation was professional. She would do her best to support a transition, but after 30 days, she would be moving on. It would be a huge loss for the facility and for Eric. Before leaving, Vickie dropped a notecard that had been left for him. From Xavier.

Taking a little sip of his coffee, he looks over the note again.

Dear Eric,

I know this is terribly old-fashioned, and I'm not typically one to wear my heart on my sleeve, but your sudden and complete disappearance is at once a cause for alarm and a deep disappointment. Are you ok? Alive? Was it something I said?

I get it. Our interactions have concluded. But please have the decency to end this like a gentleman.

-X

Eric scrolls on his phone, thinking about his painful goodbye with Vickie and the note from Xavier, hoping Jules will soon make contact. He is so deep in his own thoughts, he doesn't see Xavier's approach.

"Why did you ghost me?" Xavier asks bluntly.

Eric looks up, eyes meeting Xavier's, and motions for him to sit. "My wife saw the thread," Eric admits. "She didn't know."

"I thought you had an understanding. An arrangement."

"We kind of did. But it didn't really contemplate what we were doing. Not expressly, anyway," Eric clarifies, his voice low.

"But we never had any physical contact."

Eric nods. "Yes, I know. And I would like Jules to know. But she's not talking to me."

Xavier grimaces. "Oh no."

"Yeah," Eric says. "It's the worst thing she could possibly do. I don't handle abandonment very well."

"For the record," Xavier says, "I'm not in the business of getting attached to married men. Or getting attached at all, for that matter." Xavier pauses, considering his next words. "I've been through our text thread about a thousand times looking for a misstep. Did I say something wrong? Was I out of bounds?"

"You weren't," Eric reassures.

"I wasn't," Xavier says defensively and then pauses again. "Do you think it could have become anything more? It really felt like…"

Eric interrupts, "It did. This is on me, Xavier. Not you."

"Do you think it would help if I met her? Talked to her?"

Eric shakes his head. "I appreciate that. But that's not a good idea right now."

"I guess I was just hoping that…" Xavier trails off.

"I know," Eric says. "I felt it, too. But now is…not a good time. I didn't mean to mislead you. I promise. That was not my intention."

Xavier can see Eric's pain, and while part of him wants to stay mad, he can't. Instead, he feels his anger turn into curiosity. "So, tell me about her. What's she like?" Xavier asks.

"Jules? She's the love of my life. My most important person. I've been crazy about her since the day I got up the nerve to ask her out."

"What else?" Xavier asks. "What makes her special?"

Eric feels his heart grow warm thinking about his feelings for Jules. "She's serious until she isn't, and her laugh…"

"What about it?"

"It's my favorite sound. It's loud and unexpected. It's one of those laughs that make the people around her laugh. And when she looks at me…" Eric pauses. "When she looks at me, it feels like I'm the only person on the planet."

Xavier feels himself falling harder for Eric with every word, despite knowing it won't go any further.

"Your turn," says Eric. "You say you don't get attached to married men or otherwise. You knew I was married. I'm not shifting accountability. I take responsibility for my part in this. But what was this about for you?"

"I wish I could explain it," Xavier responds. "There is

a lot of travel in my line of work, and it's been hard to maintain any kind of relationship. With men, it's often so… transactional. That's part of why I took my current role. I'm hoping to put down some roots. And you're right. I knew you were married. I guess I wasn't expecting to get attached.

"I like to blame the travel, but if I'm being honest, I haven't found the person I want to come home to every night. When I hear the way you speak about your wife… I want to feel that way about someone someday. I want someone to feel that way about me." Xavier stands to leave. "I hope things work out with your wife, Eric."

"Yeah. Me, too. Xavier, I'm sorry," Eric says.

Xavier stops at the coffee shop door, turning back to Eric, "Yeah. Me, too."

The next morning, Alex and Eric are at the gym, their muscles straining as they lift weights. Eric's eyes are on the dumbbells in front of him, but his mind is clearly elsewhere.

Eric breaks the silence, his voice tight. "How is she?"

Alex exhales sharply, setting down his weights. "She works, comes to our house, has dinner, and goes to her room."

"Does she ask about me?" Eric asks.

"I'm sure this is hard for her, if that's what you mean. But I'm not privy to what she talks to Beth about," Alex says.

Eric nods, disappointment permeating his features. "I get it. Sorry. I don't mean to make things even more uncomfortable."

"Don't apologize," Alex says. "We are here for both of

you. We care about both of you. We just want you to get through this."

Their conversation lapses into silence, punctuated by the clanging of metal weights.

"She won't even return my texts," Eric laments.

"Oh, man," Alex says. "I don't know what to say. Maybe just give it a little more time? I just really wish…"

"Really wish what?" Eric asks.

"I really wish you would have told me what was going on. I know you're hurting, and I don't want to make it worse, but why didn't you say anything to me?"

"Alex, I…" Eric stammers. "I don't have a good answer for you. I didn't say anything because what was I going to say? I'm a selfish idiot? Check out these dick pics I've been swapping with this guy Jules knows nothing about because, you know, that's a sign of a healthy marriage? And, by the way, I liked it? Like, really liked it. Alex, I don't recognize myself. This is not who I am. Hiding things from Jules, from you. I've managed to hurt everyone I care about with the way I acted. All I can say is I'm sorry. I'm trying to figure this out."

Alex nods his head. "Just know you can talk to me about anything, ok?"

"Ok."

Eric and Alex continue their workout, and Eric rolls his eyes as he spots Jerry making his way over. "Incoming," he warns.

"He's not that bad," Alex defends.

Jerry approaches, flexing his biceps. "Dudes! Gains never sleep!"

"I stand corrected," Alex says to Eric.

"Looking good, fellas. Upper body day?" Jerry asks, grinning.

"Yes," Eric replies shortly.

"Me, too. Me, too. Plus cardio. Need to stay lean." Jerry slaps his abdomen.

"What can we do for you, Jerry?" Alex asks.

"Claire wanted me to let you know you're invited to our anniversary get-together this weekend. At the bar with the jukebox. And before you ask, Eric. Yes, Jules is invited. Hopefully, whatever is going on with you two will be over by then. Women, right?" Jerry's flippant remarks cause Eric to flinch. "Hey, is it because of what happened between you and Madelyn? She'll be there too, you know."

"Jerry! What the hell?" Alex is appalled.

Jerry looks confused, "What?!"

"Man," Alex says, "sometimes you really don't know how to read a room."

"Yeah. Claire says that, too," Jerry replies, looking around. "A treadmill just opened up. Gotta run."

Eric and Alex exhale a sigh of relief at Jerry's departure. "Man. What is with that guy?" Alex mutters, watching Jerry jog away. "He's the proverbial bull in a China shop."

"I don't know about the bull part," Eric responds with a smirk.

Alex looks at him, eyebrow raised. "Is that a sex thing?"

Eric finds himself laughing for the first time in days. "Yes, Alex. It is."

Alex laughs along, "I have so much to learn…"

Kyra returns home from work to find John in the kitchen, plating dinner. Kyra walks over and plants a soft kiss on his cheek. "Hey, babe."

John grins, returning her affection with a quick peck on her lips. "Hey."

Kyra inhales, "This smells great."

"Let's eat while it's hot."

The two sit and take their first bites. "Delish," she compliments.

John smiles in return.

"I meant to tell you," Kyra says. "We got invited to Claire and Jerry's one-year anniversary party."

"Is that a thing?"

"For Claire, it is," Kyra says.

John chuckles, "Ahh. I see."

"Jules and Eric are also invited," Kyra adds.

"Does that mean things are better with them?"

"Nope. Not even a little. They haven't spoken since the cookout," Kyra replies.

John exhales, shaking his head. "Man."

"Yeah," Kyra responds.

"I hope that never happens to us," John says, reaching out to hold Kyra's hand.

"Same," Kyra replies, squeezing his hand in return and then letting go. "I still can't believe it's happening to them. I know you don't know them well yet. They were the model couple. Always communicating. No secrets. I never, ever saw anything like this coming."

The room falls quiet as they continue their meal. John wipes the corners of his mouth with a napkin and looks up into Kyra's eyes. "You know you can tell me anything."

"I know," Kyra responds, her voice soft. She can feel panic building in her chest, but she pushes it down. Now is not the time or place. She's not even sure what she would say, how she would tell him.

"No. Really. You can talk to me about anything. I don't want us to have secrets. I don't ever want what's happening to Jules and Eric to happen to us."

"Me, neither," Kyra replies.

John lifts his glass, "To no secrets."

Kyra swallows the lump in her throat and clinks her glass against his. "To no secrets."

Across town, in the quiet dining room of Beth and Alex's house, Beth, Alex, and Jules are near the end of dinner. The only sound is silverware clinking against plates. Kevin is out with his girlfriend, and Mason is watching a movie at a friend's.

Jules, finished, starts to rise. "Thank you for dinner. Let me get the table cleared."

"Just leave the dishes in the sink," Beth says. "I'll take care of the rest."

Jules nods. "Ok."

"Want to watch TV with us?" Alex asks.

"I'm good. I just need some alone time. Good night, you two."

"Good night," Beth and Alex reply almost in unison.

Jules exits, and Beth and Alex hear the door to her room click closed.

"I worked out with Eric today," Alex begins.

Beth turns to him. "Yeah? I've been worried about him. How is he?"

"Horrible," Alex says.

"Did he ask about Jules?"

"Of course," Alex sighs, rubbing a hand over his face. "This is awful. I mean, I get it. Eric screwed up. But her stonewalling him like this… I'm worried he's going to lose his mind."

"I know," Beth says. "I know she doesn't want to make anything worse."

"This isn't making anything better," Alex points out.

Beth shrugs. "I think she just needs a little more time."

"Jerry was at the gym, as well. He invited us to their anniversary party."

"Yeah. Claire mentioned it, too."

"I really hope they at least talk by then."

"That makes two of us," Beth replies.

Later that evening, Beth walks down the hallway. The light is still on in the guest room, the soft glow seeping out from under the door.

Beth knocks, voice soft, "Hey, Jules. Can I come in?"

"Of course," Jules replies. Jules is sitting up in bed, her phone in her lap.

"Talk to me," Beth says, sitting on the edge of the bed.

"I'm not sure what to say," Jules replies.

"Have you responded to Eric?"

Jules shakes her head.

"He's going crazy, by the way," Beth informs her.

Jules' expression drops, tears welling in her eyes. "I know. It's just… I'm afraid if I talk to him before I'm ready, before I get my emotions under control, I will only make things worse."

Beth takes Jules' hand, "I will support you in whatever decision you make. But you are both in new territory, and not communicating isn't helping. The only way out of this is through, and that means you have to find a way to talk to him and figure this out."

"I know," Jules whispers.

Beth stands, leans over, and kisses Jules on the forehead. "Try to get some rest."

Beth leaves, closing the door behind her, and Jules picks up her phone. There are several messages, all from Eric.

Jules. Please. Just talk to me.

A photo of Daisy is captioned with, 'We miss you.'

Alright, well, good night. I hope we can talk tomorrow.

I get it. You need your space. I'm here when you're ready.

I was really hoping to hear from you today. Even just a text to let me know you've seen my messages.

C'mon Jules. Please? Just let me try to explain.

Jules' fingers hover over the keypad, starting to tap out a response. She types and deletes. Over and over. Nothing comes out right. Frustrated, Jules puts her phone aside, shuts off the light, and tries to drift into sweet unconsciousness. While she stares at the back of her eyelids, it occurs to her that there is someone else she can talk to, someone who might have some helpful advice.

⏀

The next day, Jules sits alone at a table for two, mid-workday. The tables around her are full with the lunchtime crowd. She sips an iced tea, watches the doorway, and waves at Elena when she sees her enter. Jules stands to greet her, and the women lightly hug and plant a kiss on each other's cheeks.

"Thanks so much for meeting me," Jules starts, "please, sit."

Elena takes a seat, places the cloth napkin in her lap, and smiles. "Of course. I was happy to hear from you." They each peruse the menu and order salads, dressing on the side.

"Excellent choice," the waitstaff confirms and steps away.

"How have you been?" Elena asks. "It was so fun to run into you at the cookout. Small world."

Jules replies, "It was nice to run into you, too, but that day didn't go well for me. In fact, that's the reason I asked you here. I was hoping I could talk to you."

Concern washes over Elena's features, and she immediately changes her tone to soft and caring. "Sure. What's up?"

"When everyone was outside while John and Kyra were making their speech, I was videoing it on Eric's phone. A message popped up, and I opened it, and there were texts. Lots of them. And photos. The thread was between Eric and another man. Someone I don't know. I had no idea that was happening."

"Ouch."

"Yes."

"What did Eric say?"

"I've been too upset to talk to him about it. I don't even know where to start. We've never had secrets before and never anything like this. And it's not just this. I'm finding that since we've started…"

"Exploring?"

"Yes, thank you. Since we've started exploring, I'm changing, too. My desires are…"

"Running wild?"

"Yes." Jules feels relief at Elena validating her confusing feelings.

Elena gives a small nod of acknowledgement and thinks for a moment before speaking. "This journey you're on, it's not for the faint of heart. When you start to open yourselves up to these types of experiences, you don't always know how they are going to go or what feelings are going to come up. New turn-ons, new turn-offs. Some healthy, some…"

"Some questionable."

"Yes. Some questionable. And every person is different, every couple is different, every interaction is different. What might be comfortable in one context will have you losing your sanity in another. When Miles and I started down this path, we had a lot to work through. I'd get jealous if one of his lovers would call during dinner time. He'd get upset if someone other than him bought me a piece of jewelry. I wasn't sure we were going to make it."

"But you two are so close."

"We are. But we had to figure a lot out. And most of it comes down to communication."

"That's a big part of it," Jules says. "We promised we'd communicate, and that fell apart here."

"Then I'd suggest you find out why. I can see you're hurt, and I'm sorry about that, but here's what I can tell you. If you decide to continue down this road, a few dirty pics are the least of it. You have to decide what you can and can't handle because it all comes at a price. All of it. The bigger question here is whether those pics are worth the price of your marriage."

"It's about trust," Jules says defensively.

"You can make it about trust," Elena continues. "You can make it about whatever you want. And I'm not suggesting you put your head in the sand and pretend like nothing happened. Clearly, something went wrong. But my suggestion would be to give yourself a little more time to calm your feelings and then find out, from Eric, what happened. Then you can decide if it's something you can live with or not. As for the new urges you're feeling, your new turn-ons, the genie is out of the bottle on those. Trying to ignore those comes at an even greater price."

"So what do you do about that?" Jules asks.

"You find ways to express yourself that don't wreck your relationship."

"Easier said than done. And we're off to a dreadful start." Jules' shoulders slump.

"I'm sorry. I know this probably feels a little harsh. But I wish someone had told me these things when Miles and I started."

Their salads arrive, and Jules picks at her food. Looking

up, Jules addresses Elena once more. "You said all of this comes at a price."

Elena nods in acknowledgment.

"Is it worth it?" Jules asks.

"Only you can answer that," Elena responds. "But here," Elena opens her purse and pulls out a business card for a couples' crisis center. "This place might help."

∽

The following days flow like water through a sieve, each day a stream of moments carrying Jules and Eric further apart. Their lives become a time-lapse, moving separately in parallel, paths never crossing. Jules' interactions with Beth and Alex are polite but clipped. Conversations are limited to pleasantries. She finds herself just going through the motions at work, finding it difficult to focus.

For Eric, it's like his world shifts from high color saturation to muted tones. Both he and Daisy occupy a space of waiting, longing. The hole Jules left feels like it gets bigger every day. Eric, too, has trouble focusing on work. He continues to message Jules several times a day. When Alex inquires as to whether Jules has responded, the answer is always no.

Life, however, moves on. Kyra and John continue to grow closer as more boxes get unpacked. Beth and Alex drop Mason off for a week at sleep-away camp and start getting Kevin ready for college. Claire is a ball of energy, ensuring every detail is perfect for the upcoming anniversary party, inviting just about everyone she runs into.

The night of Claire and Jerry's party arrives, and Eric

and Jules, respectively, agonize in private as to whether they will go. Eric desperately wants to see Jules but is unsure of his emotional state. A million questions run through his mind. *How will she react when she sees me? What if she doesn't go? Is our marriage over?* His thoughts are a runaway train of scenarios that has him on edge, but he pulls himself together. He knows he has to at least try.

It is not until Jules steps into the living room of Beth and Alex's house, wearing a little black dress, that her decision is made.

"Look at you!" Beth exclaims.

"You guys ready?" Jules asks, her hands smoothing over the fabric of her dress.

Beth gives Jules a once-over. "We're ready. Are you ready? Everyone is going to be there."

Jules knows that the 'everyone' Beth is referring to includes Eric. Jules squares her shoulders, her expression resolute. "I can't keep hiding forever."

"You look great, Jules. I'm so glad you're coming," Alex adds, reaching for his car keys. "We should head out."

Alex finds a spot right by the bar, pulls in, and parks. He and Beth open the car doors and step out, but Jules freezes.

"I don't think I want to go in."

Beth gets back in the car and faces Jules. Her face is serious. "Ok, Jules. You know how much I love you."

"I do."

"Go talk to your husband before this does permanent damage."

Jules' shoulders drop. "I don't know where to start. I'm afraid I will just make things worse."

"This certainly isn't making things better."

"But those texts…"

"Yes. They were a lot. But all of this has been a lot."

"You're not wrong. I'm just so mad."

"So?"

"What do you mean, so?"

"So, you're mad. So what? Eric is mad, too. He has hurt feelings, too. Just like you."

"Are you taking his side?" Jules can feel her walls coming up, but Beth is ready for the defensiveness coming her way. She knows her best friend well.

"I'm taking the side of your relationship. Go hear him out. Whatever you decide to do, I will support you. But go hear what he has to say."

"Alright. I'll be in. I just need a minute."

"Ok. I will see you in there."

Beth turns to face Alex, and they share a look before heading inside.

◈

The atmosphere at the bar is already in full swing. Balloon letters announcing 'HAPPY ANNIVERSARY' bob under the ceiling. The guests are encouraged to don whimsical paper hats as an homage to the first-anniversary theme. Claire and Jerry welcome their friends and acquaintances with open arms. Madelyn is in the corner, nursing a cocktail. Charlie is at the bar, a few seats away from Eric. Beth and Alex make their entrance, the absence of Jules instantly noted by Eric. He shares a wave with Alex, who joins Eric at the bar.

"She's coming, man. She just needs a few minutes," Alex reassures Eric, who exhales sharply and swallows a shot of whiskey.

"I don't think I've ever been this nervous," Eric says, his hands wrapping tightly around the shot glass.

"Just take a deep breath," Alex counsels, patting Eric on the back.

Eric watches the door like a hawk and springs to his feet as Jules walks in. He starts to approach, but anxiety overtakes him. He can feel himself sweating through his shirt and has trouble breathing. He bolts to the men's room just as Jules surveys the crowd, looking for but not finding him.

Kyra and John make their entrance next. Alex moves through the room to greet them.

"Kyra! Great to see you. John! Hey, man."

"Alex! Nice to see you!" John says. "What have you, um, been up to?"

"Oh, you know. The usual," Alex replies. The two continue with small talk, and Kyra breaks away, weaving her way toward Jules. "There you are! Look at you!" Kyra eyes Jules' dress.

"Not too much?" Jules asks.

"You look fantastic," Kyra assures her.

"Thank you. I'm so glad to see you," Jules says.

"I'm so glad you're out. Have you seen Eric yet?" Kyra asks.

"I haven't. Have you seen him?" Jules asks, a knot of apprehension tight in her stomach.

"No. We just got here." Kyra scans the crowd and

announces, "Frick. Charlie is here. At the bar," gesturing subtly in Charlie's direction.

Jules's eyes widen. "What?"

"Yeah. I should have known. This is her favorite bar. Did you know she was going to be here?" Kyra questions, a crease forming between her eyebrows.

"I don't know anything anymore," Jules says with a shrug.

"It's okay," Kyra reassures herself. "I'm with John."

Beth sidles up to Kyra and Jules, her gaze flickering toward the bar. "Is that Charlie at the bar?"

Jules nods. "It sure is."

Beth shifts her focus to Kyra. "You okay?"

"I'm okay," Kyra says, ignoring her quickening pulse. "You okay?"

"I'm okay," Beth assures her before turning to Jules. "Eric is here. Alex saw him already."

"I haven't seen him yet."

Beth places a comforting hand on Jules' arm. "You got this."

"Do I?" Jules scans the crowd for Eric, who is nowhere to be found.

Across the room, Charlie spots John and walks over to him while Kyra is chatting with Beth and Jules. Kyra makes eye contact with Charlie, and Charlie looks away. The noise level rises as even more guests arrive, crowding the space. Shots are passed, and the guests get rowdier. Sloppier. Quickly.

On the small, elevated stage, Claire wears an elaborate paper crown and taps the microphone to get the crowd's attention. "Hey, y'all. Thanks so much for being here. Jerry, come on over and stand next to your lawful, wedded wife."

Jerry raises his glass, downs a shot, then another. "Yes, dear. Coming, dear," he responds, drawing laughter from the crowd as he makes his way onto the stage.

Feeling overwhelmed by Charlie's presence, Kyra turns to Beth. "I need to get some air." She slips out through the side door, leaving Beth and Jules alone in the crowd. Charlie watches Kyra leave.

Claire, now joined by Jerry on stage, continues. "As y'all know, I got to marry my soul mate one year ago. And while it may seem a little silly, I think it is important to take the time to celebrate love. Wouldn't y'all agree?" The crowd breaks into applause, clapping and cheering.

"And as y'all also know," Claire's smile broadens, "we traditionally celebrate first wedding anniversaries with paper." She bends down to pick up a wrapped present, the rustle of paper filling the air as she hands it to Jerry.

Outside the bar, the side door swings open. It's Charlie. The noise of the bar rises before falling again as the door swings shut behind her. Charlie and Kyra lock eyes. The world goes still for a moment before Kyra steps forward, pressing herself against Charlie and kissing her with a fervor that consumes them both.

Inside the bar, the festivities go on. A drunk Jerry unwraps his gift—a hand-drawn sketch capturing a moment from their wedding. Holding it aloft for the crowd to see, a chorus of applause and coos rises in response.

"Thank you. This is really…really nice. I, uh, got you something, too," Jerry slurs, fumbling in his pocket to retrieve a folded piece of paper. He hands it to a giddy Claire, who unfolds it and quickly scans the contents. The color drains from her face.

"Are you freaking kidding me?!" Claire's voice rings out, reverberating across the room.

Jerry blinks in confusion. "What?! It's funny!"

Claire, anger flaring, drops the paper to the floor. The word "THREESOME?" glares up at them, scrawled in bold black marker.

"Funny?! You think a threesome is funny?" Claire's voice is thick with outrage.

Unfazed, Jerry locks eyes with Madelyn in the crowd. He pantomimes a phone to his ear, points in her direction, and winks. "I mean. It's what I'd like for our anniversary, but also, yeah. It's funny."

Claire storms off, furious and embarrassed. The guests are unsure how to respond.

John, sensing something amiss, looks around but cannot find Kyra. He makes his way to the side door to search for her, and as he pulls the door open, he sees Kyra and Charlie locked in an embrace against the wall.

"Kyra? Charlie? What the..." John stammers, then turns to go back inside.

"John!" Kyra calls out. Charlie breaks away and follows John back into the bar, Kyra a few steps behind.

John stops and turns to face Charlie, his face just a few inches from hers. "What the fuck, Charlie? You're my best friend... You know I love her!"

"Yeah?" Charlie says. "Well, I love her, too!"

Kyra reaches out to grab John by the arm, but he shrugs her off, nearly knocking her over.

Charlie yells, "Hey!" Fury blazes in each of their eyes, and their fists clench.

Beth sees what is happening and motions for Alex and Jules to follow her over. Jules is still trying, unsuccessfully, to look for Eric.

Eric stands in the muted glow of a dimly lit public restroom. The muffled undercurrent of music and woozy, intoxicated voices seep through the narrow perimeter of light that surrounds the locked door. His hands grip the cold edges of the bright white porcelain sink, eyes clenched shut, as a swirl of emotions move through him. He was hoping the alcohol would calm his nerves.

Beads of sweat pearl at his hairline, his breath is shallow, throat dry. His chin lifts to meet his reflection in the mirror, and his dark undereye circles make him look older than his 44 years. He can see his heartbeat pulse in the pale blue vein of his right temple when a loud pounding comes through the door.

"You done in there?"

"Just a minute!" Eric counters with an unsteady timbre in his voice. His gaze drifts down to his left finger and settles on his wedding band. With a deep inhale and sharp exhale, Eric unlocks the door to face the unknown ahead.

Eric looks out over the crowd and sees John and Charlie standing off, chest to chest, nostrils flaring. Beth, Alex, and Jules are close by, with Jules' arm protectively around Kyra. Moving swiftly through the crowd, Eric approaches just as John pulls his elbow back, gearing up to throw a punch at

Charlie, but before he can swing, Beth intervenes. She lands a right hook to John's jaw with the force of a prizefighter, and he hits the floor. Out like a light. Everyone, including Beth, is stunned. Beth rubs her knuckles, and Alex's gaze locks onto hers.

"I am so freaking turned on by you right now," he exclaims. A smile spreads across Beth's face as she winks back at him. Kyra slips out from under Jules' arm and backs away, flush with embarrassment, anger, and confusion.

Charlie sees her back away and calls out, "Kyra!" but Kyra just shakes her head and leaves the bar. Alone.

Eric and Jules come face to face for the first time since the barbeque.

"Jules. Please. I know I messed up," Eric says, his voice raw. "Can we just talk?"

Jules and Eric make their way outside, passing the bouncers on their way to remove John from the bar. They take a seat on the curb.

"Nothing physical happened," Eric begins. "I promise. I know what it looks like, and I know what you must be thinking."

"Help me understand."

"I wish I could. It started out innocently enough. He's new in town. He recognized me from the gym one day at the coffee shop. We walked for a bit and exchanged numbers. All friendly. Above board. Then, a gym check-in turned into a selfie. And the selfies got more…"

"Graphic?"

"Yes. Graphic."

"And you just kept going? Did you not think I would find out?" Jules asks.

"It was stupid. I was stupid. It started out as flirting and got out of hand. I see that now. I don't know why I got carried away, but I did. I'm not proud of it. And I didn't mean for you to find out the way that you did."

"Why didn't you tell me?"

"I don't know. Because I'm an idiot. But also because it felt private. Not that I want to keep things from you. I don't. But once it escalated, I wasn't sure how to bring it up."

"Were you punishing me? For what happened with Miles and Elena?"

"I don't know. Maybe? Or maybe I liked having something to myself? I don't have a good answer for this. What I know is that I'm sorry. I didn't mean for things to get out of control. I promise you, nothing physical has happened. But I need to be honest with you. There was something in me that needed to be seen like that."

"Do you have feelings for him?"

"Jules, I have feelings for everybody. But nothing like the feelings I have for you."

Jules wants to understand, wants to be understanding, but the weight of what Eric is saying is too much in this moment. The realization that Eric will never be, and never was, just hers. That this wasn't just play for him; it was also emotions. Attachment. All of the sadness and anger she's felt since the barbeque crystallizes into fear. *How could I have been so foolish? What have I done?* She feels herself emotionally distancing, shutting down. Eric sees it, too.

"Jules, please. Stay with me. Don't put the walls up. I need you. I love you," Eric pleads.

"I thought I was ready to talk to you," she says, standing. "I thought I could handle this. I... I need to go."

CHAPTER 7

LIKE A BULLET TO THE BACK

BETH IS CLOSE to the front of the very long line at the coffee shop at 7:30 am. The midweek bustle is well underway, and Beth is engaged in her phone, reviewing messages that came in overnight, preparing for the workday ahead.

"Beth!" she hears and looks up, spotting Claire waving at her from a table in the corner, Madelyn seated next to her. Beth waves back and walks over after placing her order.

"Claire. Madelyn. How are you?" Beth says as she approaches, pasting a smile on her face.

"Really good!" Claire responds. "How are you? How are the boys? Kevin must be home from college. How was his freshman year?"

"The house is a complete mess. The laundry room stinks like dirty socks and gym clothes, the milk carton in the fridge is constantly empty, and it's noisy as hell. It's glorious," Beth answers with a wide grin. "Kevin had a terrific first year. He made all A's and a B, and he is working at my office again this summer. Mason is off to sleep away camp in a few weeks." Beth pauses, noticing a glint of sparkle coming from Madelyn's left ring finger. "Madelyn! What is that? Is that from the guy you met at Claire's party?" she asks.

Madelyn holds out her hand for Beth to admire the engagement ring.

"His ex-wife," Madelyn says with a smirk. "She's with me now. We're eloping,"

Beth nods, taking the information in, and Madelyn adds, "I guess I just needed to find the right girl."

"Can y'all believe it's been a year?" Claire sighs. "Jerry and I are coming right up on our second anniversary. No party this time, though. I'm still recovering from the last one…"

"That was something," is all Beth can add.

"Yes, it was." Madelyn chuckles.

"I'm happy for you, Madelyn," Beth says.

"Thank you," Madelyn replies, admiring her ring.

"I miss our little coffee visits after gym class," Claire shares.

Beth avoids responding, and Madelyn shifts subjects. "How's Kyra?" Madelyn asks. "Is she back in town?"

"Charlie is wrapping up her project in Amsterdam, and they should be back soon for a visit," Beth answers.

"Well, please send them my best," Claire says. "And Jules, also."

"Me, too," Madelyn adds.

"I sure will," Beth says.

Jules is wrapped in a fluffy white terry towel, drying her short new haircut, fresh and clean from a shower. Elena, wearing only a thong, watches from the bathroom door and smiles at Jules in the mirror.

"Good morning," Elena says.

"Good morning," Jules replies, blushing. "That was some night…"

"It was," Elena responds, smile widening. "Stay for coffee? Miles is up and in the kitchen."

"I wish I could," says Jules. "I need to head out. New partner meeting this morning."

"Liking the new firm?" Elena asks.

"Loving it. Much better fit. No more babysitting," Jules says.

"That's great," Elena replies. "I'll have Miles make your coffee in a to-go cup. We can't send you off to work uncaffeinated."

Jules crosses the bathroom and plants a lingering kiss on Elena's lips. "That sounds perfect."

Eric, shirtless and in pajama bottoms, hair still mussed from sleep, takes the creamer from the fridge and opens the cabinet door. His hand reaches for, but then skips, the "World's Best Dog Mom" mug and, instead, he takes out two plain ceramic ones. Daisy thumps her tail as Eric pours the coffee, and Xavier emerges, clean-shaven in khakis and a chambray button down, and takes a seat at the kitchen island.

"Your coffee is so damn good," Xavier says as Eric hands him his cup. Eric winks and grins in return, leaning back against the counter.

Daisy's ears perk up, and she trots over to the door, which Eric and Xavier hear open and then close. Jules crouches down to scratch under Daisy's chin, then stands, walks into the kitchen, and kisses Eric on the lips.

"Good morning, you two," she says.

"Good morning," Eric says. "Good night?"

"Mmmm hmmm," Jules murmurs, looking from Eric to Xavier. "You?"

"Yes, ma'am," Xavier says, cheeks warming.

"Don't let me interrupt," Jules says. "I stopped by to pick up a few things before heading into the office."

"How's it going over there?" Xavier asks. "You know my feelings are still hurt that you didn't come work with me. We could've taken over the private equity world."

Jules shoots Xavier a look and teases, "Not sure how I would have handled the conflict of interest screening. 'Married to the boyfriend of an existing partner' isn't an option on the disclosure form."

"Fair enough." Xavier laughs, taking a sip of his coffee. "Feeling good about the move?"

"Very. I like this firm a lot. It's the right place for me," Jules says.

"Well, things finally fell apart with Peter," Xavier continues. "I'm sure he was a titan back in his day, but once you left, it was clear who had the horsepower. I think he underestimated how much weight you were carrying and overestimated the strength of his associates. And Dylan…

Dylan is just a disaster. We tried to make it work, but we just couldn't. We walked."

Jules refrains from commenting and quickly brushes away the slight smile that slips across her lips.

Eric pivots topics, "Are Kyra and Charlie back?"

"They're back this weekend," Jules responds. "I can't wait to see them. Xavier, we are having them over for dinner Saturday. Beth and Alex are coming, too. Do you want to join us?"

"I wish I could. I have plans," Xavier says. "Thanks for including me, though."

"We'll miss you," Jules and Eric say in unison.

"Someone, please, take this plate away from me," Kyra says, "I can't stop eating these ravioli."

"That makes two of us," Beth adds. "Eric, these really should come with a warning label."

Eric smiles at the compliment, and Daisy pokes her head out from under the dining table, hoping for a ravioli to fall on the floor. Jules leans forward and refills everyone's wine glass. *What a difference a year makes,* she thinks to herself, looking around the table.

Alex turns to Charlie. "How's the jet lag? You must be exhausted."

"We took cat naps this afternoon," Charlie responds. "We are determined to stay up till at least 10 tonight. Get back on schedule. Plus, we need to get caught up on everything we missed this year."

"Hold your horses, my friend," Beth says. "First things

first. Other than some texts from Kyra letting us know that she was ok, with you, and spending the year in Amsterdam, we don't know what happened after that night."

Kyra and Charlie share a look before Kyra starts. "That was a rough night, and after the confrontation with John, I had a lot of sorting out to do. I couldn't go back to John's, that much I knew. It wasn't fair to him, and it wasn't fair to me. I stayed with my brother Tommy to try to get my head straight, but all I could think about was," Kyra looks at Charlie, "you."

"I knew my feelings for Kyra had become much bigger than I was admitting to myself," Charlie continues. "The attraction was just too strong. Put us within five feet of each other, and…"

"You don't have to tell me," Jules says. "I caught the two of you making out in the bathroom, remember?"

"But John was my best friend," Charlie says, the guilt heavy in her voice. "That night, I thought I lost them both. Once we were out of the bar, Kyra went straight to Tommy's, and I went home. It was brutal. Kyra asked for space, and I gave it to her. So, I was alone."

"I know what that's like," Eric says. "It's awful."

"It is," Charlie replies. "A few more days passed, and I got a call from one of my colleagues overseas. An assignment came through in Amsterdam. Great clients. Great project. I took it as my sign to get out of town for a bit."

"You had just gotten back, though," Alex says.

"Yes, and I'd already made a mess of things. I thought the best course of action for everyone would be for me to leave town. It came together quickly. I got everything organized, I got my plane ticket…" Charlie pauses before continuing, the memory still stirring up emotions even though it's been a year.

⁓

Charlie sat on a barstool, her back to the entrance of Pilar Bar. Someone pumped the jukebox full of quarters, and Chris Isaak's *Wicked Game* filled the air, crackly with the sound of needle on vinyl. *I hate this song*, Charlie thought to herself, nursing her third old fashioned. The bartender left Charlie alone with her thoughts and her glass. She wasn't in the mood for idle chit-chat. Instead, she read through the texts she'd exchanged with John a few days after the anniversary party.

> Charlie: I'm an idiot.
> John: You are.
> Charlie: But I'm not sorry. I mean, I'm sorry I went behind your back and hurt your feelings. For that, I am sorry. But I'm not sorry I had feelings for Kyra.
> John: Why are you even texting me?
> Charlie: Because you're my friend. My best friend. Even if I'm not yours.
> John: Well, if you see Kyra, tell her her stuff is boxed up and in the garage.
> Charlie: She's not with you?
> John: No. Haven't seen or heard from her since that night. You?
> Charlie: Nothing.
> John: This sucks.

Charlie: This sucks.

John: I'm not ready to be friends with you right now. I don't know if I'll ever be.

Charlie: I'll be here if and when you're ready.

I did it again, Charlie thought to herself as she swirled her drink around the giant ice cube. *I screwed everything up. Again. Why can't I get this right? Why do I just keep hurting people? And me?* Charlie finished her drink and signaled for another one. The song ended, and the record changed to *Ain't No Sunshine* by Bill Withers. Charlie rolled her eyes to the ceiling and dropped her head into her hands. *You've got to be fucking kidding me.*

The door to the bar opened and then closed again, the noise of the street mingling briefly with the sounds of the jukebox. Without looking up, Charlie heard the feet of the bar stool next to her skid a few inches backward and felt someone take the seat. Out of the corner of her eye, she saw a red and pink paper valentine slide into view. Stapled to it was a clear plastic bag overflowing with lollipops and candy hearts.

⁓

Kyra picks up where Charlie leaves off. "I was out of my old apartment and had no place to live. I got that huge commission from closing that big deal, so I had plenty of cash. When I saw Charlie at the bar that day, I had already decided I wanted to be with her. I knew I had to be with her. So, when she told me her plans…"

"She became part of them," Charlie finishes, smiling.

"Whatever happened with John?" Beth asks Kyra.

"It took a while for me to reach out to him, but I did," Kyra replies. "I owed him an apology for how I treated him. I wasn't honest about my feelings–not with myself and not with him. It was a hard conversation, but not a complicated one. After the party, there was no going back. I loved the feeling of security that John brought to the relationship, and he didn't deserve what happened. I still feel horrible about how that part went. But it was never going to work. When he and I spoke, we both knew it was for the best. It helped that I was already in Amsterdam. We both needed the space."

"So, did you hang out at the Bulldog? The redlight district? How many space cakes did you eat?" Alex asks.

"Yes, yes, and lots," Kyra replies, laughing. "Enough about us." Kyra looks at Jules, "Catch me up…"

Jules' mind travels back to the morning after the anniversary party.

Early dawn light peeked through the bedroom window of Beth's and Alex's guest room, and Jules couldn't stay in bed any longer. She rose, put her workout clothes on and earbuds in, and stepped outside to run. She needed to clear her head after last night, after seeing Eric at the party. She needed to get her thoughts straight. The sun was coming up, and the light in the sky was pale pink. The neighborhood was quiet, still very much asleep. With no destination in mind, Jules wound through the streets, increasing her pace once her muscles warmed up. She let her legs take her, her body lead her, her breath carry her. Stride after stride.

She turned the corner to a coffee shop just as they were flipping the closed sign to open. She slowed her pace and stepped inside, approaching the counter for a water. As she was paying, the coffee shop door opened, and Xavier walked in.

"Julia? Good morning. Looks like you've already gotten a workout in."

"Xavier, hi," Julia said, taking out her earbuds and hoping he wouldn't notice how red and puffy her eyes were. "Is this your neighborhood?"

"Yes," Xavier responded, "and I'm addicted to the coffee here. I've been meaning to reach out so we can get the kick-off meeting scheduled. We are excited to get started. What are you listening to? Anything good?"

"Just a running mix," Jules said, stepping aside so Xavier could order. As he reached forward to pay, she saw it. The Patek Phillipe watch. Metal band. Blue face. Jules felt her breath catch, but she was able to maintain her composure. "Xavier, do you have a few minutes? Would you like to sit with me?"

"Yes. Let's grab a table." They chose a table in the corner and got situated with their drinks. Jules started, "Tell me, you're new in town, yes?"

"Correct. Moved here for the job. I really like it so far."

"It's a wonderful place to live. Have you been able to make friends?"

"Here and there. I've met some people at the gym."

Jules nodded, took a sip of water, and continued, "Are you married? Seeing anyone?"

Xavier shook his head. "Not married. Haven't found the

right person yet. I was texting with someone promising, but that didn't work out. You? Married? Kids?"

"No kids. Married, though. I've been with Eric since grad school." She saw Xavier's expression freeze when she said Eric's name.

"It's nice that you've been married so long," Xavier said, his voice a little shaky. "Our business isn't kind to marriages. The long hours, the travel. You must have something really special."

"Yes. Yes, I do." Jules didn't take her eyes off Xavier.

"Yeah, the person I was texting with was married. Things escalated quickly. Quicker than either of us expected, I think. There was definitely some chemistry there, but nothing happened in real life. I guess you could call it heavy flirting."

"Heavy flirting? So that's a thing?"

"In this case, yes," Xavier looks up and returns Jules' gaze. "He broke it off when his wife found out. I guess things went a little too far before he could explain. One thing he made clear, though. He loves her. More than anything. I certainly wouldn't want to be responsible for interfering with that, Jules."

Jules noticed that he didn't call her Julia. She knew he knew.

Xavier finished his coffee and stood up to leave. "I'm really glad I ran into you this morning."

"Yes," Jules said, "me, too. I'll see you around, Xavier."

Xavier left, and Jules leaned back in her chair, thinking about their exchange. Somehow, it helped that she already knew him, already liked him. She could see what Eric saw and why Eric enjoyed his attention. Putting a face and a name to those images seemed to make things sting a little less. Jules finished her water and dialed Beth.

Alex picked up. "Hey, Jules."

"Hey, Alex. How's Rocky Balboa?"

"Icing her knuckles. That was some hit, wasn't it?"

"Yeah. That was crazy. Is she ok?"

"More than ok," Alex winked at Beth and shadow-boxed, "I'm going to put you on speaker and leave you two to it."

Kevin spoke up before Beth got on the line. "Aunt Jules!"

"Hey, Kev."

"Did you see Beth knock that guy out?" he asked.

"I did indeed," Jules replied.

"Was it awesome?" Kevin asked.

"Extremely. Your mom is a force of nature. Now, please put her on," Jules answered as she smiled to herself.

"Hey, Jules," Beth said. "Good morning. You were out early."

"Yes. I couldn't stay in bed any longer. I needed to run. You ok?"

"I might've fractured my hand on John's face," Beth replied. "But it was totally worth it."

"Eye of the tiger, babe," Jules said. "How was the rest of the night?"

"Let's see. The bouncers kicked John out soon after you left."

"I'm sure," Jules said. "What about Kyra? Is she ok?"

"I don't know yet. I know she didn't go home with John. I was planning on checking in with her a little later."

"I'll give her a call as well. Do you know if she left with Charlie?"

"Not sure," Beth replied. "Charlie made her feelings quite plain. I'm sure Kyra has a lot to figure out."

"That's an understatement. What about Claire? Did she recover from Jerry's threesome comment?" Jules asked.

"I think so. I think if you're married to Jerry, public humiliation becomes a regular occurrence. By the end of the night, she was back by his side and keeping him on a short leash," Beth responded.

"On brand for Claire," Jules said.

"Most definitely. And I think Madelyn went home with one of Jerry's creepy friends."

"Also on brand," Jules said, and Beth laughed at Jules' remark.

"More importantly," Beth continued, "how are you? I saw you walk outside with Eric, but then the light was on in the guest room when we got home. What happened?"

"It didn't go well. I thought I was ready to talk to him, but I wasn't. When he started to explain what happened, I just couldn't take it. It was too much. I have a lot I need to work through, too. And then there was this morning…"

"What happened this morning?" Beth asked.

"The mystery man in the pics is no longer a mystery," Jules replied.

"Who is it?"

"It's someone I know from another firm. His name is Xavier. I recognized his watch from one of the photos."

"Are you kidding me?" Beth said.

"Not kidding," Jules said. "I ran into him this morning at the coffee shop."

"No way. How did that go? Does he know you know?"

Jules considered her words before responding. "Better than you would have expected. And yes, he knows I know. I can't really explain it, but somehow, I feel better. A little better, at least."

"I guess that's what counts," Beth said. "I need to go change my ice pack. Are you on your way back here?"

"Yes. I'm heading back now. See you in a bit." Jules hung up and walked the rest of the way home.

∽

"So, you actually knew him!" Kyra says, reaching for the wine and refilling her glass. "Now, this is the guy from the firm you were thinking of partnering with, right? The one from that networking event?" Kyra asks.

"Good memory," Jules says. "Yes. And the timing was serendipitous. That was right before things blew up, and I changed firms."

"It was only a matter of time before that was going to happen," Beth says. "I'm surprised you lasted as long as you did."

"Yeah," Jules says, thinking back to that day. "I hit my limit."

∽

"Well, Julia, you did it. We lost the deal. We got outbid," Will sneered, cheeks hot. He came ready for battle. Peter and the rest of the team looked on from their seats around the conference table, awaiting Jules' response.

"It wasn't our deal," Jules said. "And I'm still not convinced it was a good one."

"You don't know that. It could have been great."

Jules took a deep breath. *Boy, this is tiresome,* she thought to herself. "Maybe," she said. "We'll never know."

Dylan squared off his shoulders and looked directly at Jules. "You're so smug," he said, tone aggressive. "Losing that deal is going to cost us."

Jules leaned back in her chair and folded her arms in front of her chest. "We've gotten where we are today, as a firm, because of our financial discipline. We don't cave and make bad deals based on manufactured competitive pressure. We go over every number with a fine-toothed comb, and if the deal doesn't meet our criteria, we pass. If someone else takes it in the meantime, so be it. If you weren't so sloppy," she looked at Dylan, Will, and Hunter, "perhaps we would have had the analysis we needed to move more quickly. But nothing in what you presented was compelling, and frankly, I'm sick of doing your work. You're upset about losing a deal? Blame yourself."

Dylan opened his mouth, but no words came out. He looked to Peter, "Aren't you going to say something?"

Jules turned to face Peter expectantly.

Peter glared at Dylan. "This meeting is over. Go back to your offices."

The associates exited the conference room. Jules and Peter remained in their seats.

"What the hell was that?" Peter hissed at Jules once the associates left.

"I could ask you the same thing," Jules hissed back. "They look to you for how to behave, and you let them act like children. This isn't a firm anymore, Peter. It's a daycare. I'll say the same thing to you that I said to them. You don't like how things are going? Blame yourself."

"What has gotten into you?"

"This isn't what I signed up for, Peter." Jules dropped her gaze and took a breath. "We've done a lot of great work together. A lot of great deals." She looked up again, making eye contact. "But I'm out."

"Julia, no. Wait…"

Jules stood, walked back to her office, and took a seat at her desk. She looked around, taking it all in one last time, then put the framed photo of Eric and Daisy in her bag and left.

∽

"So, everything was in flux," Charlie says.

"Yes. Everything I thought was so solid was shifting. My marriage. My work. But I understood things a little better after that," Jules says, taking another sip of wine. "More importantly, I knew what I needed to do next."

"What we needed to do next," Eric adds, taking Jules' hand.

⚰

Eric and Jules arrived separately. The location felt remote despite being about an hour out of the city. There was a heavy iron gate at the entrance, monitored by a call box and a camera.

There was a crushed gravel walking path between the parking lot and the facility, and the facility itself was surrounded by pine trees. The shade from the boughs and smell of the pine needles were cooling, calming. The building was modern, wood and glass, symmetrical. The serenity of the grounds cloaked the level of personalized crisis management taking place inside, patient by patient.

Staff wore tailored black scrubs, physicians wore white coats. Jules and Eric were brought to their own separate intake rooms shortly after checking into the facility. Their bags were brought to their respective suites on different floors.

Both Jules and Eric were provided with extensive paperwork to complete in advance. Medical history, psychological history, the feelings that brought them here, what they were hoping to achieve. They each had a therapist assigned to them, qualified and experienced in working couples through difficulties, finding a path forward. After verifying the information provided through the intake forms, Eric and Jules received a consent form, which each read and signed.

It was Elena's recommendation that brought Eric and Jules here, and Dr. Layton supported the decision. What had worked in the past was no longer sufficient. Preparatory treatments would begin that day and progress throughout the week and over the coming months. They would start with lozenges and, once ready, would move to intravenous.

≪⧸

"What was it like?" Kyra asks, looking at both Eric and Jules.

"Yeah," Beth says. "You don't really talk about it."

Jules closes her eyes for a moment and remembers.

You are awake.

This is the first sensation that enters your awareness after the slight sting of the injection. Your eyes are open, and you are awake. There is ambient music in the background, nothing you recognize, nothing you feel compelled to recognize. You are aware of your body feeling heavy but you do not feel heavy. Instead, you rise.

You have come to know this feeling in your preparatory sessions, though this is a little different than the effects of the bitter lozenges. The softness. The calmness. That is familiar. The feeling of weightlessness is new; this feeling of being pulled upward.

You are keenly aware of the emotions that brought you to this place. To this treatment room. To this therapist, who is now seated in a chair in the corner across from where you are lying down, a blanket on top of you. You have no inclination to move.

The lozenges were an introduction. A path into the deep and immovable rage and sadness that enveloped you like a thick fog. All of those feelings are currently present. You can't yet see them, but you can feel them. You flutter your eyelids closed.

With your eyes closed, the rage and sadness each take on a visual quality. They have color, opacity, and texture, and swell like blooms of ink. You keep moving upward, toward them, until you are among them. Awash in your emotions.

You exhale, and you rise. You inhale, and you rise.

The visuals shift to black and white snow, like changing channels on an old television set, and there is Eric's face, turning toward you at City Hall, hands slightly trembling as he unfolds the paper where he's written his vows. You see his nervousness in the shallowness of his breath, his excitement in the quiver in his lips, and his love in the sparkle of his eyes. That love, you now remember, is for you. You become aware of pressure where your heart should be, like a balloon, that both aches and soothes. The rage melts. You feel safe again to love him. You feel safe again to miss him. You feel these feelings grow bigger and bigger, and the sadness, so thick and so dense, pixelates. It's still there, but it no longer feels suffocating. There is space now for you to breathe through it.

Tears stream down your cheeks as you return to your physical form.

"I wish I could describe it without boring you to death," Jules says, opening her eyes. "I'm not even sure I can put it into words. But it saved me."

Eric puts his arm around Jules and kisses her temple. "It saved us. It was after that session that Jules and I made our first real contact."

Eric woke up to a text message from Jules.

I feel ready to talk. No pressure. Just know that I'm ready when you are.

The response from Eric came almost immediately.

I was hoping you were ready. I'll come to you.

A few minutes later, Eric tapped lightly on the door of Jules' suite, and she invited him in. It was a carbon copy of the suite he was staying in, a small sitting room in front of a bedroom, large windows looking out into the wooded areas. The color palette was neutral, the design clean and symmetrical. Comforting.

"Please sit," Jules said, motioning to the sofa. They sat, facing one another.

"That was crazy," Eric said.

"Wild," Jules agreed.

"I've missed you," he said.

"Me, too," she replied.

Jules referred to the written guidelines they were given for if and when they felt ready to re-engage.

"I invited this conversation," Jules said. "So, if you are comfortable, please share first. I will listen."

Eric stood, poured himself a glass of water, drank, sat, and, after a deep breath, began.

"Here is what I now know. It was fear. All along, I was operating from a place of fear. Not just that I would lose you. Lose us. Fear that I wouldn't get to experience what you were getting to experience. Get to express myself the way I was perceiving you expressing yourself. Which turned to envy, like a competition, and then anger, embarrassment, and shame. But the root was, is, fear.

"I didn't think I was doing anything wrong at first. And I'm not just talking about the exchange with Xavier. I thought I was supporting you when I wasn't speaking up or saying how I really felt. I thought I was being a good husband. But I wasn't being honest. I wasn't honest about how what we were doing was making me feel, about how those feelings were informing my behavior. I wasn't being honest with you. Or with myself.

"And then things escalated with Xavier even though there was never any physical contact. Which I know is no excuse. I didn't know what to say or how to address it. I am so sorry for hurting you. For putting what we have at risk.

"And yet, I have this overwhelming need for you to trust me. To love me. I know it makes no sense after what I've done. I want you to love me for being honest so that I can be honest with you. I want you to trust me so I can be trustworthy with you. More to the point, I can't be afraid anymore that you will reject me, or judge me, or shut me out. I've gone along with a lot of this out of fear that you wouldn't love me if I spoke up, slowed things down, or just didn't want to do them. Or do some of them my way. If we can move through this, and I want more than anything in this world for us to move through this, this is what I need."

Eric paused and then concluded, "Thank you for listening."

"Thank you for sharing," Jules said.

"Too much?" Eric asked.

"Not at all," Jules replied. "My turn?"

"Yes," Eric said. "Please."

"What I learned about myself, in my sessions, is that my primary emotions were rage and sadness. There were a lot of other emotions as well, but the big ones, the ones that were swallowing me whole, were rage and sadness. Both stemmed from the same thing. An overwhelming sense of loss. Loss of a loving family. Loss of acceptance. Loss of parts of myself, loss of not knowing parts of myself. Not knowing if I will ever know all the parts of myself. Eric, what I've come to realize is that it's not you I don't trust. It's me…"

❧

"Over the next several months," Eric continues, "we had additional sessions and worked through our emotions. Together. No hedging. No incomplete truths. The commitment was that if we were going to love one another, we were going to love one another completely. All of it. Even the parts that made us uncomfortable."

"That's when the real test began," Jules says. "Bandaids. Ripped. Off."

❧

"Jules!" said Elena. She was seated at the same table they shared at lunch about ten months ago and stood to greet Jules when she arrived at the restaurant. "So nice to see you again. It feels like it's been ages."

"It does," Jules said, kissing Elena on the cheek before sitting. "I have so much to catch you up on. You look stunning. How are you and Miles?"

"I'm great. Miles is great. I was excited to hear from you. Last we spoke, you and Eric were still…sorting things out."

"Yes," Jules said. "It's been a lot these past several months. But, first, I want to thank you."

"How so?" asked Elena.

"The facility you recommended," Jules responded. "It rescued us."

"It's a very special place."

"It is."

"I've never experienced anything like that before," Jules admitted. "Neither had Eric."

"Ketamine is a game changer," Elena said, nodding in agreement.

"Incredibly powerful. It's made the work more possible if that makes sense."

"It does. It helps get your thoughts out of the way so you can see. Reframe."

"That's a good way to describe it," Jules agreed and then added, "Goodness gracious. If the lozenges were a path to experience your emotions more objectively, the injections were a lifeline."

Elena laughed. "Not for the faint of heart."

"Understatement of the year," Jules replied.

"So, tell me," Elena continued. "What did you get clear on? For yourself and for your relationship?"

"That's such an awfully big question with such a deceptively simple answer. It goes back to what we talked about all those months ago. Being brave. I thought I was being brave. But I wasn't," Jules said. "There is no such thing as 'mostly honest' when it comes to this. When it comes to living a full life. And that's what we were doing. That's what I was doing. We were being mostly honest, but not completely honest. Which means we were lying. To ourselves and to each other. Don't get me wrong. We were well-intentioned. But these aren't the kinds of lies that can be overlooked, like, 'I didn't say anything because I didn't want to ruin the surprise party' or keeping the confidence of a friend. This was impacting what we did or didn't know about ourselves or about each other. This was impacting our ability to trust ourselves. To trust each other.

"The little flashbacks you get in the sessions, the downloads, or whatever you want to call them, those were catalyzing. You start to see, or in my case, remember, the moments when you decided, or accepted, or were treated like your needs don't matter. Your wants don't matter. Whether that's to fit in, or keep the peace, or get love. There was always a consequence, something more important. And so, you hide. Or override. Or you bury parts of yourself and tell yourself it's not a big deal. But it is a big deal. It made me so sad. So angry. I was enraged. Mostly at myself."

Jules took a sip from her water glass and continued. "It goes deeper. You do the work. You get honest with yourself. You get honest with your partner, and you put yourself out there in the bravest way possible because you are not just asking them to accept you, to accept all of you. You are asking them to love you. To love all of you. And you will love all of them in return. Learning to trust that… That's where we are."

Elena reached across the table and squeezed Jules' hand. "Well said."

"Thank you," said Jules. "I'm in a good place. We're in a good place."

"Does this mean you've closed the relationship?" Elena asked.

"These past several months, yes. While we were working

through everything. Ultimately, though, that's not who we are."

"I see," said Elena. "What does that mean for you?"

Jules took a deep breath. "I'd like to re-engage. With you and Miles. Just me. How do you feel about that?"

"Eric is on board? You've both decided you are going to pursue your needs separately?" Elena asks.

"Yes. We are going to trust each other and do this separately. Eric is on board."

Elena leaned back in her chair and smiled widely at Jules. "In that case, buckle up. We're going to have a lot of fun."

≈

"How did it go with Elena?" Eric called out to Jules as she walked through the front door.

"Well. It was so good to see her," Jules replied, leaning down to pet Daisy, then walking to the kitchen, kissing Eric on the cheek, and taking a seat at the island.

"And?" Eric asked.

"And it's a go," Jules said, smiling. "I will schedule for the same night you plan to meet Xavier. How are you feeling about that?"

"About Xavier? Nervous. Excited. At the very least, I will get to explain myself and apologize again. Properly. I'm just glad he agreed to see me. To entertain the conversation. And I'm happy for you. I think you are in good hands with Miles and Elena."

"Whew," Jules said. "We're doing this."

"We're doing this."

~

Kyra reaches for the wine bottle and says, "Wow, you two. You have me on pins and needles. I'm going to need a refill to hear the rest of this."

Beth slides her glass toward Kyra. "That makes two of us. Kyra, fill me up."

"No kissing and telling at the dinner table," Jules says, "but it was a big leap for both of us. None of us knew if things would work out in real life. The best we could do was put ourselves out there and try."

~

Jules pulled into the driveway at Miles' and Elena's house the following Saturday evening. She and Eric had one last conversation before she left to make sure they were both okay with what was about to happen. They talked about their respective fears, needs, and desires, but mostly, they spoke about being supportive of one another. Loving one another. They each worked hard to get to this moment, confident enough in themselves, each other, and their relationship so they could have these experiences. Independently. They would take things one step at a time, they agreed. They also agreed that tonight represented a very big step.

Florence and the Machine streamed from the car speakers as she sang along with the lyrics while checking her makeup one last time in the rearview mirror: "Happiness. Hit her. Like a train on a track."

"Ready," she said out loud before cutting the engine and walking up the entryway. Miles and Elena opened the front door before Jules had a chance to knock.

"Welcome," they said with grins on their faces. Jules grinned in return. "We made some drinks and light snacks," Elena said. "Come on in."

"It's so nice to see you again," Miles said, leading Jules into the living room.

"Thank you. You, too," Jules replied, taking a seat in one of the upholstered chairs.

"How have you been these past months?" Miles asked, pouring drinks for all three of them and then taking a seat next to Elena.

"A lot of change," Jules replied. "But good change. I took some time off and now I have a new job. Eric and I are in a good place. Things are good. How are you?"

"We're good. Work is good. Elena is great…" Miles replied, and then the room went quiet. "This is always the awkward part," Miles said.

"It doesn't have to be," Elena said. "We're all adults. We know why we are here. Jules, we have you till about midnight, yes?"

"Yes," said Jules.

The air thickened with anticipation.

"Elena," Miles said. "I would very much like to watch you undress Jules."

Elena's expression turned crafty. "I would very much like to do that for you, Miles. Jules, would you like that?"

Jules felt her lips start to tremble with excitement. "Yes."

"Remember, Jules," Elena said, guiding Jules by the hand to stand up, "you're in control. Once you say no, it's a no. Agreed?"

"Agreed."

Jules wore a black, semi-sheer blouse tucked into form-fitting jeans with a black leather belt and black pumps.

"Start with the blouse," Miles suggested.

Elena stood facing Jules, brushing the hair off Jules' forehead and nuzzling her neck. Elena loved this part, feeling Jules' pulse quicken, goosebumps rising, in response to her touch. Elena took the folds of Jules' collar between her fingers and slowly traced the seam down to the buttons, stopping at the top. Elena licked her lips. "Shall we begin?"

Jules nodded her head yes.

"Yes, what?" Elena asked.

"Yes, please," Jules whispered, leaning into Elena for a deep kiss. Elena resisted the urge to rip Jules' blouse open and, instead, went button, by button, by button. By the time Elena reached her waist, Jules couldn't take it anymore. Jules undid the remaining buttons herself, dropped her blouse on the floor, and stood in front of Elena in her jeans, pumps, and black lace bra. "Ready when you are," said Jules.

Miles joined Elena and Jules, and all three took turns tasting each other while their remaining clothes came off.

"You have such nice lips," Miles said to Jules, tracing them with his fingertips.

"Doesn't she?" Elena added before kneeling and taking the head of Miles' cock into her mouth, running her tongue along his shaft. "Jules, care to join me?"

Jules smiled and kneeled, kissing Elena and then taking Miles into her mouth. Miles leaned his head back and moaned, saying, "Let's take this to the couch." Miles sat with his knees wide, Jules kneeling in front of him, rubbing his cock across her breasts before putting him back in her mouth. Elena stood on the couch, straddling Miles, while he buried his face between her legs. Jules could smell how wet Elena was. Taste the saltiness of Miles. It made her mouth water.

Jules reached up and stroked Elena's outer folds with her thumb, feeling Miles' tongue as it slid past. Elena felt like hot silk under Jules' touch. She looked down to smile at Jules and then turned, taking a seat next to Miles, legs wide. Jules leaned up to kiss Elena's mouth, letting her taste her husband on Jules' lips, and then worked her way down her chest before taking her into her mouth. Elena was salty and juicy.

Miles moved behind Jules and took her into his mouth from behind, alternating fingers and tongue inside of her. Jules rolled her hips while drinking in Elena.

"I'd like to be inside of you," Miles said to Jules, "Would that be alright?"

Jules lifted her head and said, "Yes."

"Yes, what?" Elena said.

"Yes, please," replied Jules, making eye contact with Elena, then taking Elena back into her mouth. Miles slipped on a condom, and Jules gasped when he entered her. His movements were controlled. Practiced. He cupped Jules' bottom with his hands and smiled at Elena. Elena smiled in return. "I think she likes it, Miles," Elena said.

"It appears so," he replied.

"She's not to orgasm until I say so," Elena said, which caused Jules to grind harder into Miles.

"Understood," he replied, slowing his pace, softening his pressure.

"Keep her steady. I'll be right back," Elena said, and then she stood and walked upstairs. A few minutes later, she returned with a strap-on. "I picked this up for you, Jules," Elena said. "Do you like it?"

Jules nodded her head yes.

"I want you to ride me, and I want you to come. I want to feel you running all over my stomach."

Jules felt like a wild animal. "Get on your back," Jules said.

Elena laid down, back flat to the floor, and Jules mounted her. The stiffness of the strap-on hit all the right places, and Jules rocked her hips, tension building. Miles lay down next to Elena, and they both watched Jules writhe and moan. Jules' tone dropped, heavy with breath, and Elena said, "Now come for me."

Jules shuddered as the pressure inside of her grew, and then she leaned up and came, hot liquid pouring out of her and onto Elena's stomach. Jules closed her eyes to catch her breath.

"You are so lovely," said Elena, reaching up to touch Jules' face. Jules kissed Elena's palm in response. "Now me," Elena said. "Jules, I want you on the couch behind me. Miles, I want you kneeling in front of me."

"Gladly," Miles said.

"Most definitely," Jules said, wiping the sweat off her forehead.

Elena sat between Jules' legs on the sofa and leaned back against her chest. Miles knelt in front of Elena, entering her. Jules hugged Elena from behind, holding her breasts and kissing her neck as Miles moved inside her.

Jules felt Elena's body tense and relax under all the sensations, and Elena's moans grew louder in Jules' ear. Miles held Elena's knees wide as he pushed into her, moving his hips, keeping his breath measured. Elena's body rolled with pleasure as her orgasm hit, and Miles leaned down to kiss both her and Jules. "Keep going," Elena said, pressing her hand to Miles' chest, and Miles obliged, bringing Elena to a second and then third peak before reaching his own.

Jules adored every single second.

✿

Eric stood to greet Xavier at the restaurant. Eric picked a place that was both quiet and private, so he and Xavier could talk.

"Thank you for coming," Eric said. "I wasn't sure you would."

"It piqued my curiosity to hear from you after all this time," Xavier said, taking a seat across from Eric. "I thought I would at least run into you at the gym or the coffee shop. And then Julia left Peter's firm. It's like you both vanished."

"I had a lot of work to do, personally. We both did. It's been intense these past several months." Eric paused before continuing. "But also really good. Look, Xavier, let me start by apologizing once more for how things went between us. I let myself get carried away in a way that wasn't honest or fair to anyone involved. I am so sorry. That's not who I am."

Xavier felt himself soften toward Eric. He didn't know what to expect when he heard from him again, and his guard was up. *Fool me once*, Xavier thought to himself on the drive over. But here was Eric, so handsome and so sincere.

"No hard feelings, Eric. I know things got confusing,"

Xavier said. He took a case out of his pocket, put on tortoise shell framed glasses, and picked up the menu, "So now that we got the small talk out of the way…"

Eric laughed and felt his pulse quicken. *As if Xavier isn't sexy enough.*

A server approached, and they ordered drinks; whiskey neat for Eric, vodka soda for Xavier. "Tell me," Eric said after the server left, "how have you been?"

"It's been a busy several months for me as well. I settled into my apartment, settled into the job."

"Have you been seeing anyone?" Eric asked tentatively.

"Nothing serious," Xavier replied, making eye contact. "Tell me about the work you did these past several months."

"Ketamine therapy."

"Really?"

"Really."

"What was that like?"

Eric closed his eyes for a moment, remembering.

"It's hard to put into words, but it was beautiful," Eric said. "It helped me in ways I couldn't have ever imagined. It was like being set free."

"How interesting," Xavier said, taking a sip of his drink. Eric found himself envious of the glass, wanting to know what it would feel like to have Xavier's lips on him.

"Things worked out with you and Julia?" Xavier asked, tilting his head toward Eric's wedding band.

"Yes. Thankfully. We are in a really good place," Eric replied.

"Is that what you brought me here to tell me?" Xavier asked.

"Kind of. But not in the way you might think," Eric said.

"How's that?" said Xavier.

"I apologized for how I treated you, but I won't apologize for how I felt about you. How I still feel about you. I would understand if you want nothing to do with me after how things went, but I'm not that person anymore. I know you want a big relationship someday, and that's not something I can give you. But I think we can be friends. I think we can be more than friends if you're open to it."

"What are you trying to tell me?" Xavier asked.

"Jules and I have known about each other's sexuality and preferences since our very first date. ENM had been something we talked about for years without really knowing how to do it. We went in unprepared. In every possible way. It brought out sides of me that I didn't know existed and, frankly, didn't like. Same with Jules. Reckless is the best word I can use to describe it," Eric answered. "A big part of the work we did was to come to terms with that, come to terms with who we are as individuals and as partners. But also acknowledge that we are not the other's everything. We've known that all along, intellectually. So, the question was whether there is enough trust for us to handle it emotionally."

"Eric," Xavier said, leaning back in his chair, "I'm happy for you and Jules, but I'm not interested in being an experiment."

"You wouldn't be. That's what I'm trying to tell you. I'd like to start again. Differently this time. You know I'm married, and that is, and will always be my primary relationship.

But I think I can be a good friend to you. And I'd like you to be a good friend to me."

"And Jules is alright with this?"

"She is," Eric replied.

"What happens if we fall in love?"

"Make no mistake," Eric held eye contact with Xavier, "I have every intention of loving you."

Xavier felt his heart pound. This was not at all what he was expecting. "I need a minute," he said and stood and walked to the restroom.

Eric finished his drink and signaled the server for another. *This is what honesty feels like*, he reminded himself. He knew putting himself out there with Xavier would feel risky and that there was a good chance Xavier would walk away from what he was proposing. But he hoped he wouldn't. He hoped he would give Eric another chance. Eric felt his phone buzz with an incoming text, and his breath caught when he read it:

X: You want me? Come get me.

Eric left cash on the table to cover the tab, finished his second drink in one swallow, and walked directly to the restroom, the front of his jeans feeling noticeably tighter. With the door barely closed behind him, his lips met Xavier's, their first kiss wet, urgent. Eric reached his fingers into Xavier's dark hair, pulling his head back and kissing his neck. Eric could feel Xavier's pulse against his tongue. Xavier's lips met Eric's again, and, holding each other's gaze, Eric reached between Xavier's legs, and Xavier reached between Eric's. Their breath turned ragged, primal.

"On your knees," Eric said, pushing Xavier's head down.

"Like this?" Xavier said, unzipping Eric's pants, taking him into his hands, then taking him into his mouth.

Eric ran his fingers along Xavier's jawline, then pushed deeper into Xavier's throat. "Like this," Eric said, leaning his head back with pleasure. "I want to come in that pretty mouth of yours," he said, and Xavier sucked harder, finishing him.

"My turn," Eric said, pushing Xavier's back against the bathroom door and kneeling in front of him. Eric held Xavier's cock with both hands, stroking. Xavier bit his bottom lip in anticipation, a heavy moan escaping his lips when Eric's hot mouth finally came around him.

"Yes," he whispered, "yes." Eric moved slowly at first, then faster. He loved the feeling of Xavier in his mouth, what he tasted like when he finished.

"So that's a yes to trying again?" said Eric.

"That's a yes," said Xavier.

༄

It was just about midnight when Eric pulled into the driveway, and the lights were already on. Daisy was perched at the front door, tail wagging, waiting to greet him when he stepped in, and he leaned over to scratch behind her ears. "That's my sweet girl," he murmured, "now where's your mom?"

Eric heard the shower running and paused at the bathroom entryway. Jules was naked and covered in soap and steam; he could see her through the glass. He hardened at the sight of her, and as if she could feel his eyes on her, she turned to look at him and traced a heart with her finger.

"Get in here," she said and watched him brush his teeth and undress before joining her under the hot water.

"Good night?" he asked, lathering himself up.

"Very good night," Jules responded. "Elena and Miles send their warmest regards. You? Everything go ok with Xavier?"

"Better than I could have ever imagined," Eric said, smiling.

Jules smiled in return. "How do you feel?" she asked.

"Turned on," he replied, chest rising and falling. The air in the shower took on a charged quality, almost electric.

"I was hoping you'd say that," said Jules, pressing into him, pulling him into a deep kiss. He ran his hands up and down her body.

"I need you," he said, turning Jules to face the shower wall, back facing him. Jules tilted at the waist, hands on the shower wall, and pushed her bottom against him, feeling him slick against her.

"I need you," she said.

"Is this what you need?" he said, pushing into her.

"Yes," she said with a gasp.

"Louder."

"Yes," Jules cried and felt Eric get harder.

Eric pulled out of Jules and slid two fingers inside her. "You first," he said, hearing her exhales grow louder. "Tell me," Eric said.

"I love you," Jules breathed out.

"Tell me," Eric repeated, pulsing his fingers, feeling the pressure inside of Jules building.

"More than anything," Jules whimpered.

"Mmmmm…" Eric murmured. "You feel so…ready."

Jules nodded her head yes.

"You love me?" Eric asked.

Jules nodded again and pushed into his fingers.

"Show me," he said, pulling his fingers out as Jules splashed all over him.

"You," Jules said, looking back at Eric, "I want you."

Eric grabbed Jules' hips and pushed into her, controlling her rhythm with his hands. He wanted this moment to stretch out, to last. He watched the rivulets of water from the shower head run rivers down Jules' spine, and his heart… His heart felt full.

Every part of Eric's body trembled as he peaked, from his toes to his hairline, quaking with sensation, with pleasure, with love. Jules turned, took Eric into her arms, and pressed her heart to his.

"You," she said.

"You," he said.

"It wasn't easy. There were plenty of times that I worried we wouldn't make it. But with the help of some great therapy and a lot of hard work, we've managed to get ourselves to a really good place," Eric says, finishing his glass of wine.

"That's right," Jules replies, putting her arm around Eric and leaning over to kiss his temple. "I'm a lucky girl," Jules says.

"That makes two of us," Eric whispers into Jules' ear.

Charlie covers a yawn with her hands. "I'm so sorry, everyone. I'm fading. I need to get to bed."

"Absolutely," Eric says. "You guys go ahead. We'll clear."

"You sure?" Charlie says, standing.

"Positive," Jules says.

"Thank you," Kyra says, following Charlie. "We'll host next time."

"Sounds good," Beth says. "We're heading home, too. Mason has a friend over, and Kevin is supposed to be keeping an eye on them. Need to make sure they didn't set the house on fire."

"Oh, man," Alex groans. "We haven't heard about the space cakes yet!"

"Next time," Charlie assures Alex, laughing.

"We'll walk you out," Jules says.

~

Jules shuttles the last of the dishes into the kitchen from the dining room as Eric loads the dishwasher, Daisy lying at his feet. She turns the volume up on the speakers. *Woman* by Mumford and Sons plays, and she sways to the music.

"Dinner was excellent," Jules says.

"It was fun having everyone here," Eric says, watching Jules dance, then taking her into his arms and joining her.

"I'm so glad Kyra and Charlie are back," says Jules.

"They seem really happy. Sounds like Amsterdam was the right move for both of them," Eric adds.

"Sounds like it. You know, talking about this past year, realizing how much has changed, how much we've changed…"

"Yeah," Eric agrees. "It's been a lot."

"Was it worth it, you think? All of the hurt? The uncertainty?"

"Do I wish we could have avoided those parts? Yes. Of course. I never wanted to hurt you. I never wanted to feel hurt. But I'm glad we were able to face it. Grow through it. Become who we are now. And, given who we are, we will change again, and we will work through that, whatever it might be. But this much I know. Because of what we went through, I know what it means to be loved. Completely. And I know what it means to love. Completely. I wouldn't change that for anything. I love you, Jules," Eric says.

"I love you more."

AUTHOR'S NOTE / ACKNOWLEDGEMENTS

For those of you carrying stories inside you: don't wait for others to open your query, acknowledge your outreach, respond, or validate your work. There's no time for that—it only delays getting your stories into readers' hands. Consider this your encouragement: be fearless with your work.

Everyone's artistic path is their own. Knowing your strengths and weaknesses is key to building the right team around you. Personally, I kissed a lot of frogs before assembling my small but mighty team. Special thanks to Natasha Marie Rajendram of Scott Editorial, whose editing expertise sharpened both my story and my writing. Having a trusted set of eyes that honored my voice and narrative goals was a gift.

Thank you also to Robynne and the Damonza team for crafting a stunning cover and formatting. To Kate Rock and her team, your marketing talents are helping me reach readers far and wide—thank you. And to Jane Friedman: though we've never met, your newsletters and recommendations were invaluable to me as a new author. If our paths ever cross, I'll gladly buy you a drink.

Now more than ever, we need diverse, unafraid, empowering voices. If you feel called to write, *write*. If you feel called to share your stories, *share them*. Please, share them. Urgently.

ABOUT ELISS KACEY

Eliss Kacey is a compelling storyteller celebrated for her ability to weave sharp humor, emotional depth, and thought-provoking insights into contemporary relationships. In her debut novel, See More of Your Friends, Eliss delivers a captivating exploration of sexual identity, diving deep into the complexities of love, acceptance, and the human experience. Her work boldly examines modern relationships, desire, and societal norms, offering stories that challenge conventions while remaining deeply relatable.

With a talent for crafting vibrant characters and authentic conflicts, Eliss strikes the perfect balance between laugh-out-loud humor and poignant reflection. Her writing resonates with readers who crave narratives that push boundaries, spark meaningful conversations, and explore the intricacies of what it means to be human.

Based in the United States, Eliss lives with her partner and finds inspiration in the world around her. When she's not writing, she's traveling, always seeking the humor, heart, and stories that shape everyday life.

For more about Eliss Kacey, visit
elisskacey.com.

For more about Flight Risk Press, visit
flightriskpress.com.

BOOK CLUB/READER'S GUIDE

1. Did you have a favorite character or relationship in the story? If so, who or which? Why? What about the character or relationship made them/it your favorite?

2. Which scene(s) in the book made you feel something? What were those feelings? Is there something in your experience that resonated with the scene(s) you identified?

3. Are you in touch with your deepest desires? Can you write them down? Can you say them out loud? To yourself? To your partner(s)? To your trusted circle?

4. Do your deepest desires scare you? Excite you? Confuse you? All of the above? Are you able to unpack your responses for yourself? What is it about your desires that make you feel what you feel?

5. If you currently don't act on your desires, why? What do you think the impact would be if you did? What is not acting on your desires doing to your emotional state? What, if anything, would need to change for you to act on your desires?

6. Which characters did you want to know more about?

www.ingramcontent.com/pod-product-compliance
Lightning Source LLC
Chambersburg PA
CBHW050025120726

47903CB00006B/1911